GENERAL JOHN REGAN

GEORGE A. BIRMINGHAM

ZINC READ

Published by
This edition copyright © 2024 by Zinc Read
Design and setting By Zinc Read
Email- zincread@gmail.com
ISBN-978-93-6124-197-0

CONTENTS

CHAPTER I

The Irish police barrack is invariably clean, occasionally picturesque, but it is never comfortable. The living-room, in which the men spend their spare time, is furnished with rigid simplicity. There is a table, sometimes two tables, but they have iron legs. There are benches to sit on, very narrow, and these also have iron legs. Iron is, of course, harder than wood. Men who are forced to look at it and rub their legs against it at meal times are likely to obtain a stern, martial spirit. Wood, even oak, might in the long run have an enervating effect on their minds. The Government knows this, and if it were possible to have tables and benches with iron tops as well as iron legs police barracks in Ireland would be furnished with them. On the walls of the living-room are stands for arms. Here are ranged the short carbines with which, in extreme emergencies, the police shoot at the other inhabitants of Ireland. The sight of these weapons serves to remind the men that they form a military force.

Near the carbines hang a few pairs of handcuffs, unobtrusively, because no one wants to emphasize the fact that the police in Ireland have to deal with ordinary wrong doers as well as with turbulent mobs. Ornament of every kind is rigorously excluded from these rooms. It is all very well to aim at the development of the aesthetic faculty for children by putting pictures and scraggy geraniums in pots into schoolrooms. No one wants a policeman to be artistic. But the love of the beautiful breaks out occasionally, even in policemen who live in barracks. Constable Moriarty, for instance, had a passion for music. He whistled better than any man in Ballymoy, and spent much of his leisure in working up thrilling variations of popular tunes.

Being confined by the call of duty to the living-room of the barrack in Ballymoy for a whole morning, he had accomplished a series of runs and trills through which the air of "The Minstrel Boy" seemed to struggle for expression. His attention was fixed on this composition, and not at all on the newspaper which lay across his knees.

At twelve o'clock he rose from the bench on which he was sitting and allowed the newspaper to fall in a crumpled heap on the floor at his feet. He stretched himself and yawned. Then he glanced round the barrack-room with an air of weariness. Sergeant Colgan, his tunic unbuttoned, his grey flannel shirt open at the neck, dozed uncomfortably in a corner. Moriarty looked at him enviously. The sergeant was much the older man of the two, and was besides of portly figure. Sleep came easily to him under the most unpromising circumstances. Moriarty was not more than twenty four years of age. He was mentally and physically an active man. Before he went to work on "The Minstrel Boy" he had wooed sleep in vain. Even a three days' old copy of the *Weekly Freeman* had brought him no more than a series of stupefying yawns. If a man cannot go to sleep over a back number of a weekly paper there is no use his trying to go to sleep at all. He may as well whistle tunes.

Moriarty left the living-room in which the sergeant slept and went out to the door of the barrack. He stared across the market square. The sun shone pitilessly. Except for a fat white dog, which lay asleep in the gutter opposite the shop of Kerrigan, the butcher, no living thing was to be seen. Hot days are so rare in west of Ireland towns that the people succumb to them at once. Business, unless it happens to be market day, absolutely ceases in a town like Ballymoy when the thermometer registers anything over eighty degrees. Moriarty stretched himself again and yawned. He looked at the illustrated poster which hung on a board beside the barrack door. It proclaimed the attractiveness of service in the British army. It moved him to no interest, because he had seen it every day since he first came to Ballymoy. The gaudy uniforms depicted on it excited no envy in his mind. His own uniform was of sober colouring, but it taught him all he wanted to know about the discomfort of such clothes in hot weather. His eyes wandered from the poster and remained fixed for some time on the front of the office of the *Connacht Advocate*. The door was shut and the window blind was pulled down. An imaginative man might have pictured Mr. Thaddeus Gallagher, the editor, penning ferocious attacks upon landlords at his desk inside, or demonstrating, in spite of the high temperature, the desperate wickedness of all critics of the Irish Party. But Moriarty was by temperament a realist. He suspected that Thaddeus Gallagher, divested of his coat and waistcoat, was asleep, with his feet on the office table. Next to the newspaper office was the Imperial Hotel, owned and managed by Mr. Doyle. Its door was open, so that any one with sufficient energy for such activity might go in and get a drink at the bar. Moriarty gazed at the front of the hotel for a long time, so long that the glare of light reflected from its whitewashed walls brought water to his eyes. Then he turned and looked into the barrack again. Beside him, just outside the door of the living-room, hung a small framed notice, which stated that Constable Moriarty was on guard. He looked at it. Then he peeped into the living-room and satisfied himself that the sergeant was still sound asleep. It was exceedingly unlikely that Mr. Gregg, the District Inspector of the Police, would visit the barrack on such a very hot day. Moriarty buttoned his tunic, put his forage cap on his head, and stepped out of the barrack.

He crossed the square towards Doyle's Hotel. A hostile critic of the Royal Irish Constabulary—and there are such critics even of this excellent body of men—might have suspected Moriarty of adventuring in search of a drink. The great heat of the day and the extreme dulness of keeping guard over a barrack which no one ever attacks might have excused a longing for bottled porter. It would have been unfair to blame Moriarty if he had entered the bar of the hotel and wakened Mr. Doyle. But he did no more than glance through the open door. He satisfied himself that Mr. Doyle, like the sergeant and Mr. Thaddeus Gallagher, was sound asleep. Then he passed on and turned down a narrow laneway at the side of the hotel.

This led him into the yard at the back of the hotel. A man of delicate sensibilities would have shrunk from entering Mr. Doyle's yard on a hot day. It was exceedingly dirty, and there were a great many decaying things all over it, besides a manure heap in one corner and a pig-stye in another. But Constable Moriarty had no objection to bad smells. He sat down on the low wall of the pig-stye and whistled "Kathleen Mavourneen." He worked through the tune twice creditably, but without attempting variations. He was just beginning it a third time when a door at the back of the hotel opened and a girl came out. Moriarty stopped whistling and grinned at her amiably. She was a very pretty girl, but she was nearly as dirty as the yard. Her short skirt was spotted and stained from waist-band to the ragged fringe where there had once been a hem. Her boots were caked with dry mud. They were several sizes too large for her and seemed likely to fall off when she lifted her feet from the ground. A pink cotton blouse was untidily fastened at her neck with a brass safety pin. Her hair hung in a thick pig-tail down her back. In the higher ranks of society in Connacht, as elsewhere, girls are generally anxious to pose as young women at the earliest possible moment. They roll up their hair and fasten it with hairpins as soon as their mothers allow them. But girls of the peasant class in the west of Ireland put off the advance of womanhood as long as they can. Wiser than their more fashionable sisters, they dread the cares and responsibilities of adult life. Up to the age of twenty, twenty-one, or twenty-two, they still wear their hair in pig-tails and keep their skirts above their ankles.

"Is that you, Mary Ellen?" said Constable Moriarty.

The girl stood still. She was carrying a bucket full of a thick yellow liquid in her right hand. She allowed it to rest against her leg. A small portion of its contents slopped over and still further stained her skirt. She looked at Constable Moriarty out of the corners of her eyes for a moment. Then she went on again towards the pig-stye. She had large brown eyes with thick lashes. Her hair was still in a pig-tail, and her skirt was far from covering the tops of her boots; but she had a precocious understanding of the art of looking at a man out of the corners of her eyes. Moriarty was agreeably thrilled by her glance.

"Is it the pig you're going to feed?" he asked.

"It is," said Mary Ellen.

A very chivalrous man, or one trained in the conventions of what is called polite society, might have left his seat on the wall and helped the girl to carry the bucket across the yard. Moriarty did neither the one nor the other. Mary Ellen did not expect that he would. It was her business and not his to feed the pigs. Besides, the bucket was very full. That its contents should stain her dress did not matter. It would have been a much more serious thing if any of the yellow slop had trickled down Constable Moriarty's beautiful trousers.

She reached the pig-stye, lifted the bucket, and tipped the contents into a wooden trough. Constable Moriarty, still seated on the wall, watched her admiringly. Her sleeves were rolled up above the elbows. She had very well-shaped, plump, brown arms.

"There's many a man," he said, "might be glad enough to be that pig."

Mary Ellen looked up at him with an air of innocent astonishment.

"Why would he then?" she said.

"The way he'd have you bringing his dinner to him," said Moriarty.

This compliment must have been very gratifying to Mary Ellen, but she made no reply to it. She set down the empty bucket on the ground and rubbed her hands slowly on the sides of her skirt Moriarty probably felt that he had done as much as could be expected of him in the way of pretty speeches. He whistled "Kathleen Mavourneen" through once while Mary Ellen wiped her hands dry. She picked up her bucket again and turned to go away.

"Tell me this now," said Moriarty. "Did ever you have your fortune told?"

"I did not," she said.

"It's what I'm good at," said Moriarty, "is telling fortunes. There was an aunt of mine one time that was terrible skilful at it. It was her taught me."

"It's a pity she had no more sense."

"If you was to sit up on the wall beside me," said Moriarty, "and if you was to lend me the loan of your hand for one minute— —"

"Get out," said Mary Ellen.

"You'd be surprised, so you would," said Moriarty, "at the things I'd tell you."

"I might."

"You would."

"But I won't be," said Mary Ellen, "for I've more to do than to be listening to you."

"Where's the hurry?" said Moriarty. "Sure the day's long."

The affair might have ended in a manner pleasant to Moriarty and interesting to the pig. The attraction of the occult would in all probability have overcome Mary Ellen's maidenly suspicions. She might not have sat upon the wall. She would have almost certainly have yielded her sticky hand if a sudden sound had not startled Moriarty. A motorcar hooted at the far end of the village street. Moriarty jumped off the wall.

"There's one of them motorcars," he said, "and the fellow that's in her will be stopping at the barrack for to ask his way to somewhere. It's a curious thing, so it is, that them motor drivers never knows the way to the place they're going to, and it's always the police they ask, as if the police had nothing to do but to attend to them. I'll have to be off."

He left the yard, hurried down the narrow lane, and crossed the road to the barrack. Just as he reached it the car, a large, opulent-looking vehicle, stopped outside Doyle's Hotel. Moriarty went into the barrack and wakened the sergeant. He had a keen sense of his duty towards his superior officer. It would not have been kind or right to allow the sergeant to sleep through an event so unusual as the stopping of a handsome motor outside the door of the Imperial Hotel.

The car was a large one, but it carried only a single traveller. He was a lean, sharp-faced man, clean shaven, with very piercing hard grey eyes. He blew three blasts on the horn of his motor. Then Mr. Doyle came out of the door. He blinked irritably at the stranger. The strong sunlight affected his eyes, and the rude way in which he had been awakened from his sleep overcame for a moment the natural instinct of the hotel keeper. All hotel keepers are civil to possible guests. Otherwise they would not succeed in their business. Mr. Doyle knew this, but he scarcely realised at first that the gentleman in the motorcar might be a guest. His was not a tourist's hotel and he had been very sound asleep.

"Say," said the stranger, "are you the proprietor?"

"I am," said Doyle.

"Can I register?" said the motorist.

The word was strange to Doyle, Guests at his hotel were very few. A commercial traveller stopped a night with him occasionally, trying to push the sale of drapery goods or boots in Ballymoy. An official of a minor kind, an instructor in agriculture, or a young lady sent out to better the lot of domestic fowls, was stranded now and then in Ballymoy and therefore obliged to spend the night in Doyle's hotel. But such chance strangers merely asked for rooms and food. They did not want to "register."

"Can you what?" said Doyle.

"Register," said the stranger.

"I don't know can you," said Doyle. "This is a backward place, but you might try them at the police barrack. The sergeant's an obliging man, and if the thing can be done I wouldn't doubt but he'd do it for you."

"You don't kind of catch on to my meaning," said the stranger. "What I want is to stop a day or two in your hotel."

Doyle suddenly realised the possibilities of the situation.

"You can do that of course," he said, "and welcome. I'd be glad if we had a gentleman like yourself every day of the week."

He turned as he spoke and shouted for Mary Ellen.

"Business pretty stagnant?" said the stranger.

"You may say that. Mary Ellen, Mary Ellen! Come here, I say."

The stranger got out of his car. He looked up and down the empty street.

"Guess," he said, "since I travelled in this slumbrous old country of yours I've seen considerable stagnation, but this licks the worst I've struck yet. Your town pretty well fathoms the depths. Are the folks here alive at all?"

"They are, of course."

Doyle looked round him as he spoke. He saw a good deal that the stranger missed. Sergeant Colgan and Constable Moriarty standing well back inside the barrack door, were visible, dim figures in the shadow, keenly alert, surveying the stranger. Young Kerrigan, the butcher's son, crouched, half concealed, behind the body of a dead sheep which hung from a hook outside the door of his father's shop. He too was watching. One side of the window blind of the *Connacht Eagle* office was pulled aside. Thaddeus Gallagher was without doubt peering at the motorcar through a corner of the window. Three small boys were lurking among the packing cases which stood outside a shop further down the street. Doyle felt justified in repeating his statement that many of the inhabitants of Ballymoy were alive.

"There is," he said, "many a one that's alive enough, though I don't say but that business might be brighter. Mary Ellen, I say, come here."

Mary Ellen appeared at the door of the hotel. She had improved her appearance slightly by putting on an apron. But she had not found time to wash her face. This was not her fault. Washing is a serious business. In Mary Ellen's case it would have taken a long time if it were to be in the least effective. Doyle's call was urgent.

"Why didn't you come when you heard me calling you?" he said.

Mary Ellen looked at him with a gentle tolerant smile. She belonged to a race which had discovered the folly of being in a hurry about anything. She knew that Doyle was not really in a hurry, though he pretended to be.

"Amn't I coming?" she said.

Then she looked at the stranger. He, being a stranger and apparently a man of some other nation, might perhaps really be in a hurry. Such people sometimes are. But his eccentricities in no way mattered to Mary Ellen. The wisdom of the ages was hers. The Irish have it. So have eastern peoples. They will survive when the fussy races have worn themselves out. She gave the stranger one glance of half contemptuous pity and then looked at the motorcar.

"Now that you are here," said Doyle severely, "will you make yourself useful?"

Mary Ellen stared at the motorcar. Her beautiful brown eyes opened very wide. Her mouth opened slightly and expanded in a smile. A long line of the black transferred from the kitchen kettle to her cheek reached from her ear to the point of her chin. It was broken as her smile broadened and finally part of it was lost in the hollow of a dimple which appeared. Mary Ellen had never before seen so splendid a motor.

"Will you stop grinning," said Doyle, "and take the gentleman's things into the house?"

"My name," said the stranger, "is Billing, Horace P. Billing."

"Do you hear that now?" said Doyle to Mary Ellen.

She approached the motorcar cautiously, still smiling. Mr. Billing handed out two bags and then a photographic camera with tripod legs, strapped together. Doyle took one of the bags. Mary Ellen took the other. Mr. Billing himself carried the camera.

"It occurs to me," said Mr. Billing, "that this town kind of cries out to be wakened up a bit."

"I wouldn't say," said Doyle, "but it might be the better of it."

Mary Ellen turned round and looked at Mr. Billing. She felt that he was likely, if he were really bent on waking up the town, to begin with her. It did not please her to be wakened up. She looked at Mr. Billing anxiously. She wanted to know whether he were the kind of man who would be able to rouse her to unusual activity.

"Where I come from," said Mr. Billing, "I'm reckoned to hustle quite considerable. I'd rather like to try if I could get a move on your folks."'

"You can try," said Doyle. "I'd be glad if you'd try, for the place wants it."

No harm could possibly come of the effort; and it was likely to occupy Mr. Billing for several days. The prospect was gratifying to Doyle. A guest who travelled in a very large motorcar might be made to pay heavily for his rooms and his meals.

Five small boys came out of different houses up and down the street. When Mr. Billing, Doyle and Mary Ellen entered the hotel the boys drifted together towards the motorcar. They walked all round it. They peered cautiously into it. The boldest of them prodded the tyres with his fingers. The window of the office of the *Connacht Eagle* was opened, and Mr. Thaddeus Gallagher looked out Young Kerrigan emerged from the shelter of the body of the dead sheep and stood outside the shop. His father joined him. Both of them stared at the motorcar. Sergeant Colgan, followed by Constable Moriarty, stepped out of the police barrack and stalked majestically across the street. The sergeant frowned heavily at the small boys.

"Be off out of that, every one of yez," he said.

The small boys retreated at once. The law, in spite of all that is said to the contrary, is greatly respected in the west of Ireland. Sergeant Colgan would have made it respected anywhere. His appearance was far more impressive than that of any judge in his robes of office. Constable Moriarty, who was more than six feet high, was impressive too.

"That's a fine car," said the sergeant.

"It is," said Moriarty, "as fine a one as ever I seen."

"The man that owns it will be a high up man," said the sergeant.

"He will," said Moriarty.

The sergeant looked into the car. He gazed at the steering-wheel with interest. He glanced intelligently at the levers. His eyes rested finally on a speedometer.

"The like of that," he said, pointing it out to Moriarty, "is what I never seen before."

"I've heard of them," said Moriarty.

"There's a clock along with it," said the sergeant.

"The man that owns it," said Moriarty, "must have a power of money."

CHAPTER II

Doyle came out of the hotel. He joined the sergeant and Moriarty at the motorcar.

"Good-morning, sergeant," he said. "It's a fine day, thanks be to God. The people will only have themselves to thank if they don't get their hay saved this weather."

"What I'm after saying to Constable Moriarty," said the sergeant, "is that that's a fine car."

"You may say that," said Doyle.

"It'll be some high up gentleman that owns it," said the sergeant.

He paused. It was plainly the duty of Doyle to give some information about his guest. But Doyle remained silent.

"He'll have a power of money, whoever he is," said Moriarty.

He and the sergeant looked at Doyle and waited. Doyle still remained silent. The door of the office of the *Connacht Eagle* opened and Thaddeus Gallagher shambled along the street. He was a tall, grizzled man, exceedingly lean and ill-shaven. His clothes, which were shabby, hung round him in desponding folds. His appearance would have led a stranger to suppose that the *Connacht Eagle* was not a paying property. He greeted Sergeant Colgan and Moriarty with friendly warmth. When he had nothing else to write leading articles about he usually denounced the police, accusing them of various crimes, from the simple swearing away of the liberties of innocent men to the debauching of the morals of the young women of Ballymoy. But this civic zeal did not prevent his being on perfectly friendly terms with the members of the force. Nor did his strong writing rouse any feeling of resentment in the mind of the sergeant. He and Moriarty welcomed the editor warmly and invited him to inspect the car.

Thaddeus Gallagher looked at the car critically. He rubbed his hand along the dusty mud guard, opened and shut one of the doors, stroked the bulb of the horn cautiously, and then turned to Doyle.

"Is it the Lord-Lieutenant you have within in the hotel?" he asked.

He spoke with a fine suggestion of scorn in his voice. As a prominent local politician Thaddeus Gallagher was obliged to be contemptuous of Lords-Lieutenant. Doyle looked offended and at first made no reply. Sergeant Colgan, acting as peacemaker, spoke in a noncommittal, but soothing tone.

"It might be," he said, "it very well might be."

"It is not then," said Doyle. "Nor it's not the Chief Secretary."

"If it's not," said Gallagher, "it's some other of them fellows out of Dublin Castle."

"It's a high up gentleman surely," said Sergeant Colgan.

"And one that has money to spare," added Constable Moriarty. "It could be that he's one of the bosses of the Congested Districts Board. Them ones is well paid and has motors kept for them along with their salaries, so they tell me anyway."

Then Mary Ellen came out of the hotel. She stood at a little distance and smiled pleasantly at Constable Moriarty. Doyle turned on her.

"What is it that you want now, Mary Ellen?" he said. "Why aren't you within attending on the gentleman?"

"Sure I am," said Mary Ellen.

"You are not," said Doyle. "Don't I see you standing there grinning at Constable Moriarty?"

"He's after asking for his dinner," said Mary Ellen.

She referred of course to Mr. Billing. The suggestion that she was grinning at Moriarty was unworthy of her notice.

"And if he is," said Doyle, "why don't you give it to him?"

"What'll I give him?"

"Give him chops," said Doyle. "And if there's no chops in the house—and there may not be—run across to Kerrigan the butcher and ask him for a couple. It'll be quicker than killing a chicken; but that's what you'll have to do in the latter end if Kerrigan has no chops."

"It was only this morning," said Sergeant Colgan hopefully, "that Kerrigan killed a sheep."

Mary Ellen crossed the street towards Kerrigan's shop. Constable Moriarty winked at her as she passed. Mary Ellen was a good girl. She took no notice of the wink. The sergeant, unfortunately, did.

"Come along out of this, Constable Moriarty," he said. "Have you no duties to perform that you can afford to be standing there all day making faces at Mary Ellen? Come along now if you don't want me to report you."

Sergeant Colgan, though Gallagher insinuated evil things about him, was a man with a strict sense of propriety. He must have wanted very much to hear something more about Doyle's guest, but he marched off up the street followed by Moriarty. Doyle and Gallagher watched them until they were out of sight. Then Gallagher spoke again.

"If he isn't the Lord-Lieutenant," he said, "and if he isn't the Chief Secretary, will you tell me who he is?"

"It's my opinion," said Doyle, "that he's a Yank."

"I don't know that I've much of an opinion of Yanks," said Gallagher. "It's in my mind that the country would be better if there was fewer of them came back to us. What I say is this: What good are they? What do they do, only upset the minds of the people, teaching them to be disrespectful to the clergy and to use language the like of which decent people ought not to use?"

"It's my opinion that he is a Yank anyway," said Doyle.

Mary Ellen returned from Kerrigan's shop. She carried a small parcel, wrapped in newspaper. It contained two chops for Mr. Billing's dinner.

"Mary Ellen," said Doyle, "is it your opinion that the gentleman within is a Yank?"

"He might be," said Mary Ellen.

"Go you on in then," said Doyle, "and be cooking them chops for him. Why would you keep him waiting for his dinner and him maybe faint with the hunger?"

"And why would you say he was a Yank?" said Gallagher.

"Why would I say it? You'd say it yourself, Thady Gallagher if so be you'd heard the way he was talking. 'Is there a live man in the place at all?' says he, meaning Ballymoy. 'It's waking up you want.' says he."

"Did he? The devil take him," said Gallagher.

"'And I've a good mind to try and wake you up myself,' said he. 'I'm reckoned middling good at waking people up where I come from,' says he."

"Let him try," said Gallagher. "Let him try if it pleases him. We'll teach him."

Gallagher spoke with an impressive display of truculent self-confidence. He had at the moment no doubt whatever that he could subdue Mr. Billing or any other insolent American. His opportunity came almost at once. Mr. Billing appeared at the door of the hotel. He looked extraordinarily cool and competent. He also looked rather severe. His forehead was puckered to a frown. It seemed that he was slightly annoyed about something. Gallagher feared that his last remark might have been overheard. He shrank back a little, putting Doyle between him and Mr. Billing.

"Say," said Mr. Billing, "is there any way of getting a move on that hired girl of yours? It'll be time for breakfast to-morrow morning before she brings my lunch if some one doesn't hustle her a bit."

"Mary Ellen," shouted Doyle. "Mary Ellen, will you hurry up now and cook the gentleman's dinner?" Then he sank his voice. "She's frying the chops this minute," he said. "If you was to stand at the kitchen door you'd hear them in the pan."

Thaddeus Gallagher, reassured and confident that Mr. Billing had not overheard his threat, stepped forward and stood bowing, his hat in his hands. Wealthy Americans may be objectionable, but they are rare in the west of Ireland. Gallagher felt that he would like to know Mr. Billing. Doyle introduced him.

"This is Mr. Gallagher," he said. "Mr. Thaddeus Gallagher, J. P."

Mr. Billing bowed courteously and shook hands with Mr. Gallagher.

"Proud to meet you, sir," he said. "Proud to meet any prominent citizen of this section."

"Mr. Thady Gallagher," said Doyle, "is the proprietor of the *Connacht Eagle,* our principal newspaper."

The Connacht Eagle was, in fact, the only newspaper in Ballymoy. It was the only newspaper published within a radius of forty miles from Ballymoy.

It could therefore be quite truthfully called the principal one. Mr. Billing shook Thady Gallagher's hand again.

"I'm a newspaper man myself," he said. "I control two-thirds of the press in the state where I belong."

Thady Gallagher seemed greatly impressed by this statement. Doyle felt more than ever that his new guest was a man who ought to be treated with all possible consideration.

"It could be," he said, "that them chops would be ready for you now, and if you'll tell the girl what it is you'd like to drink——"

"When I've finished my lunch," said Mr. Billing, "I'd like to take a stroll round this section. There are some things I want to see. Perhaps Mr. Gallagher will come with me, if he can spare the time."

"Thady Gallagher will be pleased," said Doyle. "And as for sparing the time, he has plenty of that. You'll go with the gentleman, won't you, Thady?"

"I will, of course," said Gallagher.

"And there's no man knows the neighbourhood better," said Doyle. "There isn't one in it, man, woman, or child, that he isn't acquainted with, and anything there might be to tell about their fathers or mothers before them, Thady Gallagher is well fit to tell it to you.".

"What I'd like to be shown first," said Mr. Billing, "is the statue to the memory of General John Regan."

Doyle looked at Gallagher doubtfully. Gallagher edged away a little. He seemed inclined to take shelter again behind Doyle.

"The statue?" said Doyle.

"Statue or other memorial," said Mr. Billing.

"With regard to the statue— —" said Doyle slowly.

Then he turned round and caught Gallagher by the arm.

"Speak up, Thady Gallagher," he said, "and tell the gentleman about the statue."

"With reference to the statue— —" said Gallagher.

"Yes," said Mr. Billing encouragingly, "the statue to General John Regan."

"With reference to the statue of the deceased general," said Gallagher.

"What he's wanting to say," said Doyle, "is that at the present time there's no statue to the General, not in Ballymoy, anyway."

"You surprise me some," said Mr. Billing.

"It's what there ought to be," said Doyle, "and that's a fact."

"Is Ballymoy such a nursery of heroes," said Mr. Billing, "that you can afford to neglect the memory of the great General, the patriot statesman, the deliverer of Bolivia?"

"Speak up, Thady," said Doyle, "and tell the gentleman why there's no statue to the General in Ballymoy."

Gallagher cleared his throat and began to speak. At first his words came to him slowly; but as he warmed to his subject he became fluent and even eloquent.

"It's on account of the way we find ourselves situated in this country at the present time," he said. "It's not the hearts of the people that's at fault. There isn't one, not the poorest man among us, that wouldn't be willing to do honour to the memory of the great men of the past that died on the scaffold in defence of the liberty of the people. It's the cursed system of Castle Government and the tyranny of the landlords, and the way the people is driven off their farms by the rack-renting flunkeys of the rent office. How is the country to prosper, and how is statues to be erected to them that deserve statues, so long as the people isn't able to call their souls their own? But, glory be to God, it won't be so for long! We have Home Rule as good as got, and when we have it— —"

Gallagher might have gone on speaking for a long time. He was a man of tried and practised eloquence. He had arrived without much effort at his favourite subject. Fragments of old speeches, glowing periods, oft-repeated perorations thronged confusedly on his memory. Mr. Billing seemed to be listening with sympathy and admiration. It might be a long time before such a favourable opportunity for making a speech came to Gallagher again. Unfortunately he was interrupted. Mary Ellen had come, unperceived, out of the hotel. She was at Mr. Billing's elbow just when Gallagher reached his prophecy about Home Rule. She spoke without the slightest regard for the orator's feelings.

"The chops is fried," she said.

Doyle had often heard his friend make speeches before. He had no wish to be subjected to unnecessary oratory on a very hot day. He supported Mary Ellen's appeal.

"It would be as well for you," he said, "to go and eat them, the way they won't be getting cold on you."

Mr. Billing saw the wisdom of this advice at once. He turned to go into the hotel. But he evidently wanted to hear more of Thady Gallagher's speech.

"When I've finished my lunch," he said, "I shall look forward to a long talk with Mr. Gallagher. I want to gather together all the local traditions which survive about the boyhood of the great General. I'm writing his biography, gentlemen. I need say no more."

"Mary Ellen," said Doyle, "whatever the gentleman fancies in the way of a drink, will you see that he gets it?"

Mary Ellen, smiling pleasantly, walked in front of Mr. Billing and conducted him to the small ill-lighted room which Doyle called the Commercial Room of his hotel. There, on a very dirty table cloth, were a knife and fork, a plate which held two chops with a quantity of grease round them, and a dish with five pallid potatoes in it. The meal was not appetising. On a very hot day it was almost repulsive. But Mr. Billing was either really hungry or he was a man of unusual determination. He sat down to his chops with a smile.

"I guess," he said, "that whisky is the drink you're most likely to have in this hotel?"

"There's porter," said Mary Ellen, "and there's minerals, and there's ginger cordial."

"If I'm here for a week," said Mr. Billing, "I'll put you wise in the matter of making cocktails. A Saratoga cocktail is a drink— —"

"Is it whisky I'll bring you now?" said Mary Ellen.

She was a girl of sense and wisdom. She was no more inclined to listen to Mr. Billing's panegyric of the Saratoga cocktail than to Thady Gallagher's patriotic denunciation of the flunkeys of the rent office. Without waiting for an answer she went away and brought Mr. Billing the usual quantity of Irish whisky in the bottom of a tumbler with a bottle of soda water.

Doyle and Thady Gallagher, left alone in the street, stared at each other in silence. It was Doyle who spoke first:

"What you want, Thady," he said, "is a drop of something to drink, to revive the courage in you."

"What sort of a fellow is that at all?" said Thady hoarsely.

"A pint of porter, now," said Doyle, "or a drop of spirits. You want it this minute, and you'll want it more before, you're through with the job that you have on hand."

He led the way into the bar and provided Thady with a satisfying draught. Thady emptied the tumbler without drawing breath. Then he took his pipe from his pocket and lit it.

"Mr. Doyle," he said, "you're a man I've a liking for and always had. What's more, you're a man I respect, and it isn't everyone that I would say that to."

"The same to you," said Doyle, "and may you live long to enjoy it. Will you have another drop?"

"I don't mind if I do," said Thady.

Doyle filled up the empty tumbler. As he did so Gallagher spoke with serious deliberation.

"Seeing that you're a man I've every confidence in, I'd be glad if you'd tell me this. Who was General John Regan? For I never heard tell of him."

"It'll be better for you, Thady, to know something about him be the same more or less, before the gentleman within has finished his dinner. He'll be asking questions of you the whole of the rest of the day."

"Let him ask."

"And you'll have to be answering him, for he'll not rest contented without you do."

"There's no Regans here," said Gallagher, "and what's more there never was."

"There's no statue anyway," said Doyle, "nor there won't be."

"I don't know that there'd be any harm in a statue," said Gallagher. "What has me bothered is who the General was."

"There'll be no statue," said Doyle. "It's all very well to be talking, but the rates is too high already without an extra penny in the pound for a statue that nobody wants."

"I wouldn't be in favour of a statue myself," said Gallagher, "unless, of course, the gentleman was to pay for it himself, and he might."

"Of course if he was to pay for it, it would be different. By the look of the motorcar he came in I'd say he'd plenty of money."

The idea that Mr. Billing could pay for a statue was a pleasant one, and it was always possible that he might do so. He appeared to be very anxious that there should be a statue.

"There's some men," said Doyle hopefully, "that has no sense in the way they spend what money they've got."

Mr. Gallagher admitted with a sigh that there are such men. He himself had no money, or very little. If, as he hoped, he succeeded in becoming a Member of Parliament, he would have money, large quantities of it, a full £400 a year. He would have more sense than to spend any of it in erecting statues. Doyle, on the other hand, had money. He lent it freely, at a high rate of interest, to the other inhabitants of Ballymoy. This was his idea of the proper use of money. To spend it on works of public utility or sentimental value, struck him as very foolish.

"I'd be glad, all the same," said Gallagher, "if I knew who the General was that he's talking about."

"It could be," said Doyle hopefully, "that he was one of them ones that fought against the Government at the time of Wolfe Tone."

"He might, of course. But the gentleman was saying something about Bolivia."

"Where's that at all?" said Doyle.

Thady Gallagher did not know. Editors of newspapers are supposed to know everything and have succeeded in impressing the public with the idea that they do, but there are probably a few things about which even the ablest editor has to refer to encyclopedias; and Gallagher was not by any means at the top of his profession. The *Connacht Eagle* was indeed a paper which exercised a very great influence on the minds of those who read it, more influence, perhaps, than even *The Times* has on its subscribers. For the readers of Gallagher's leading articles and columns of news were still in that primitive stage of culture in which every statement made in print is accepted as certainly true, whereas the subscribers to *The Times* have been educated into an unworthy kind of scepticism. Also the readers of the *Connacht Eagle* read little or nothing else, while those who read *The Times* usually glance at one or two other papers as well, and even waste their time and unsettle their minds by dipping into books. Thus, in spite of the fact that *The Times* appears every day, and the *Connacht Eagle* only once a week, it is likely that the Irish paper exercises more real influence than the English one—produces, that is to say, more definite effect upon the opinions of men who have votes. The editor of *The Times* would perhaps scarcely recognise Thady Gallagher as a fellow journalist. He may know—would probably in any case be ashamed to admit that he did not know—where Bolivia is. Thady Gallagher did not know, and was prepared to confess his ignorance in private to his friend. Yet Gallagher was in reality the more important man of the two.

"I know as much about Bolivia," he said, "as I do about the General, and that's nothing at all."

"I'm glad it's you and not me," said Doyle, "that he took the fancy to go out walking with."

"I suppose now," said Gallagher, "that you wouldn't come along with us."

"I will not," said Doyle, "so you may make your mind easy about that."

"I don't see what harm it would do you."

"I've things to look after," said Doyle, "and anyway I don't fancy spending my time talking about a dead General that nobody ever heard of."

"It's what I feel myself," said Gallagher.

"You may feel it," said Doyle, "but you'll have to go with him. It was you he asked and not me."

CHAPTER III

Dr. Lucius O'Grady is the only medical man in Ballymoy. Whatever money there is to be won by the practice of the art of healing in the neighbourhood, Dr. O'Grady wins and has all to himself. Unfortunately it is not nearly sufficient for his needs. He is not married and so cannot plead a wife and family as excuses for getting into debt. But he is a man of imaginative mind with an optimistic outlook upon life. Men of this kind hardly ever live within their incomes, however large their incomes are; and Dr. O'Grady's was really small. The dullard does not want things which the man of lively imagination feels that he must have. The sour man of gloomy disposition is forever haunted by the possibility of misfortune. He hoards whatever pittance he may earn. Dr. O'Grady had good spirits and a delightful confidence in life. He spent all, and more than all he had, feeling sure that the near future held some great good fortune for him—a deadly epidemic perhaps, which would send all the people of Ballymoy flocking to his surgery, or a post under the new Insurance Act The very qualities of mind which made him improvident made him also immensely popular. Everybody liked him. Even his creditors found it hard to speak harshly to him. He owed money to Doyle; but Doyle, though as keen as any man living on getting what was due to him, refrained from hurrying Dr. O'Grady over much. He grumbled a great deal, but he allowed the account in the shop attached to the hotel to run on. He even advanced sums of hard cash when some distant creditor, a Dublin tailor, for instance, who did not appreciate the doctor's personal charm, became importunate. Between what was due in the shop for tea, sugar, whisky, tobacco, and other necessaries, and the money actually lent, Dr. O'Grady owed Doyle rather more than £60. He owed Gallagher more than £1, being five years' subscription to the *Connacht Eagle*. He owed a substantial sum to Kerrigan, the butcher. He owed something to every other shopkeeper in Ballymoy. The only people to whom he did not owe money were Major Kent, Mr. Gregg, the District Inspector of Police, and Mr. Ford, the stipendiary magistrate. No one could have owed money to Mr. Ford because he was a hard and suspicious man who never lent anything. Nobody could have borrowed from Mr. Gregg, because Mr. Gregg, who had just got married, had no money to lend. Major Kent had a little money and would have lent it to Dr. O'Grady, would, in fact, have given it to him without any hope of ever getting it back again, but the doctor refused to borrow from him. He had a conscientious objection to victimising his personal friends. Doyle, so he explained, lived very largely by lending money, and therefore offered himself as fair game to the impecunious borrower. The shopkeepers throve on a system of credit. They were fair game too. Major Kent was in a different case. To borrow from him was to take a mean advantage of the good nature of a simple, unprofessional man.

Major Kent and Dr. O'Grady walked into Ballymoy together at about half past two on the day of Mr. Billing's arrival. They had lunched at Portsmouth Lodge, the Major's house. Dr. O'Grady had given his opinion of a new filly which the Major had bought a few days before. It was a very unfavourable opinion, and the Major, who had the greatest confidence in the doctor's judgment, was duly depressed.

"If I were you, Major," said the doctor, "I'd sell that one at once. She's no good."

"I'd sell her fast enough," said the Major gloomily, "if I could find a buyer."

"It was £30 you gave for her in the fair?" said the doctor.

"It was; and if you're right about her she's not worth the half of it. She's not worth £12."

"I happen to know that fellow Geraghty," said the doctor. "The man who stuck you with her. He's a patient of mine. I pulled him through his last attack of d. t.'s so I know all there is to know about him. He'd stick an archangel. If he happened to be selling him a pair of wings it would turn out afterwards that the feathers were dropping out."

"If you know him," said the Major, "you know a blackguard."

"After sticking you with the filly," said the doctor, "he spent the evening drinking in the hotel."

"He would."

"And the more he drank the bigger the price was that he said he got from you. When Doyle turned him out in the end he was saying that he had your cheque for £60 in his pocket. I don't suppose Doyle believed that. Nobody would. But he probably thinks you gave £40 or £45."

"All I gave was £30. But I don't see that it matters what Doyle believes."

"It does matter," said Dr. O'Grady. "If Doyle believes you gave £40 for the filly, and if you were to offer her to him for £35 he'd think he was getting a bargain and he'd jump at it. Doyle's just the kind of fool who thinks he knows all about horses and so he's quite an easy man to stick. Come on now, and we'll try."

Major Kent was in all ordinary affairs of life a strictly honourable man. But horses are not ordinary affairs. It is on record that a bishop, an Irishman and therefore intensely religious, once sold a thoroughly unsound horse to an archdeacon for a large price. The archdeacon had a high opinion of the bishop beforehand, regarding him as a saintly man of childlike simplicity. He had a much higher opinion of him after he understood the failings of the animal he had bought. He then respected the bishop for his shrewdness. Horse-dealing is a thing apart from all other buying and selling. Honesty, in the common sense of the word, does not enter into it. Therefore, Major Kent was quite ready to defraud Doyle if he could. He and Dr. O'Grady walked into Ballymoy together for the purpose.

They reached the corner of the market square and caught sight of Mr. Billing's large motorcar standing outside the hotel. Doyle and Gallagher, who had stopped drinking, were standing near it.

"If Doyle's bought that motor," said the Major, "he won't look at the filly."

"He hasn't," said the doctor. "What would he do with the motor if he had it? All the same it's queer. I don't know what it's doing there. Nobody with money enough to own a car like that could possibly be stopping at Doyle's Hotel. Come along and let's find out about it."

They hurried across the square and greeted Doyle and Gallagher.

"Whose is the big motor?" said Dr. O'Grady.

"It belongs to an American gentleman," said Doyle, "who's within in the hotel. We're waiting for him this minute. He's getting his camera, and when he has it got he's going round with Thady Gallagher to photograph the town."

Gallagher took Major Kent by the arm and drew him apart.

"Major," he said, "can you tell me who was General John Regan?"

"Never heard of him," said the Major, "but if he owns that car he must be a middling well-off man."

"Look here, Doyle," said Dr. O'Grady, "you know that filly the Major bought at the fair."

"I've heard of her," said Doyle.

"Well, as it happens," said Dr. O'Grady, "she turns out to be a bit too good for what he wants. His idea was to get something to do a bit of carting, and it turns out that this one is—well, she has breeding. Now, look here, Doyle———"

He led Doyle apart just out of earshot of the Major and Gallagher.

"I owe you a trifle, don't I, Doyle?"

"As near as I can go to it without looking at my books," said Doyle, "you owe me £60, and I'd be thankful if so be that it's quite convenient to you——"

"It isn't a bit convenient," said Dr. O'Grady, "but I quite admit that I owe the money. Now what I suggest is this. I've persuaded the Major to let you have that filly cheap, dirt cheap. It will be found money to you, Doyle, if you get her at the price the Major's going to name, and you may be able to knock a pound or two off that. Under these circumstances and seeing that I'm putting the chance in your way—it isn't everyone that could, but I'm a friend of the Major's and he trusts me—I think you ought to stop talking about the trifle I owe you. I'm sick of the subject."

"You're not near as sick of it as I am," said Doyle, "and I don't know that I want the filly."

"You do want her," said Dr. O'Grady. "You want anything that you can make money out of. Hullo! Who's that?"

Mr. Billing, carrying his camera, appeared at the door of the hotel.

"It's the American gentleman that owns the motorcar," said Doyle. "Tell me this now, doctor. Did ever you hear of General John Regan?"

"Of course I did," said Dr. O'Grady. "He's a well-known millionaire, just the sort of man to be touring the country in a big motor. Go you off now and settle with the Major about the filly. I'll entertain the General for you."

"For God's sake, doctor, be careful what you say," said Doyle in a whisper. "The General's dead this twenty years and it's a statue there ought to be to his memory. So that fellow's after saying, any way."

"Oh, all right," said Dr. O'Grady. "It's just the same thing. I'll manage. You go and settle with the Major."

He approached Mr. Billing jauntily.

"Delighted to meet you, sir," he said. "Delighted to welcome you to Ballymoy. You'll find it a most interesting locality. My name is O'Grady, Lucius O'Grady, M.D."

Mr. Billing took off his hat, laid down his camera, and shook hands with the doctor.

"Mine is Billing," he said. "Horace P. Billing. I come from America. My object in visiting Ballymoy——"

"The poor old General, of course," said Dr. O'Grady. "We thought you'd be sure to come sooner or later. Your uncle, wasn't he, or great uncle? I forget."

Mr. Billing seemed surprised, very much surprised. He dropped Dr. O'Grady's hand abruptly and stared at him. Then he recovered himself with an effort.

"I can't claim relationship with that great man," he said.

"That's a pity," said Dr. O'Grady.

"I'm his biographer," said Mr. Billing. "I'm engaged in writing the first complete life of the founder of the Bolivian Republic. I have come to Ballymoy— —"

"You couldn't possibly have come to a better place."

Dr. O'Grady was not a literary man, but he had an idea that people who write books seek out quiet places in which they are not likely to be over excited while engaged in their trying work. Ballymoy seemed to him a suitable place for anyone engaged in writing a biography.

"It surprises me some," said Mr. Billing, "to find that you've no statue erected to the memory of the General. I'd have thought— —"

"The matter is under discussion," said Dr. O'Grady. "Our Urban District Council is alive to its duty in the matter. At the last meeting—let me see now, was it the last meeting? Gallagher! Thady Gallagher! Come here for a minute."

Thady Gallagher, who had been acting as umpire in an animated wrangle between Doyle and Major Kent, shambled across to the door of the hotel where Dr. O'Grady and Mr. Billing were standing.

"Was it the last meeting of the Urban District Council," said Dr. O'Grady, "or was it the last but one, that you were discussing the erection of a statue to General John Regan?"

He did not venture to wink as he asked the question, but Gallagher was quite quick-witted enough to give the proper answer.

"It was the last meeting," he said.

"There was a slight difference of opinion among the members," said Dr. O'Grady, "as to the form which the memorial was to take. Some of them wanted a life-size statue in white marble. Mr. Gallagher here was more in favour of a drinking fountain. It was you who wanted the fountain wasn't it, Thady?"

"It was," said Gallagher.

"As a cheaper form of memorial," said Dr. O'Grady, "so as to spare the rates as far as possible."

"That's right," said Gallagher.

"If you will allow me to say so," said Mr. Billing, "the question of expense ought not to be allowed to stand in your way. I myself will gladly promise— —"

Mr. Billing hesitated for a moment. It was not clear whether he meant to promise a handsome subscription or merely to say that he would help in collecting the necessary money. Dr. O'Grady thought it well to assume at once that a subscription had been promised.

"Good," he said, "take note of that, Thady, and announce it to the Urban District Council at the next meeting. Mr. Billing will hand over his subscription to the treasurer as soon as one is appointed. You can arrange about a proper vote of thanks being passed."

Mr. Billing seemed quite pleased at this interpretation of his unfinished sentence. He went on to make another promise.

"And I think I may safely guarantee," he said, "on behalf of the people of Bolivia— —they can never forget— —"

"They oughtn't to," said the doctor. "After all he did more for them than he ever did for us."

"He was born here," said Mr. Billing, "and that's something to be proud of."

"And we are proud of it. Thady Gallagher is having an article in his paper next week saying how much we appreciate the dear old General. Aren't you, Thady?"

"I am, of course," said Gallagher.

Then, lest he should be committed any further, Gallagher slipped away and joined Major Kent and Doyle. They were standing together near the motorcar in high debate as to whether the price of the filly was to be £30 or £34. The Major had abated one pound of the price he asked at first. Doyle had, so far, resisted every effort to induce him to make an advance upon his original offer. They were both enjoying themselves greatly. But Gallagher interrupted them.

"The doctor knows all about him," he said, "thanks be to God he's— —"

"She's a filly," said Doyle, "and I know as much about her as the doctor does."

He had for the moment forgotten his American guest, and was thinking only of the animal which Major Kent was trying to sell him.

"It's the General I'm talking about," said Gallagher in an aggrieved tone, "and the doctor says there's to be an article on the paper about him next week. But if there is the doctor may write it himself. It'll be easy for him seeing he knows who the General was."

"He does not know any more than the rest of us," said Doyle. "Didn't he say a minute ago he was a well-known millionaire?"

"He knows now, anyway," said Gallagher, "and what's more he says that the Urban District Council has been talking about erecting a statue to him."

"Erecting a statue to who?" said the Major.

"To General John Regan, of course," said Gallagher.

"But sure there was no such talk," said Doyle, "not that I heard of, anyway."

"There was not," said Gallagher, "but there will be now; and there might have been. There's no denying that there might have been."

"Doyle," said the Major anxiously. "We must finish settling the price of the filly later on. I'm nervous, I'm confoundedly nervous about what the doctor may be doing. You never know what wild idea he may take into his head, or what he may let us all in for."

"He's all right," said Gallagher. "Don't I tell you he's arranging with the American gentleman?"

"He may be getting us all into some mess or other. You never know what the doctor will be at. He's so infernally imaginative."

Mr. Billing and Dr. O'Grady had left the door of the hotel. They were standing together in the middle of the square almost opposite the police barrack. Major Kent hurried towards them. Doyle and Gallagher followed him slowly.

"What's this talk about a statue?" said Doyle. "Didn't I tell you before that I'd agree to no statue? Isn't the rates high enough already without that? And don't I have to pay more of them than any other man in the town?"

"There'll be no addition to the rates," said Gallagher. "The way the doctor was fixing it up it'll be the American gentleman that'll pay for the statue. He's just after saying he will, and the Urban District Council is to pass a vote of thanks to him, which is what they'll be glad to do, and I'll draw it up myself."

"Of course," said Doyle, slightly mollified, "if he pays the cost of it there'll be no objection to the statue. But are you sure now that he's fit? Statues cost a deal."

"Look at the motorcar he came in," said Gallagher.

The motor seemed conclusive evidence. It was a very splendid vehicle. Doyle hurried forward. A stranger who proposed to spend large sums of money in the town deserved to be treated with every kind of politeness and respect. A statue still struck Doyle as an exceedingly useless thing; but he was not without hope that Mr. Billing might be persuaded to give his money, if he really wanted to give money, to some more sensible object.

Dr. O'Grady introduced Major Kent to Mr. Billing.

"Our principal resident gentleman," he said, "a J. P. and a strong Unionist. Gallagher, of course, is a Home Ruler. But these little political differences of opinion don't really matter. They're both equally keen on doing their duty to the memory of the great General."

"What's that?" said the Major. "What General are you talking about?"

"General John Regan," said Dr. O'Grady.

"Who? What?" said the Major.

"Don't give yourself away now, Major," said Dr. O'Grady, in a whisper. "Don't let Mr. Billing find out that you've never heard of the General. You ought to have heard of him. The Major," he said aloud, "isn't as well up in the General's history as he might be. He hasn't studied the details of his campaigns; but he quite agrees with the rest of us that there ought to be a statue to his memory."

"Dr. O'Grady has just informed me," said Mr. Billing, "that the centre of this square is the site that has been selected by your Urban District Council."

"The very spot we're standing on at the present moment," said Dr. O'Grady. "The Major has promised £5, which shows how keen he is on the project. Don't say you haven't, Major. We all know that you're a modest man, doing good by stealth and blushing to find it known. But a public subscription can't be kept secret. Sooner or later the list of subscribers will have to be published. Doyle," he looked round as he spoke and saw Doyle and Gallagher standing near him. "Doyle has promised another £5. He ought to be giving more, and I daresay he will in the end. He's a much richer man than the Major, though he doesn't look it. Gallagher is good for another pound. It doesn't sound much from a newspaper editor, but it's as much as he can afford. Half the advertisements in his paper aren't paid for at all. Father McCormack—he's the parish priest, and we haven't asked him yet, but he'll put down his name for £10 at least. He always supports every kind of good work liberally."

"Gentlemen," said Mr. Billing, "you may put me down for five hundred dollars."

Doyle and Gallagher drew pieces of paper and pencils from their pockets. They did sums rapidly, Doyle on the back of an old envelope,

Gallagher on a sheet of paper already covered with shorthand notes. Dr. O'Grady worked his sum in his head. He arrived at his answer first.

"A hundred pounds!" he said. "A generous subscription!"

"It's more than a hundred," said Doyle. "What do you make it, Thady?"

"Counting 4s. 2d. to the dollar," said Gallagher, "it comes to———"

"There's a halfpenny along with that," said Doyle, "as often as not."

"Anyway," said Gallagher, "it won't be less than £104 3s. 4d."

"The Urban District Council," said Doyle, "will take a delight in passing that vote of thanks to Mr. Billing at its next meeting, and it'll be a good strong vote, won't it, Thady?"

"As strong as ever any one that was passed about the landlords," said Gallagher, "only different, of course, mighty different."

"Look here, O'Grady," said Major Kent. "What do you mean by saying that I'm going to subscribe £5? Who is this General you're all talking about?"

"Do shut up, Major," said Dr. O'Grady. "Everything's all right if you'll only keep quiet. As you've got a camera with you, Mr. Billing," he went on, "you might like to take a photograph of that house opposite you. It was there that the great General——"

"Glory be to God," said Gallagher, "it's the police barrack!"

"The birthplace of the great General?" said Mr. Billing, taking off his hat.

"Not exactly," said Dr. O'Grady. "Thady Gallagher will show you his birthplace this afternoon. This is the house in which he spent his early youth, up to the age of eleven years."

"Excuse me," said Mr. Billing. "I'll just get my camera. A view of that house will be most interesting. I certainly ought to have it for my biography."

He crossed the road to the hotel and picked up his camera. He carried it to the middle of the square and set up the tripod legs. Then he screwed the camera into its place.

"O'Grady," said Major Kent, angrily. "I don't want to make a public exposure of you before a total stranger, but if you don't stop trying to make fools of us all———"

"I don't know what you're talking about, Major," said the doctor. "I'm not making a fool of anyone. I'm helping to persuade Mr. Billing to erect a statue in this town. You can't deny that a statue would be an improvement to the place."

"A statue!" said the Major. "Who to?"

"Good Heavens!" said Dr. O'Grady, "haven't you grasped that yet? To General John Regan."

Mr. Billing had his head under a black cloth. He was screwing the lens of his camera backwards and forwards and appeared to be entirely absorbed in his photography.

"Tell me now, doctor," said Doyle, "before we go further into the matter—— Mind you, I'm not saying a word against what you're doing, but I'd be glad to know who was General John Regan."

"If I'm to show the American gentleman the birthplace of the General," said Gallagher, "I'll need to know where it is. Will you tell me this now, doctor, where was the General born?"

"I haven't time," said Dr. O'Grady, "to give you all elementary lectures on modern history; and I certainly haven't the temper to spend all day hammering into your heads simple facts which——"

"Facts!" said the Major.

"Go home, Major," said Dr. O'Grady. "You've no tact, and in an affair of this kind where the highest kind of diplomacy is necessary, you're not only useless, you're actually dangerous. Now, Doyle, do you or do you not want to have the handling of that American gentleman's £100? You do, of course. Very well then. Leave the matter in my hands and don't annoy me by asking frivolous questions. Thady, the birthplace of the General is one of those ruined cottages—it doesn't in the least matter which—on the grass farm where Doyle has his cattle ever since you and your League prevented anyone else taking the place. You ought to have known that without bothering me. Good Heavens! Here's the police sergeant coming to ask questions now."

Sergeant Colgan and Constable Moriarty were approaching at a rapid walk.

"Begging your pardon, doctor," said the sergeant, "but is that a camera that the gentleman has, and is he thinking of taking a picture of the barrack?"

"He is," said the doctor, "but he's not photographing it as a barrack at all. He's doing it in an entirely different spirit. So there's no necessity for you to start any theory about his being a German spy, or to raise stupid objections."

"I wasn't thinking of objecting," said the sergeant. "It makes no matter to me what notion he has in his head. But what Constable Moriarty was saying to me this minute——" he hesitated, and then added, "speak up now, Moriarty."

"What the sergeant said to me," said Moriarty, "as soon as ever he seen the gentleman with the camera——"

"It wasn't me passed the remark," said the sergeant, "but yourself. I'll not have it put out that I was the one——"

Mr. Billing, standing bare-headed beside his camera, squeezed a yellow bulb and clicked the shutter of his lens. He turned smiling.

"A successful photograph, I hope, gentlemen," he said. "The people of Bolivia will be interested to see it. It will adorn the first volume of the General's life."

"There!" said Dr. O'Grady to Sergeant Colgan. "That comes of not speaking out promptly. The photograph is taken now and whatever remark it was that you or Moriarty made will be entirely wasted."

"It's a pity, so it is," said the sergeant, "for what Constable Moriarty was after saying——"

"What the sergeant said," said Moriarty, "is that he'd be glad if the gentleman would take him along with the barrack."

"It's not often," said the sergeant, "that we have anyone taking photographs round in these parts, and Constable Moriarty would have been pleased to be took on account of being able to send the photo after to a young lady that he is acquainted with up in Dublin."

"There's no young lady up in Dublin," said Moriarty sulkily.

Dr. O'Grady was a man of quick sympathy and a kind heart. He realised at once that both Sergeant Colgan and Constable Moriarty wanted to have their photographs taken.

"Go over to the door of the barrack," he said, "and arrange yourselves in such a way as to look as ornamental as possible. I'll try to get the gentleman to take another photograph."

Mr. Billing had slipped his dark slide into his pocket, and was unscrewing his camera from its stand. Dr. O'Grady called to him.

"I'm afraid," he said, "that you got your photograph wrong."

"Mistake about the house," said Mr. Billing. "Well, it can't be helped. Which is the right one?"

"Not exactly that," said Dr. O'Grady. "You've got the proper house, but the Major has just reminded me——"

"I did not," said Major Kent.

"Well, if it wasn't you it was Thady. Thady Gallagher has just reminded me that the top storey wasn't built when the General lived there. The Government added it afterwards when the place was bought for a police barrack. What you ought to do if you want to get the thing absolutely right is to take another photograph and make sure that the top storey doesn't come into it."

"I'm greatly obliged to you," said Mr. Billing. "I'll expose a second plate."

He arranged his camera again. Sergeant Colgan and Moriarty settled themselves in stiff attitudes, one on each side of the barrack door.

"Am I to take the two policemen as well?" said Mr. Billing, looking out from beneath his black cloth.

"You may as well," said Dr. O'Grady. "It will interest the Bolivians to see how this country is overrun with what Thady Gallagher calls the armed forces of an alien power."

"What I say is this," said Thady Gallagher, grasping at his opportunity, "so long as the people of this country is kept in subjection and the cursed system of landlordism is supported——"

"Look here, O'Grady," said Major Kent, angrily, "I can't be expected to stand this."

"It's all right, Major," said Dr. O'Grady. "It's only poor old Thady. You know jolly well he doesn't mean a word of it."

"As long as the sacredness of our homes is invaded," said Gallagher, "and the virtues of our families corrupted by the overfed minions of the landlord class——"

"Oh, do shut up, Thady," said the doctor. "We all know that stuff off by heart, and you must try to recollect that the Major's a Unionist. He can't be expected to listen to you peaceably; and if we don't run this statue business on strictly non-political lines we'll never be able to carry it through."

"Whisht now, Thady, whisht," said Doyle soothingly; "sure the sergeant is doing you no harm."

Mr. Billing clicked his shutter again. Sergeant Colgan and Constable Moriarty relapsed from their strained attitudes and breathed freely.

"Got the lower storey all right?" said Dr. O'Grady. "Good. I daresay now you'd like to toddle around with Thady Gallagher and see the General's birthplace. I'm sorry I can't go with you myself, but I happen to be rather busy. There are two old women with rheumatism expecting bottles from me in the course of the afternoon."

"I'll fold up the camera," said Mr. Billing, "and start at once."

"Doctor," said Gallagher anxiously, "what'll I do when he starts asking me questions about the General?"

"Answer him, of course," said Dr. O'Grady.

"How can I, when I never heard tell of the General till to-day. For the love of God, doctor dear, will you tell me who he was?"

"Thady," said the doctor, "I'm ashamed of you. Aren't you a politician? You are, and well you know it. Aren't you a newspaper editor? You are, there's no use denying it. Don't you spend your whole life either talking or writing on subjects that you know nothing about? You do. And what on earth's the use of your pretending now that you can't answer a few simple questions about General John Regan? There now, he's got his camera folded up and he's waiting for you. Be off at once."

CHAPTER IV

Motorcars are even yet far from common in the west of Ireland. They are not, for instance, used in elections as they are in England. There very seldom are elections in the west of Ireland; but even if these entertainments were, as frequent as elsewhere motorcars would not be used in them. This is partly because the Irish voter is recognised as incorruptible, not the kind of man who would allow his vote to be influenced by a ride in an unaccustomed vehicle; partly because the west of Ireland candidate for Parliament is not rich enough to keep a motorcar himself, and has no friends or supporters who could lend him anything more expensive than a horse. Therefore motor drives are an unknown luxury to most Connacht men. Thady Gallagher, though he was a newspaper editor, had never travelled even in the side car of a motor-cycle. When Mr. Billing made it clear that he meant to go to the General's birthplace in his large car everybody felt slightly envious of Gallagher, and Doyle wished that he had not refused to join the expedition. Gallagher himself was not elated by his good fortune. He was embarrassed and depressed. He cast an appealing glance at Doyle.

"What am I to do, at all?" he said. "What am I to say to him when——?"

"If you've any sense," said Doyle, "you'll take a good long drive now you have the chance. He doesn't know the way. What's to hinder you from taking him round every road within ten miles of the town?"

But the prospect did not cheer Gallagher. He tried to grasp Dr. O'Grady's arm as he passed him. But the doctor shook him off impatiently. He even attempted an appeal to Major Kent, quite vainly. The Major was still smarting under the rhetorical denunciation of landlords. He would not at that moment have gone a step out of his way to rescue Gallagher from drowning.

The moment the motorcar was out of sight Major Kent and Doyle turned hotly on Dr. O'Grady.

"What the devil do you mean, O'Grady," said the Major, "by talking in this absurd way? You know perfectly well——"

Doyle spoke at the same time.

"It's a curious thing, so it is, doctor," he said. "It's a curious thing that you'd be letting me in for £5 when you know the loss I'm in on account of you already. I'd have thought——"

Dr. O'Grady interrupted them both.

"Suppose you agree to split the difference," he said, "and say £32 10s. for the filly. It's a pity to see two men like you losing your tempers over a bargain."

"It's not the bargain," said Doyle, "that has my temper riz. It's— —"

"Doyle can have the filly if he likes," said the Major, "at £32 10s. I don't want to go on wrangling about that. What I want to know— —"

"I'll take her," said Doyle.

Major Kent smiled faintly. He was getting out of what threatened to be a very bad bargain with an actual gain of £2 10s. He began to recover command of his temper. Doyle also smiled. He believed that he was buying for £32 10s. an animal for which Major Kent had paid £40 three days before. He felt kindly disposed towards Dr. O'Grady, who had put the chance of such a bargain in his way.

"Now, Major," said the doctor, "you trot along to my house while I speak a word or two to Doyle. I'll be round with you in about ten minutes, and give you some tea."

"But about that General?" said the Major, "I'd rather like to know— —"

He still wanted to know about General John Regan. But the tone in which he asked for information had changed. He no longer seemed to threaten.

"I'll explain all that to you if you'll only do as I tell you," said Dr. O'Grady. "At present I can't because I'm going to explain it to Doyle."

"Why can't you explain it to both of us at once?" said the Major. "That is to say if there is any explanation of the way you've been going on."

"There are two explanations," said Dr. O'Grady, "one for you and one for Doyle. I can't give them both at once, because they're different. I should have thought you'd have seen that for yourself."

"I don't see how there can be two explanations," said the Major, "not two true ones. But of course they're neither of them that."

"They're both quite true," said Dr. O'Grady, "but they're different, of course, because you and Doyle look at everything from such different points of view. Now do trot along, Major, and don't interrupt me any more. That American may be back at any moment. I don't believe Gallagher will be able to keep him in play for very long."

He took Major Kent by the shoulders as he spoke and pushed him some little way along the street. Then he returned to Doyle.

"Now then, Doyle," he said, "you've done pretty well over that filly. Strictly speaking, you owe me £7 10s. But I'm not going to say a word about that."

"Seeing that you owe me £60," said Doyle, "it'll maybe be as well for you not."

"What I do want to talk about," said Dr. O'Grady, "is General John Regan."

"If you tell me who he was," said Doyle, "I'll be content."

"I don't see that it matters in the least to you who he was. Look here now, Doyle. You're a business man, and among other things you sell whisky. Now suppose someone was to walk into your hotel and tell you to forward ten dozen bottles of whisky—the best you had—to his aunt, and supposing that he told his aunt's name was Regan, would you go questioning and cross-questioning every man you met as to whether there really was an old lady called Miss Regan at the address he gave you?"

"I would not," said Doyle. "So long as I got my money I wouldn't care whether the fellow ever had an aunt, or what sort of a name there might be to her if he had."

"Well, this is exactly the same sort of case. Here's a man who wants a statue for a dead General, and is perfectly willing to pay for it. Why should you bother your head about who the statue is supposed to represent? £100 is £100, I suppose, even if there never was a Regan in the world; and there have been, plenty of them."

"I see that," said Doyle. "I see that, now you put it to me. And I don't deny but there's a lot in what you say. But what I don't see is this: I'd make something out of the whisky for the gentleman's aunt, but I don't understand how I'm to make a penny out of the statue."

"You'll be treasurer of the fund," said Dr. O'Grady, "and I needn't tell you that in all these cases the treasurer—well, there might be a little balance in hand at the end. There often is. Nobody ever inquires about those balances. If the treasurers are fools they lie in the banks and nobody ever gets any good of them. But you're not a fool, Doyle."

"I am not; and of course, there has been balances of the kind you speak of before now. I wouldn't say but—looking at the matter in that way—and besides there'd be a commission from the fellow that got the contract for the statue. And with regard to the £5 that my name's down for— —"

"Come now, Doyle. Don't pretend to be stupider than you are. You know perfectly well that every public fund has to be started by somebody with a respectable looking subscription. I put it to you now as a business man, did you ever hear of a case in which a subscription of that kind was actually paid? It appears in the published list and it encourages other people, but——"

"Say no more, doctor," said Doyle. "Say no more."

"I shall count on you then, Doyle, to help me in every way you possibly can. It's all for your own good. And you won't be doing anybody any harm."

"There's just one thing more," said Doyle.

"Out with it. And be as quick as you can. I've still got to soothe the Major's scruples."

"If you don't mind my asking the question," said Doyle, "what are you going to make out of it yourself?"

"That's a delicate point. I might tell you I'm going into the business for the fun of the thing; but you wouldn't believe that."

"I would not," said Doyle, winking slowly.

"I was afraid you wouldn't. It's true, as it happens. That's just exactly why I am running this statue. It offers me a little excitement and variety. But as you won't believe it I'll have to make up some sort of a lie that you will believe. I owe you about £60, don't I?"

"You do, doctor, but I'd be the last man in Ireland to press you for the money if——"

"Very well. If I put £20 into your pocket over this statue, in addition to the £7 10s. you're making on the filly, I'll expect you to stop talking about what I owe you for the next six months. You see some sense in that, don't you?"

"I do."

"And it satisfies you as a reason for my taking all the trouble that I'm going to take."

"It does, of course. Why wouldn't it?"

"Very well. Believe it. But if the matter ever comes up again you'll remember, Doyle, that I offered you the truth and you wouldn't have it. I didn't attempt to impose on you with that lie until you insisted that I should."

Doyle grinned. He did not for a moment believe that Dr. O'Grady was going to give himself a great deal of trouble in the matter of General John Regan's statue without gaining something by it. But he admired the way in which the doctor, even when apparently cornered, succeeded in keeping up appearances.

"If Gallagher gets tangled up in any difficulty," said Dr. O'Grady, as he said good-bye to Doyle, "send him straight round to me. Don't you attempt to extricate him or you'll make matters worse. I shall be at home for the next two hours. It will take me that time at least to talk sense into the Major."

When he got back to his own house Dr. O'Grady found his friend in a state of badly repressed impatience.

"That seems to have been a pretty long explanation which you gave to Doyle," said the Major. "I hope mine will turn out to be a bit shorter."

"That," said Dr. O'Grady, "will entirely depend on yourself, Major. If you were a really intelligent man no explanation whatever would be necessary. You'd grasp the situation for yourself. If you were even fairly intelligent a short explanation would be quite sufficient. If, as I fear, you are downright stupid I may have to spend an hour or two talking to you."

"I don't see the slightest necessity for that," said the Major. "You've only got to give a simple answer to a perfectly plain question. Who was General John Regan? You answer that, and no further explanation will be necessary."

"I'm afraid it will," said Dr. O'Grady. "Even if I tell you all I know about the General you'll still want to heckle me and generally upset my plans."

"No, I won't, O'Grady. I promise you I won't. Just tell me all you know about this General and I won't say another word."

"Very well," said Dr. O'Grady. "I don't know anything at all about the General. I never heard of him in my life until to-day."

Major Kent gasped. Then he grew suddenly red in the face. Then he spluttered explosively. Then he burst into violent speech.

"And what the devil do you mean, O'Grady, by ——? I'm hanged if I ever heard of such——"

"There you are," said Dr. O'Grady. "I knew you wouldn't be satisfied. I've told you all I know about the General, and so far from saying nothing more, you begin to curse in the most frightful way."

"That's all very well," said the Major, "but if there's no such person as that General——"

"I didn't say that. I said I knew nothing about him. I'm a well educated man, Major, far better educated than you are. But there are thousands and thousands of quite eminent people still alive whose names I've never heard, and when it comes to dead people there are probably millions, scattered up and down through history books, whom

I know nothing about. They may all be quite famous in their own localities and may thoroughly deserve statues. It's not their fault that I know nothing about them."

"But we don't any of us know anything about this General. I don't. Doyle doesn't. You don't. Why on earth should we put up a statue to him?"

"Why shouldn't we allow that American—Billing or whatever his name is—to put up a statue if he likes? He wants to. Why shouldn't he?"

"Why should he put it up here?" said the Major. "What brings him to Ballymoy?"

"I expect," said Dr. O'Grady—"mind, I don't know for certain—but I expect that he's come to the wrong place, mixed up Ballymoy with some other town, with the town in which Regan was really born. This General of his was evidently a pretty big pot in his way, and if he had been born in Ballymoy some of us would have heard of him."

"In that case," said the Major, "we ought to tell Billing of his mistake."

"Certainly not. In the first place that would be a very unkind thing to do. Nobody likes being told of their mistakes, especially when they're as full of bounce and self-confidence as this fellow Billing. It's not right to be maliciously and wantonly unkind, Major, even to dumb animals; and I can't imagine anything more cruel than to tell Billing that he's made a mistake. In the next place, why on earth should we miss the chance of getting a statue in Ballymoy? We haven't got one at present, and a good statue—we'll get quite a respectable one for Billing's £100, even if we don't subscribe a penny ourselves—will be a great ornament to the town. You may not care for statues, Major, but all really cultivated people love them. Look at Dublin! It's a city with two universities in it, and the consequence is that it's simply spotted all over with statues. Look at ancient Athens, the most cultured city the world has ever seen. The number of statues the Athenians had would surprise you. Why shouldn't we have one? It'll do us all good."

"I call it a fraud," said the Major. "It's getting money out of this fool of an American under false pretences. If this General of his wasn't born here——"

"Now do you suppose, Major, that the General himself, the original John Regan, cares a pin where his statue is?"

"Of course he doesn't. The one thing we do know about him is that he's dead. Why should he care?"

"Quite so. Then there's no fraud so far as he's concerned."

"I wasn't talking about him. I was talking about the American."

"I'm just coming to him. Billing wants a statue to the General. He wants it so much that he's prepared to pay £100 for it. He also believes that the General was born here. I think myself that he's mistaken about that; but there's no doubt he believes it. He'll be quite satisfied if we have the statue here. If we don't he'll have to go to a lot of trouble and expense looking up another birthplace for the General. When he finds one the people there may not be as civil and obliging as we are. Or they may have as many statues as they want already. I cannot for the life of me see that we're committing any kind of fraud when we're saving Billing a lot of expense, possibly a great disappointment, and allowing him to do exactly what he wants."

Major Kent sighed hopelessly.

"It's no use arguing with you," he said, "but you'll get us all into trouble before you've done. You're absolutely certain to be found out."

"Now you're beginning to talk sense," said Dr. O'Grady. "There is a certain risk of being found out. I don't deny that. What we have to do is to minimise it as far as possible. We must take care not to commit ourselves to any statement about the General's public career until we've found out all we can about him. I intend to write to Dublin to-night for every book there is about Bolivia, which is the country he liberated. In the meanwhile we're fairly safe in working up any kind of local tradition we can think of. If that sort of thing is well done there's practically no risk of discovery. Even if the stories don't exactly fit in with what's known about the General's later life, it doesn't matter. The things that are told about the boyhood of great men are all invented afterwards. Nobody expects them to be true; but biographers have to put them in to satisfy the curiosity of the public. There must be a chapter headed 'Early Days,' or 'Home Life,' or something of that kind in every biography. That's the stuff Billing expects us to supply in exchange for the statue. At the same time men like Gallagher and Doyle are appallingly stupid, and I can't say you're exactly brilliant, Major. Any of you may, in an unguarded moment——"

"I shan't," said the Major, "because I'm going straight home and don't mean to leave the house again till this whole business is over."

"I wish that were possible," said Dr. O'Grady. "I should be much easier in my mind if you weren't here at all. But unfortunately we must have you. You give an air of solid respectability to the proceedings. You inspire confidence. We can't do without you. I'll get Gregg, the District

Inspector, dragged into it too, and Ford, the Resident Magistrate, if I can."

"You won't get him. He has too much sense."

"I'll get his wife anyway. She loves a fuss of any kind."

"Some of them will give you away," said the Major. "You'll be found out."

"If Gallagher gets through this afternoon," said Dr. O'Grady, "I shall feel pretty safe. I wish I hadn't been obliged to send Gallagher off alone with Billing. Poor Thady is such an ass. But what could I do? I couldn't go myself because I had to explain the situation to you and Doyle. I shall feel deeply thankful when Thady is safely home again."

"By the way," said the Major, "what was the explanation that you gave to Doyle? It was different from my one I know. I'd rather like to hear it."

"Poor Doyle!" said Dr. O'Grady. "Do you know I felt quite sorry for him about that filly. He probably won't find out what's wrong with her for about a fortnight or three weeks. He'll be so busy over this General John Regan business that he won't have time to do anything with her. But when he does find out——"

"He'll not be the first man in Ireland," said the Major, "who's been let in over a horse, and I don't pity him."

"I do," said Dr. O'Grady, "I pitied you, Major, when you were stuck and I helped you to get out I don't see why I shouldn't pity Doyle too."

"How do you mean to get him out?" said the Major. "Perhaps you intend to palm off that filly on your American."

"Not at all," said Dr. O'Grady. "My idea is to get Doyle's money back for him out of the statue."

The Major thought this statement over and gradually came to suspect that O'Grady contemplated some dishonourable use of public money. He was just beginning to make a violent protest when the door of the room in which they were sitting opened, and Gallagher came in.

"Doctor," he said, "will you oblige me by coming over to the hotel at once and pacifying the American gentleman?"

"I thought as much," said Dr. O'Grady, jumping up. "You've muddled things somehow, Thady."

"I did the best I could," said Gallagher, "but he wouldn't rest content with young Kerrigan's wife."

"Good heavens!" said Dr. O'Grady, "what on earth have you said? Young Kerrigan hasn't got a wife."

"Sure I know that. But what was I to do? What I said was for the best. But anyway you'd better come round to the hotel, till you see for yourself the way we're in."

"Come along, Major," said Dr. O'Grady. "You'll enjoy watching us get out of this entanglement, whatever it is."

"I'm not going with you," said the Major. "I don't see any fun in standing still and listening to you telling lies to that American. It's not my idea of spending a pleasant afternoon."

"Come along," said Dr. O'Grady, taking him by the arm. "I may want you. I can't tell yet whether I shall or not, for I don't know yet what's happened. But I may."

The Major hung back.

"I'm not going," he said.

"If you don't," said Dr. O'Grady in a whisper, "I'll tell Doyle about the filly, all about her, and as you haven't got the money for her yet—well, you know what Doyle is. He's not the kind of man I'd care to trust very far when he finds out that—Oh, do come on."

It may have been this threat which overcame Major Kent's reluctance. It may have been a natural curiosity to find out what trouble Gallagher had got into with Mr. Billing: It may simply have been Dr. O'Grady's force of character which vanquished him. He allowed himself to be led away.

CHAPTER V

"Now Thady," said Dr. O'Grady, "tell me exactly what happened and what the trouble is."

"It was on account of my mentioning young Kerrigan's wife," said Gallagher.

"Young Kerrigan hasn't got a wife," said the Major.

"Better begin at the beginning," said Dr. O'Grady. "If we knew how you arrived at whatever statement you made about young Kerrigan's wife we'd be in a better position to judge what has to be done about it, Start off now at the moment when you went away in the motorcar. You went to Doyle's farm, I suppose, as I told you, so as to show Mr. Billing the General's birthplace."

"In the latter end we got there," said Gallagher, "but at the first go off I took him along the road past the workhouse."

"That wasn't quite the shortest route," said Dr. O'Grady. "In fact you began by going in exactly the opposite direction."

"After that we went round by Barney's Hill," said Gallagher, "and along the bohireen by the side of the bog, me telling him the turns he ought to take."

"What on earth did you go there for," said the Major, "if you wanted to get to Doyle's farm?"

"When we'd passed the bog," said Gallagher, "we took a twist round, like as we might be trying to cut across to the Dunbeg Road."

"You seem to have gone pretty well all around the town," said Dr. O'Grady. "I suppose you enjoyed driving about in a large motor. Was that it?"

"It was not," said Gallagher, "but I was in dread to take him to Doyle's farm not knowing what questions he might be asking about the General when we got there. I'd be glad now, doctor, if you'd tell me who the General was, for it's troublesome not knowing."

"There isn't time," said Dr. O'Grady, "to go into long explanations simply to satisfy your morbid curiosity. Go on with your story. What happened when you did get to the place? I suppose you got there in the end?"

"We did of course," said Gallagher, "and I showed him the ruin of the little houseen, the same as you told me to. 'And was it there,' says he, 'that the great General, the immortal founder of the liberties of Bolivia, first saw the light?' 'It was,' says I. So he took a leap out of the motorcar and stood in front of the old house with his hat in his hand. So I told him about the way the landlords had treated the people of this country in times past, and the way we are meaning to serve them out as soon as we have Home Rule, which is as good as got, only for the blackguards of Orangemen up in the North. I told him——"

"I'm sure you did," said Dr. O'Grady, "but you needn't go over all that to us, particularly as the Major hates that kind of talk."

"Nobody," said Gallagher, "would want to say a word that was displeasing to the Major, who is well liked in this locality and always was. If only the rest of the landlords was like him, instead of——"

"Go on about the American," said Dr. O'Grady, "did he throw stones at you while you were making that speech about Home Rule?"

"He did not," said Gallagher, "but he stood there looking at the houseen with the tears rolling down the cheeks of him——"

"What?" said Dr. O'Grady, "do you mean to tell me he cried?"

"It was like as if he was going to," said Gallagher, "and 'the patriot statesman,' says he, 'the mighty warrior,' says he, and more to that, the same as if he might be making a speech about the land and the league boys cheering him."

"I'm rather bothered about that American in some ways," said Dr. O'Grady. "Are you telling me the truth now, Thady, about what he said?"

"I am," said Gallagher. "I'd take my oath to every word of it."

"Either he's a much greater fool than he looks," said Dr. O'Grady, "or else—but I'll find that out afterwards. Go on with your story, Thady. What happened next?"

"Well, after he'd cried about a saucerful——"

"I thought you said he didn't actually cry?"

"It was like as if he was going to cry. I told you that before."

"Come on, O'Grady," said the Major. "What's the use of listening to this sort of stuff?"

"Be quiet, Major," said Dr. O'Grady. "We're just coming to the point. Go ahead, Thady. You'd just got to the saucerful of tears. When he'd emptied that out, what did he do?"

"He asked me," said Gallagher, "was there any relatives or friends of the General surviving in the locality? He had me beat there."

"I hope you told him there were several," said Dr. O'Grady.

"I did, of course. Is it likely I'd disappoint the gentleman, and him set on finding someone belonging to the General? 'Who are they?' said he. 'Tell me their names,' Well, it was there I made the mistake."

"It was a bit awkward," said Dr. O'Grady, "when you didn't know who the General was."

"What I thought to myself," said Gallagher, "was this. There might be many a one in the locality that would be glad enough to be a cousin of the General's, even if there was no money to be got out of it, and it could be that there would. But, not knowing much about the General, I wasn't easy in my mind for fear that anybody I named might be terrible angry with me after for giving them a cousin that might be some sort of a disgrace to the family— —"

"I see now," said Dr. O'Grady. "You thought it safer to name somebody who didn't exist. But what made you think of a wife for young Kerrigan?"

"It was the first thing came into my head," said Gallagher, "and I was that flustered I said it without thinking."

"Well, how did he take it?"

"He was mighty pleased, so he was. 'Take me to her,' he said. 'Take me to see her this minute,' Well, to be sure I couldn't do that."

"You could not," said Dr. O'Grady. "Could he, Major?"

"I don't see why not. He might have hired some girl for half an hour."

"No decent girl would do it," said Gallagher, "and anyway I wouldn't have had the time, for he had me in the motor again before I knew where he was and 'Show me the way to the house,' says he. 'You can't see her at the present time,' says I, 'though you may later,' 'And why not?' says he. 'The reason why you can't,' says I, 'is a delicate matter,' 'Oh!' says he. 'That's the way of it, is it? I'm glad to hear of it. The more of the stock of the old General there are in the world the better.' Well, when I seen him so pleased as all that, I thought it would be no harm to please him more. 'It's twins,' I said, 'and what's more the both of them is boys,' 'Take me to see the father,' says he. 'I'll be able to see him anyway. I'd like to shake him by the hand.'"

"Has he seen young Kerrigan?" said Dr. O'Grady.

"He has not; but he won't rest easy till he does. I wanted to run round and tell young Kerrigan the way things are, so as he'd be ready when the gentleman came. But Doyle said it would be better for me to tell you what had happened before worse came of it."

"Doyle was perfectly right Kerrigan would stand over your story all right as long as he could, but in the end he'd have had to produce the twins. That's the awkward part. If you hadn't said twins we might have managed. But there isn't a pair in the town."

"Couldn't you telegraph to Dublin?" said the Major. "For a man of your resource, O'Grady, mere twins ought not to prove a hopeless obstacle. I should think that one of the hospitals where they go in for that kind of thing would be quite glad to let you have a brace of babies in or about the same age."

O'Grady knew that this suggestion was not meant to be helpful. The Major had an objectionable habit of indulging in heavy sarcasm. He turned on him sharply.

"You'd better go home, Major. When you try to be facetious you altogether cease to be useful. You know perfectly well that there's no use talking about importing babies. What would we do with them afterwards? You couldn't expect young Kerrigan to keep them."

"I offered to go home some time ago," said the Major, "and you wouldn't let me. Now that I've heard about young Kerrigan's twins I mean to stop where I am and see what happens."

"Very well, Major. Just as you like. As long as you don't upset Billing by rolling up any of those heavy jokes of yours against him I don't mind. Here we are. I expect Doyle has Billing in the bar trying to pacify him with whisky. You'd better stay outside, Thady."

"I'd be glad of a drop then," said Gallagher wistfully. "After all the talking I did this afternoon——"

"Oh, go in if you like," said Dr. O'Grady. "Probably the safest thing for you to do is to get drunk. Here's Billing crossing the street He's just come out of Kerrigan's shop. Why on earth Doyle couldn't have kept him in play till I came.... He's sure to have found out now that young Kerrigan isn't married. This will make my explanation far more difficult than it need have been."

"It will make it impossible, I should imagine," said the Major.

Mr. Billing, his hands in his coat pockets and a large cigar between his teeth, came jauntily across the street. Dr. O'Grady greeted him.

"Good-evening, Mr. Billing," he said. "I hope you've had a pleasant and satisfactory afternoon."

Sergeant Colgan and Constable Moriarty came out of the barrack together. They joined the group opposite the hotel. Constable Moriarty was grinning broadly. He had evidently heard some version of the story about young Kerrigan's twins.

"I am sorry to find," said the doctor, "that Thady Gallagher made a mistake, and a bad one, this afternoon."

"I reckon," said Mr. Billing, "that he kind of wandered from the path of truth."

"Young Kerrigan isn't married," said the doctor.

"The twins," said Mr. Billing, "were an effort of imagination. I am a man of imagination myself, so I'm not complaining any."

"Being a newspaper editor you have to be, of course," said Dr. O'Grady. "But Gallagher's story wasn't pure imagination. It was rather what I'd call prophetic. The fact is young Kerrigan is going to be married. Gallagher only anticipated things a bit. I daresay he thought the ceremony had really taken place. He didn't mean to deceive you in any way. Did you, Thady?"

He looked round as he spoke. He wanted Gallagher to confirm what he said.

"He's within," said Constable Moriarty, grinning, "and I wouldn't say but he's having a drink. Anyway, here's Mr. Doyle."

Doyle, having supplied Gallagher with a bottle of porter, came out of the hotel. He was naturally anxious to hear Dr. O'Grady's explanation.

"The twins," said Mr. Billing, "were considerable previous."

"Not so much as you might think," said Dr. O'Grady. "Once people get married, you know, Mr. Billing, it often happens—generally in fact—not necessarily twins, but more or less that kind of thing. I can quite understand Thady making the mistake. And the girl young Kerrigan's going to marry really is a grandniece of the General's. Thady was quite right there."

"I'd like to see her," said Mr. Billing. "I'd like to take a photograph of her. The Bolivian public will be interested in a photograph of General John Regan's grandniece."

"Run and get your camera then," said Dr. O'Grady. "I'll have her ready for you by the time you're back."

Mr. Billing, looking very well satisfied and quite without suspicion, went into the hotel.

"Doyle," said Dr. O'Grady, "fetch Mary Ellen as quick as you can."

"Is it Mary Ellen?"

"It is. Get her at once, and don't argue."

"But sure Mary Ellen's not the grandniece of any General."

"She's the only grandniece we can possibly get on such short notice," said Dr. O'Grady.

"I don't know," said Sergeant Colgan, "will Mr. Gallagher be too well pleased. Mary Ellen's a cousin of his own."

"Thady will have to put up with a little inconvenience," said Dr. O'Grady. "He got us all into this mess, so he can't complain."

"I beg your pardon, doctor," said Constable Moriarty, who had stopped grinning and looked truculent, "but I'll not have it put out that Mary Ellen's going to marry young Kerrigan. He's a boy she never looked at, nor wouldn't."

"Shut up, Moriarty," said Dr. O'Grady. "If you won't call her, Doyle, I must do it myself. Mary Ellen, Mary Ellen, come here!"

"What's the use of calling Mary Ellen?" said Doyle. "The girl knows well enough she's not the niece nor the grandniece of any General. As soon as ever you face her with the American gentleman she'll be saying something, be the same more or less, that'll let him know the way things are with her."

"If I know anything of Mary Ellen," said Dr. O'Grady, "she'll not say a word more than she need on any subject. I never could drag anything beyond 'I did,' or 'I did not,' or 'I might,' out of her no matter how hard I tried, Mary Ellen! Mary Ellen! Ah! here she is."

Mary Ellen came slowly through the door of the hotel. She smiled when she saw Dr. O'Grady, smiled again and then blushed when her eyes lit on Constable Moriarty. Her face and hands were a little dirtier than they had been earlier in the day, but she had added a small, crumpled, white cap to the apron which she put on in honour of Mr. Billing. The sight of her roused all Constable Moriarty's spirit.

"I'll not have it done, doctor," he said, "so there it is for you plain and straight. I'll not stand by and see the character of a decent girl——"

"Whisht, can't you," said Mary Ellen.

"Sergeant," said Dr. O'Grady, "this isn't a matter in which the police have any business to interfere. No one is committing a crime of any sort. You'd far better send Moriarty back to the barrack before he makes a worse fool of himself than he has already."

"Get along home out of that, Moriarty," said the sergeant. "Do you want me to have to report you to the District Inspector for neglect of duty?"

The threat was a terrific one. Moriarty quailed before it. He did not actually go back to the barrack; but he retired to the background and did no more than look reproachfully at Mary Ellen whenever he thought she was looking his way.

"It's a great pity," said Dr. O'Grady, "that we haven't time to wash her face. I might do something, even without soap and water, if I had a pocket-handkerchief. Major, just lend me—— Oh hang it! I can't. Here comes Billing with his camera. Pull yourself together now, Mary Ellen, and try to look as if you were proud of your distinguished relative. It isn't every girl of your age who has a General for a great uncle."

Mr. Billing approached. The corners of his lips were twitching in a curious way. Dr. O'Grady looked at him suspiciously. A casual observer might have supposed that Mr. Billing was trying hard not to smile.

"This," said Dr. O'Grady, pointing to Mary Ellen, "is the grandniece, the only surviving relative, of General John Regan."

"You surprise me," said Mr. Billing. "When I recollect that she cooked chops for my luncheon to-day I'm amazed."

"The General wouldn't have thought a bit the worse of her for that," said Dr. O'Grady. "A true democrat, the General, if ever there was one. I daresay he often cooked chops himself, when campaigning I mean, and was jolly glad to get chops to cook."

"So you," said Mr. Billing, addressing Mary Ellen, "are the grandniece of the great General?"

"I might be," she said.

"And I am to have the privilege—gentlemen, please stand a little aside. I wish to——"

Mr. Billing set up his camera and put his head under the black cloth. Constable Moriarty sidled up to Major Kent. Nothing had been said about Mary Ellen's marriage with young Kerrigan. He felt that he had been unnecessarily alarmed.

"I beg your pardon, Major," he said, "but maybe if you asked the gentleman he'd give me a copy of the photo when it's took."

"Talk to the doctor about that," said the Major. "He's managing this show. I've nothing to do with it."

"I'd be backward about asking the doctor," said Moriarty, "on account of what passed between us a minute ago when I thought he was wanting to take away the girl's character."

Mr. Billing completed his arrangements and stood beside his camera ready to release the shutter.

"You're quite sure," said Dr. O'Grady, "that you wouldn't care to have her face washed?"

"Certain," said Mr. Billing. "The General was a genuine democrat if ever there was one. He wouldn't have thought a bit the worse of her for having a dirty face."

Dr. O'Grady started slightly and then looked questioningly at Mr. Billing. It struck him that there was something suspicious about this repetition of his words. He glanced at the Major, at Doyle, and then at the two policemen. They all seemed completely absorbed in the taking of the photograph. Mr. Billing's last remark had not struck them as in any way odd.

The shutter clicked. One of Mary Ellen's sweetest smiles was secured on the sensitive plate. Constable Moriarty, greatly daring, asked Mr. Billing for a print of the photograph. Mr. Billing promised him a copy of the life of General John Regan when it appeared. He said that there would be a full page reproduction of Mary Ellen's portrait in the second volume.

"The Major and I must be off," said Dr. O'Grady, "but if I may call on you to-morrow morning, Mr. Billing, I should like to make arrangements about the public meeting. We want to have you at it."

"The meeting?" said Doyle.

"The meeting about the statue," said Dr. O'Grady. "By the way, Doyle, you might call on Father McCormack this evening." He spoke with a glance at Mr. Billing which he hoped that Doyle would interpret correctly. "You'd better remind him that he's to take the chair. He promised a week ago, but he may have forgotten. That's the worst of these good-natured men," he added, speaking directly to Mr. Billing. "They promise anything, and then it's ten to one they forget all about it."

"I'm not quite sure," said Mr. Billing, "that my arrangements will allow me——"

"Oh, they will if you squeeze them a bit. Arrangements are extraordinary pliable things if you handle them firmly, and we'd like to have you. A speech from you about the General would be most interesting. It would stimulate the whole population. Wouldn't it, Major?"

"I'd like to hear it," said the Major.

"Good-bye then, for the present," said Dr. O'Grady. "Come along, Major. By the way, Doyle, if Thady takes a drop too much to drink, and he may, don't let him start boring Mr. Billing about Home Rule."

He took Major Kent by the arm and walked off. Until they passed the end of the street and were well out on the lonely road which led to the Major's house, neither of them spoke. Then the Major broke the silence.

"I hope, O'Grady, that you're satisfied with that performance."

"To tell you the truth, Major, I'm not."

"I'm surprised to hear that," said the Major. "You've told the most outrageous lies I ever heard. You've—-"

"I gave the only possible explanation of a rather difficult situation."

"You've made a laughing stock of a respectable girl."

"I've given Mary Ellen a great uncle that she ought to be proud to own. That's not what's bothering me."

"What is, then?"

"That American," said the doctor. "I don't at all like the way he's going on. He's not by any means a fool——"

"He must be or he wouldn't have swallowed all those lies you told him in the way he did. How could Mary Ellen possibly be———?"

"That's just it," said Dr. O'Grady. "He swallowed what I said far too easily. The situation, owing to Thady Gallagher's want of presence of mind, was complex, desperately complex. I got out of it as well as any man could, but I don't deny that the explanation I gave—particularly that part about Mary Ellen being engaged to young Kerrigan, was a bit strained. I expected the American would have shied. But he didn't. He swallowed it whole without so much as a choke. Now I don't think that was quite natural. The fact is, Major, I'm uneasy about Billing. It struck me that there was something rather odd in the way he repeated my words about the General being a genuine democrat. He gave me the impression that he was—well, trying to make fools of us."

"You were certainly trying to make a fool of him."

"I don't quite understand his game," said Dr. O'Grady, "if he has a game. I may be wronging him. He may be simply an idiot, a well-meaning idiot with a craze for statues."

"He must be," said the Major. "Nothing else would account for——"

"I doubt it," said Dr. O'Grady. "He doesn't look that kind of man. However, there's no use talking any more about it to-night. I'll be in a better position to judge when I've found out all there is to know about this General of his. I'll write for the books I've mentioned, and I'll write to a man I know in the National Library. If there's anything known about the General on this side of the Atlantic he'll ferret it out for me."

Dr. O'Grady stopped speaking. The Major supposed that he had stopped thinking about Mr. Billing's curious conduct. The doctor did indeed intend to stop thinking about it. But it is difficult to bridle thought. After walking half a mile in silence Dr. O'Grady spoke again, and his words showed that his mind was still working on the same problem.

"Americans have far too good an opinion of themselves," he said. "Billing may possibly think he's playing some kind of trick on us. He may be laughing at us in some way we don't quite understand."

"I don't know whether he's laughing or not," said the Major, "but everybody else will be very soon if you go on as you're going."

CHAPTER VI

It is very difficult to do anything of importance to the community without holding a public meeting about it. In Ireland people have got so accustomed to oratory and the resolutions which are the immediate excuse for oratory, that public meetings are absolutely necessary preliminaries to any enterprise. This is the case in all four provinces, which is one of the things which goes to show that the Irish are really a single people and not two or three different peoples, as some writers assert. The hard-headed, commercially-minded Ulsterman is just as fond of public meetings as the Connacht Celt. He would hold them, with drums and full dress speechifying, even if he were organising a secret society and arranging for a rebellion. He is perfectly right. Without a public meeting it would be impossible to enrol any large number of members for a society.

Dr. O'Grady, having lived all his life in Ireland, and being on most intimate terms with his neighbours, understood this law. He also understood that in order to make a success of a public meeting in Connacht and therefore to further the enterprise on hand, it is necessary that the parish priest should take the chair and advisable that a Member of Parliament should propose the first resolution.

He began by sending Doyle to Father McCormack. Doyle, foreseeing a possible profit for himself, did his best to persuade Father McCormack to take the chair. Father McCormack, who was a fat man and therefore good-natured, did not want to refuse Doyle. But Father McCormack was not a free agent. Behind him, somewhere, was a bishop, reputed to be austere, certainly domineering. Father McCormack was very much afraid of the bishop, therefore he hesitated. The most that Doyle could secure, after a long interview, was the promise of a definite answer the next day.

Father McCormack made use of the twenty-four hours' grace he had secured by calling on Major Kent. The Major was a Protestant, with strong anti-Papal convictions, and therefore was not, it might have been supposed, a good man to advise a priest on a delicate question of ecclesiastical etiquette. But the Major was eminently respectable, and his outlook upon life was staidly conservative. Father McCormack felt that if Major Kent thoroughly approved of the erection of a statue to General John Regan it was likely to be quite a proper thing to do.

"I'm not sure," said Father McCormack, "whether it will suit me to take the chair at this meeting the doctor's getting up or not. I'm not sure, I say. Can you tell me now, Major Kent, who's this American gentleman they're all talking about?"

"I don't know anything about him," said the Major, "but I'm bound to say he looks like a Protestant. I don't know whether that will make any difference to you or not."

"From the little I've seen of him—just across the street from the window of the Presbytery—I'd say you were right about his religion, but I needn't tell you, Major Kent, that I'm not a bigoted man. It wouldn't stop me taking the chair if he was a Protestant. It wouldn't stop me if he was a Presbyterian, and I can't say more than that. You know very well that I'd just as soon be sitting on a committee alongside of a Protestant as any ordinary kind of man. I'm not one that would let religion interfere too much."

"He seems quite respectable," said the Major. "He's been here three days now, and I never saw him drunk."

"It's not that either that's troubling me," said Father McCormack. "There's many a man gets drunk when he can, and I'd be the last to make too much out of that."

"I can't tell you any more about him," said the Major, "for that's all I know, except that he appears to be rich."

"The difficulty I'm in is on account of the bishop. He's getting to be mighty particular. I don't say he's wrong, mind you; only there it is. But sure, if no one in the place has anything to say against the American gentleman it's likely he'll turn out to be all right. But what about the fellow they want to put up the statue to?"

"General John Regan," said the Major.

"What about him? I never heard tell of him before."

"For the matter of that, nor did I."

"Who was he at all?"

"You'll have to ask Dr. O'Grady that. He's the only man who professes to know anything about him."

"As I was saying to you this minute," said Father McCormack, "I wouldn't mind if he was a Protestant."

"He hardly could be," said the Major, "with that name."

"There's many a Protestant that might be just as well deserving of a statue as maybe a bishop. But what I'm afraid of is that this fellow might be worse. For let me tell you, Major, there's worse things than

Protestants, and I'm not saying that just because I'm talking to you. I'd say it to anyone."

This gratified Major Kent, but it did not enable him to give any information about General John Regan.

"There's no use asking me about him," he said wearily. "Ask Dr. O'Grady."

"If it was to turn out at the latter end," said Faflier McCormack, "that he was one of those French atheists, or if he had any hand in hunting the nuns out of Portugal, the bishop wouldn't be too well pleased when he heard that I'd been helping to put up a statue to him."

"You'll have to ask Dr. O'Grady. It's no good asking me."

"Will you tell me this, Major Kent, and I won't ask you another question. Are you going to the meeting yourself?"

"I am."

"Well now, you're a man with a position in the place and you wouldn't be going to a meeting of the sort unless it was all right. I'm inclined to think now that if you're going—I wouldn't give a thraneen for what Doyle might do. If that fellow saw half a chance of making sixpence by going to a meeting he'd go, if it was held for the purpose of breaking the windows of the Presbytery. That's the sort of man Doyle is. And I wouldn't mind Thady Gallagher. Thady is a kind-hearted poor fellow, though he's a bit foolish at times; but he's not the sort of man you could trust. He's too fond of politics, and that's a fact. Give Thady the opportunity of making a speech and you wouldn't be able to keep him at home from a meeting, whatever sort of a meeting it might be. But it's different with you, Major Kent."

The Major was deeply touched by this eulogy; so deeply touched that he felt it wrong to leave Father McCormack under the impression that he was going to the meeting out of any feeling of admiration for General John Regan.

"The fact is," he said, "that I wouldn't go near the meeting if I could help it."

"Is there anything against that General then?"

"It's not that. It's simply that I loathe and detest all public meetings, and I wouldn't go to this one or any other if I could get out of it."

"And why can't you get out of it? A man needn't go to a meeting unless he likes."

"He must," said the Major, "I must; any man must, if Dr. O'Grady gets at him."

"That's true, too," said Father McCormack, "and I don't mind telling you that I've been keeping out of the doctor's way ever since Doyle asked me. I'd rather not see him till I have my mind made up the one way or the other."

It was unfortunate for Father McCormack that Dr. O'Grady should at that moment have walked into the Major's study without even knocking at the door. He had just received answers to his letters from four of the most eminent Irish Members of Parliament He had asked them all to attend a meeting at Ballymoy and make speeches about General John Regan. They had all refused, offering the very flimsiest excuses. Dr. O'Grady was extremely indignant.

"I don't see what on earth use there is," he blurted out, "in our keeping Members of Parliament at all. Here we are paying these fellows £400 a year each, and when we ask for a perfectly simple speech—— Oh, I beg your pardon, Father McCormack, I didn't see you were here. But I daresay you quite agree with me. Every one must."

"Father McCormack came here," said the Major, "to ask about General John Regan."

"Who is he at all?" said the priest.

"A general," said Dr. O'Grady, "Irish extraction. Born in Ballymoy. Rose to great eminence in Bolivia. Finally secured the liberty of the Republic."

"Father McCormack seems to think," said the Major, "that he was some kind of anti-clerical socialist."

"I said he might be," said Father McCormack. "I didn't say he was, for I don't know a ha'porth about him. All I said was that if he turned out to be that kind of a man it wouldn't suit me to be putting up statues to him. The Bishop wouldn't like it."

"My impression is———" said Dr. O'Grady. "Mind, I don't say I'm perfectly certain of it, but my impression is that he built a cathedral before he died. Anyhow I never heard or read a single word against his character as a religious man. He may have been a little——" Dr. O'Grady winked slowly. "You know the kind of thing I mean, Father McCormack, when he was young. Most military men are, more or less. I expect now that the Major could tell us some queer stories about the sort of thing that goes on——"

"No, I couldn't," said the Major.

"In garrison towns," said Dr. O'Grady persuasively, "and of course it's worse on active service. Come now, Major, I'm not asking you to give yourself away, but you could——"

"No, I couldn't," said the Major firmly.

"What you mean is that you wouldn't," said Dr. O'Grady. "Not while Father McCormack is listening to you anyhow. And you may take my word for it that the old General was just the same. He may have been a bit of a lad in his early days— —"

"I wouldn't mind that," said Father McCormack. "I wouldn't mind that if it was twice as much, so long— —"

"But he'd never have said anything really disrespectful in the presence of a clergyman of any denomination. Whatever his faults were—and he had faults, of course—he wasn't that kind of man. So you needn't hesitate about taking the chair at the meeting, Father McCormack. I defy the most particular bishop that ever wore a purple stock to find out anything really bad about the General."

"If I have your word for that," said Father McCormack, "I'm satisfied."

"I'm not a rich man," said Dr. O'Grady. "I can't afford to lose money, but I'll pay down £50 to any man who proves anything bad about the General. And when I say bad I don't, mean things like— —"

"I understand you," said Father McCormack.

"I mean," said Dr. O'Grady, "atheism of a blatant kind, or circulating immoral literature—Sunday papers, for instance—or wanting to turn the priests out of the schools, or not paying his dues— —"

"I understand you," said Father McCormack.

"I know what I'm talking about," said Dr. O'Grady, "for I've had a man looking up all that's known about General John Regan in the National Library in Dublin."

CHAPTER VII

At the very bottom of the main street of Ballymoy, close to the little harbour where the fishing boats nestled together in stormy weather, there is a disused mill. Corn was ground in it long ago. The farmers brought it from the country round about after the threshing was over, and the stream which now flows idly into the sea was then kept busy turning a large wheel. Since the Americans have taken to supplying Ireland with flour ready ground, bleached, and fit for immediate use, the Irish farmers have left off growing wheat. Being wise men they see no sense in toiling when other people are willing to toil instead of them. The Ballymoy mill, and many others like it, lie idle. They are slipping quietly through the gradual stages of decay and will one day become economically valuable to the country again as picturesque ruins. Few things are more attractive to tourists than ruins, and the country which possesses an abundance of them is in a fair way to grow rich easily. But it is necessary that the ruins should be properly matured. No man with an educated taste for food will eat Stilton cheese which is only half decayed. No educated tourist will take long journeys and pay hotel bills in order to look at an immature ruin. The decaying mills of Ireland have not yet reached the profitable stage of development. Their doors and windows are still boarded up. Their walls are adorned with posters instead of ivy. No aesthetic archaeologist has as yet written a book about their architecture.

The Ballymoy mill was the property of Doyle. He bought it very cheap when the previous owner, a son of the last miller, lapsed into bankruptcy. He saw no immediate prospect of making money out of it, but he was one of those men—they generally end in being moderately rich—who believe that all real property will in the end acquire a value, if only it is possessed with sufficient patience. In the meanwhile, since buildings do not eat, and so long as they remain empty are not liable for rates, the mill did not cost Doyle anything. He tried several times to organise schemes by means of which he might be able to secure a rent for the mill. When it became fashionable, eight or ten years ago, to start what are tailed "industries" in Irish provincial towns, Doyle suggested that his mill should be turned into a bacon factory. A public meeting was held with Father McCormack in the chair, and Thady Gallagher made an eloquent speech. Doyle himself offered to take shares in the new company to the amount of £5. Father McCormack, who was named as a director, also took five £1 shares. It was agreed that Doyle should be paid £30 a year for the mill. At that point the scheme broke down, mainly because no one else would take any shares at all.

A couple of years later Doyle tried again. This time he suggested a stocking manufactory. Stockings are supposed to require less capital than bacon curing, and, as worked out on paper, they promise large profits. Doyle offered the mill for £25 a year this time, and was greatly praised by Thady Gallagher in the columns of the *Connacht Eagle* for his patriotic self-sacrifice. Another large meeting was held, but once more the public, though enthusiastic about the scheme, failed to subscribe the capital. A great effort was made the next year to induce the Government to buy the building for a £1,000, with a view to turning it into a Technical School. A petition was signed by almost everyone in Ballymoy setting forth the hungry desire of the people for instruction in the arts of life. Several Members of Parliament asked the Chief Secretary searching questions on the subject of the Ballymoy Technical School. But the Chief Secretary declared himself quite unable to wring the money out of the Treasury. Thady Gallagher wrote articles and made speeches which ought to have caused acute discomfort to the Prime Minister. But Doyle found himself obliged to give up the idea of a Technical School. He waited hopefully. In the end, he felt sure, some way of utilising the old mill would be found. In the meanwhile the building, though unprofitable to Doyle was not entirely useless. Its walls, boarded doors and windows, formed the most excellent place for the display of advertisements. The circuses which visited the town in summer covered a great deal of space with their posters. When retiring members of the Urban District Council wanted to be re-elected they notified their desire by means of placards pasted on the walls of Doyle's mill. All public meetings were advertised there. Doyle himself made nothing out of these advertisements; but Thady Gallagher did. He printed the posters, and it was admitted by everyone that he did it very well.

Two days after his arrival in Ballymoy, Mr. Billing strolled down to the harbour. He was a man of restless and energetic disposition, but the visits which he received from Dr. O'Grady, and the speeches about Home Rule to which Gallagher subjected him, began to worry him. In order to soothe his nerves he used to spend an hour or two morning and evening looking at the fishermen who spent the day in contemplating their boats. There is nothing in the world more soothing than the study of a fisherman's life on shore. When he is at sea it is probably strenuous enough. But then he very seldom is at sea, and when he is he is out of sight. Having, so to speak, drunk deeply of the torpor of Ballymoy harbour, Mr. Billing turned his face towards the shore and looked at the wall of Doyle's mill. He was startled to find six new posters stuck on it in a row. They were all bright green. Mr. Billing read them with interest.

The announcement opened with a prayer, printed in large type:

"GOD SAVE IRELAND,"

GENERAL JOHN REGAN

This was repeated at the bottom of each poster in the Irish language, which Mr. Billing could not read. Next to the prayer, in very much larger type, came the words:

"A PUBLIC MEETING,"

Then, in quite small letters:

"WILL BE HELD ON TUESDAY NEXT AT 3 P. M.
IN THE MARKET SQUARE, OPPOSITE THE 'IMPERIAL HOTEL.'"

Mr. Billing read on and learned that Father McCormack would take the chair, that several distinguished Members of Parliament would address the meeting, that Mr. T. Gallagher, Chairman U. D. C., would also speak, and that—here the letters became immense—Mr. Horace P. Billing, of Bolivia, would give an account of the life of General John Regan, in whose honour it was proposed to erect a statue in Ballymoy.

Mr. Billing smiled. Then he turned and walked briskly to the hotel. He found Doyle and Thady Gallagher seated together on the bench outside the door. He addressed them cheerfully:

"Say, gentlemen," he said, "that doctor of yours seems to have got a move on this locality. The announcement of the meeting is a good thing, sure."

"The doctor," said Doyle, "is a fine man; but it would be better for him if he'd pay what he owes. I'm tired, so I am, of trying to get my money out of him."

"The doctor," said Gallagher, "has the good of the locality at heart, and whatever it might be that he takes in hand will be carried through. You may rely on the doctor."

Thady Gallagher had not yet been paid for printing the green posters. But he had every hope he would be when Mr. Billing handed over his subscription to the statue fund. He felt, it right to do all in his power to encourage Mr. Billing. Doyle, on the other hand, was becoming despondent. He did not like to see money which ought to be his frittered away on posters and the other necessary expenses of a public meeting. He was much less inclined to admire, the doctor's enterprise.

"I guess," said Mr. Billing, "that these Congressmen will draw some."

"If you mean the Members of Parliament," said Doyle, "the doctor told me this morning that they said they'd more to do than to be attending his meetings."

"It could be," said Gallagher hopefully, "that one of them might."

"They will not," said Doyle.

"We'll do without them," said Mr. Billing.

"That's what the doctor said to me," said Gallagher. "'We'll do without them, Thady,' said he, 'so long as we have Mr. Billing and Father McCormack and yourself,' meaning me, 'we'll have a good meeting if there never was a Member of Parliament near it.' And that's true too."

"If the doctor," said Doyle, "would pay what he owes instead of wasting his time over public meetings and statues and the like it would be better. Not that I'd say a word against the statue, or, for the matter of that, against the doctor, who's well liked in the town by all classes."

The Tuesday fixed for the meeting was a well chosen day. It was the occasion of one of the largest fairs held in Ballymoy during the year. The country people, small farmers and their wives, flock into the town whenever there is a fair. The streets are thronged with cattle lowing miserably. "Buyers," men whose business it is to carry the half-fed Connacht beasts to the fattening pastures of Meath and Kildare, assemble in large numbers and haggle over prices from early dawn till noon. No better occasion for the exploitation of a cause could possibly be chosen. And three o'clock was a very good hour. By that time the business of the fair is well over. The buying and selling is finished. But no one has gone home, and no one is more than partially drunk. It is safe to expect that everybody will welcome the entertainment that a meeting affords during the dull time which must intervene between the finishing of the day's business and the weary journey home.

The green posters were distributed far and wide. They adorned every gatepost and every wall sufficiently smooth to hold them within a circle of three miles radius around the town. There was some talk beforehand about the meeting. But on the whole the people displayed very little curiosity about General John Regan. It was taken for granted that he had been in some way associated with the cause of Irish Nationality, and one or two people professed to recollect that he had fought on the side of the Boers during the South African War. Whoever he was, the people were inclined to support the movement for erecting a statue to him by cheering anything which Thady Gallagher said. But they did not intend to support it in any other way. The Connacht farmer is like the rest of the human race in his dislike of being asked to subscribe to anything. He is superior to most other men in his capacity for resisting the pressure of the subscription list.

On the Saturday before the meeting Gallagher published a long article on the subject of the General in the *Connacht Eagle*. It was read, as all Gallagher's articles were, with respectful attention. Everybody expected to find out by reading it who the General was. Everyone felt, as he read it, or listened to it read aloud, that he was learning all he wanted to know, and did not discover until he came to talk the matter over afterwards with his friends that he knew no more when he had read the article than he did before.

It was not Thady Gallagher but Dr. O'Grady who wrote the article. Thady made several attempts and then gave up the matter in despair. Dr. O'Grady, though he was extremely busy at the time, had to do the writing. It was very well done, and calculated to heat to the boiling point the enthusiasm of all patriotic people. He began by praising Thomas Emmet. He passed from him to Daniel O'Connell. He recommended everyone to read John Mitchell's "Jail Journal." He described the great work done for Ireland by Charles Stewart Parnell. Then he said that General John Regan was, in his own way, at least the equal, possibly the superior, of any of the patriots he had named. He wound up the composition with the statement that it was unnecessary to recapitulate the great deeds of the General, because every Irishman worthy of the name knew all about them already.

No one read the article with more eagerness and expectation than Gallagher himself. As the day of the meeting drew nearer he was becoming more and more uncomfortable about his speech. He had not been able to find out either from Doyle or from Father McCormack anything whatever about the General. He did not want much. He was a practised orator and could make a very small amount of information go a long way in a speech, but he did want something, if it was only a date to which he might attach the General's birth or death. Doyle and the priest steadily referred him to Dr. O'Grady. From Sergeant Colgan he got nothing except a guess that the General might have been one of the Fenians. Dr. O'Grady, before the appearance of the article, promised that it would contain all that anyone needed to know. After the article was published Gallagher was ashamed to ask for further information, because he did not want to confess himself an Irishman unworthy of the name.

Doyle also was dissatisfied and became actually restive after the appearance of Saturday's *Connacht Eagle*. He was not in the least troubled by the vagueness of the leading article. He was not one of the speakers at the meeting, and it did not matter to him whether he knew anything about General John Regan or not. What annoyed him was the publication, in the advertisement columns of the paper, of a preliminary list of subscribers. In the first place such an advertisement cost money and could only be paid for out of Mr. Billing's subscription, thus further diminishing the small balance on which he was calculating as some compensation for the irrecoverable debt owed to him by Dr. O'Grady. In the second place his name appeared on the list as a donor, not of £5, but of £10. He knew perfectly well that he would not be expected to pay any subscription, but he was vaguely annoyed at the threat of such a liability.

On Sunday afternoon he called on Dr. O'Grady.

"Wasn't it agreed," he said, "that I was to be the treasurer of the fund for putting up the statue?"

"It was," said Dr. O'Grady, "and you are the treasurer. Didn't you see your name printed in the *Connacht Eagle*, 'Secretary, Dr. Lucius O'Grady. Treasurer, J. Doyle'?"

"If I'm the treasurer it's no more than right that I should have some say in the way the money's being spent, for let me tell you, doctor—and I may as well speak plain when I'm at it—I'm not satisfied. I've had some correspondence with a nephew of mine who's in that line of business himself up in Dublin, and he tells me that £100 is little enough for a statue of any size. Now I'm not saying that I want to close the account with a balance in hand——"

"It's what you do want, Doyle, whether you say it or not."

"But," said Doyle ignoring this interruption, "it wouldn't suit me if there was any debt at the latter end. For it's myself would have to pay it if there was, and that's what I'd not be inclined to do. The way you're spending money on posters and advertisements there'll be very little of the American gentleman's £100 left when it comes to buying the statue."

"I see your point all right, Doyle, but——"

"If you see it," said Doyle, "I'm surprised at you going on the way you are; but, sure, I might have known that you wouldn't care how much you'd spend or how much you'd owe at the latter end. There's that £60——"

"Don't harp on about that miserable £60," said Dr. O'Grady, "for I won't stand it. Here I am doing the very best I can to make money for you, taking no end of trouble, and all you do is to come grumbling to me day after day about some beggarly account that I happen to owe you."

"It's what I don't see is how I'm going to make a penny out of it at all, the way you're going on."

"Listen to me now, Doyle. Supposing—I just say supposing—the Government was to build a pier, a new pier, in Ballymoy, who do you think would get the contract for the job?"

"I would, of course," said Doyle, "for there'd be no other man in the town fit to take it."

"And how much do you suppose you'd make out of it?"

"What's the use of talking that way?" said Doyle. "Hasn't the Government built us two piers already, and is it likely they'd build us another?"

"That's not the point. What I'm asking you is: Supposing they did build another and you got the contract for it, how much do you suppose you'd make?"

"Well," said Doyle, "if it was a good-sized pier and if the engineer they sent down to inspect the work wasn't too smart altogether I might clear £100."

"Now, suppose," said Dr. O'Grady, "that you were able to sell the stones of that old mill of yours——"

"They're good stones, so they are."

"Exactly, and you'd expect a good price for them. Now suppose you succeeded in selling them to the Government as raw material for the pier— —"

"They'd be nice and handy for the work," said Doyle. "Whoever was to use those stones for building the pier would save a devil of a lot of expense in carting."

"That, of course, would be considered in fixing the price of the stones."

"It would," said Doyle. "It would have to be, for I wouldn't sell them without it was."

"Under those circumstances," said Dr. O'Grady, "what do you suppose you'd make?"

"I'd make a tidy penny," said Doyle.

"Very well. Add that tidy penny to the £100 profit on the pier contract and it seems to me that it would pay you to lose a couple of pounds—and I don't admit that you will lose a penny—over the statue business."

The mention of the statue brought Doyle back from a pleasant dream to the region of hard fact.

"What's the good of talking?" he said. "The Government will build no more piers here."

"I'm not so sure of that. If we were to get a hold of one of the real big men, say the Lord-Lieutenant, if we were to bring him down here and do him properly—flags, you know, Doyle, and the town band, and somebody with a bouquet of flowers for his wife, and somebody else—all respectable people, Doyle—with an illuminated address—and if we were all to stand round with our hats in our hands and cheer—in fact if we were to do all the things that those sort of fellows really like to see done— —"

"We could have flags," said Doyle, "and we could have the town band, and we could have all the rest of what you say; but what good would they be? The Lord-Lieutenant wouldn't come to Ballymoy. It's a backward place, so it is."

"I'll get to that in a minute," said Dr. O'Grady. "But just suppose now that we had him and did all the things I say, do you think he'd refuse us a simple pier when we asked for it?"

"I don't know but he would. Hasn't the Government built two piers here already? Is it likely they'd build a third?"

"Those two piers were built years and years ago," said Dr. O'Grady. "One of them is more than ten years old this minute, and they were both built by the last Government The present Lord-Lieutenant has probably never so much as heard of them. We shouldn't go out of our way to remind him of their existence. Nobody else in Ireland will remember anything about them. We'll start talking about the new pier as if it were quite an original idea that nobody had ever heard of before. We'd get it to a certainty."

Doyle was swept away by the glorious possibilities before him.

"If so be the Lord-Lieutenant was to come, and the Lady-Lieutenant with him, and more of the lords and ladies that does be attending on them up in Dublin Castle— —"

"Aides-de-camp, and people of that sort," said Dr. O'Grady. "They'd simply swarm down on us."

"There'd have to be a luncheon for them," said Doyle.

"And it would be in your hotel. I forgot about the luncheon. There'll be a pot of money to be made out of that."

"With drinks and all," said Doyle, with deep conviction. "There would. The like of them people wouldn't be contented with porter."

"Champagne," said Dr. O'Grady, "is the recognised tipple for anybody high up in the Government service. It wouldn't be respectful not to offer it."

"But he won't come," said Doyle. "What would bring him?"

"The statue will bring him."

"The statue! Talk sense, doctor. What would the like of him want to be looking at statues for? Won't he have as many as he wants in Dublin Castle, and better ones than we'd be able to show him?"

"You're missing the point, Doyle. I'm not proposing to bring him down here simply to look at a statue. I'm going to ask him to unveil it. Now as far as I know the history of Ireland—and I'm as well up in it as most men—that would be an absolutely unprecedented invitation for any Lord-Lieutenant to receive. The novelty of the thing will attract him at once. And what's more, the idea will appeal to his better nature. I needn't tell you, Doyle, that the earnest desire of every Lord-Lieutenant is to assist the material and intellectual advancement of Ireland. He's always getting opportunities of opening technical schools and industrial shows of one sort or another. They've quite ceased to attract him. But we're displaying an entirely new spirit. By erecting a public statue in a town like this we are showing that we've arrived at an advanced stage of culture. There isn't another potty little one-horse town in Ireland that has ever shown the slightest desire to set up a great and elevating work of art in its midst. You may not appreciate that aspect of the matter, Doyle, but——"

"If I was to give my opinion," said Doyle, "I'd say that statues was foolishness."

"Exactly. But the Lord-Lieutenant, when he gets our invitation will give you credit for much finer feeling. Besides he'll see that we've been studying up our past history. The name of General John Regan will mean a great deal to him although it conveys very little to you."

"It's what Thady Gallagher is always asking," said Doyle, "who was the General?"

"Gallagher ought to know," said Dr. O'Grady, "and I've told him so."

"He does not know then. Nor I don't believe Father McCormack does. Nor I don't know myself. Not that it would trouble me if there never was a General, only that you have Mary Ellen's head turned with the notion that she'll be coming into a big fortune one of these days——"

"Is she not doing her work?" said Dr. O'Grady.

"Devil the tap she's done these two days, but what she couldn't help. Not that that bothers me, for it's nothing strange. She never was one for doing much unless you stood over her and drove her into it. But what has annoyed me is the way Constable Moriarty is never out of the kitchen or the back yard. He was after her before, but he's fifty times worse since he heard the talk about her being the niece of the General. Besides the notion he has that young Kerrigan wants her, which has made him wild."

"Moriarty ought to have more sense," said Dr. O'Grady.

"He ought," said Doyle, "but he hasn't. The tunes he whistles round the house would drive you demented if so be that you listened to them; but I needn't tell you I don't do that."

"You'll have to put up with it," said Dr. O'Grady. "It won't be for very long, and you needn't mind what Mary Ellen neglects so long as she attends properly on Mr. Billing."

"She'll attend him right enough," said Doyle. "Since ever she got the notion that he was going to make a lady of her, attending on him is the one thing that she will do."

"Then you needn't bother your head about anything else."

CHAPTER VIII

There are men in the world, a great many of them—who are capable of managing details with thoroughness and efficiency. These men make admirable lieutenants and fill subordinate positions so well that towards the end of their lives they are allowed to attend full dress evening parties with medals and stars hung round their necks or pinned on their coats. There are also a good many men who are capable of conceiving great ideas and forming vast plans, but who have an unconquerable aversion to anything in the way of a detail. These men generally end their days in obscure asylums, possibly in workhouses, and their ideas, after living for a while as subject matter for jests, perish unrealised. There is also a third kind of man, fortunately a very rare kind. He is capable of conceiving great ideas, and has besides an insatiable delight in working out details. He may end his days as a victorious general, or even as an emperor. If he prefers a less ostentatious kind of reward, he will die a millionaire.

Dr. Lucius O'Grady belonged to this third class. In the face of Doyle's objection to his expenditure on posters, he was capable of conceiving on the spur of the moment and without previous meditation, the audacious and magnificent plan of bringing the Lord-Lieutenant to Ballymoy and wrestling from a reluctant treasury a sufficient sum of money to build a third pier on the beach below the town. There may have been other men in Ireland capable of making such a plan. There was certainly no one else who would have set himself, as Dr. O'Grady did, with tireless enthusiasm, to work out the details necessary to the plan's success.

As soon as Doyle left him he mounted his bicycle and rode out to the Greggs' home. Mr. Gregg, being the District Inspector of Police, was usually a very busy man. But the Government, though a hard task-master in the case of minor officials, does not insist on anyone inspecting or being inspected on Sunday afternoons. Mr. Gregg had taken advantage of the Government's respect for revealed religion, and had gone out with a fishing rod to catch trout. Mrs. Gregg was at home. Being a bride of not more than three months' standing she had nothing particular to do, and was yawning rather wearily over the fashion-plates of a ladies' paper. She seemed unaffectedly glad to see Dr. O'Grady, and at once offered to give him tea. The doctor refused the tea, and plunged into his business.

"I suppose," he said, "that you'll have no objection to presenting a bouquet to Lady Chesterton when she comes to Ballymoy?"

"Is she coming?" said Mrs. Gregg. "How splendid!"

Before marrying Mr. Gregg she had lived in a Dublin suburb. Accustomed to the rich and varied life of a metropolis she found Ballymoy a little dull. She recognised Major Kent as "a dear old boy," but he was quite unexciting. Mrs. Ford, the wife of a rather morose stipendiary magistrate, had severely snubbed Mrs. Gregg. There was no one else, and the gay frocks of Mrs. Gregg's bridal outfit were wasting their first freshness with hardly an opportunity of being worn.

"Yes," said Dr. O'Grady. "She's coming with the Lord-Lieutenant to unveil the new statue."

"How splendid!" said Mrs. Gregg again. "I heard something about the statue, but please tell me more, Dr. O'Grady. I do so want to know."

"Oh, there's nothing particular to tell about the statue. It's to be to the memory of General John Regan, and will be unveiled in the usual way."

This did not add much to the information which Mr. Gregg, who himself had gleaned what he knew from Sergeant Colgan, had already given her. But Mrs. Gregg was quite content with it. She did not, in fact, want to know anything about the statue. She only asked about it because she thought she ought to. Her mind was dwelling on the dazzling prospect of presenting a bouquet to Lady Chesterton.

"Of course I should love to," she said. "But I wonder if I could—really, I mean."

Dr. O'Grady was a man of quick intelligence. He realised at once that Mrs. Gregg had not been listening to his account of the statue, but that she was replying to his original suggestion.

"It's not the least difficult," he said. "Anyone could do it, but we'd like to have it done really well. That's the reason we're asking you."

"Don't you have to walk backwards?" said Mrs. Gregg. "I'd love to do it, of course, but I never have before."

"There's no necessity to walk at all. You simply stand in the front row of the spectators with the bouquet in your hand. Then, when she stops opposite you and smiles—she'll be warned beforehand, of course—and she's had such a lot of practice that she's sure to do it right—you curtsey and hand up the bouquet. She'll take it, and the whole thing will be over."

"Oh," said Mrs. Gregg, "is that all?"

Dr. O'Grady was conscious of a note of disappointment in her voice. He felt that he had over-emphasized the simplicity of the performance. Mrs. Gregg would have preferred a longer ceremony. He did his best to make such amends as were still possible.

"Of course," he said, "your photograph will be in all the illustrated papers afterwards, and there will be a long description of your dress in *The Irish Times*."

"I'd love to do it," said Mrs. Gregg.

"Very well, then," said Dr. O'Grady, "we'll consider that settled."

Leaving Mrs. Gregg, he rode on to Major Kent's house. The Major, like all men who are over forty years of age, who have good consciences and balances in their banks, spent his Sunday afternoons sleeping in an armchair. No one likes being awakened, either in a bedroom by a servant, in a railway carriage by a ticket collector, or on a Sunday afternoon by a friend. The Major answered Dr. O'Grady's greeting snappishly.

"If you've come," he said, "to ask me to make a speech at that meeting of yours on Tuesday, you may go straight home again, for I won't do it."

"I'm not such a fool," said Dr. O'Grady pleasantly, "as to ask you to do any such thing. I know jolly well you couldn't. Even if you could and would, we shouldn't want you. We have Father McCormack, and Thady Gallagher, besides the American. That's as much as any audience could stand!"

"If it isn't that you want," said the Major, "what is it?"

"It's a pity you're in such an uncommonly bad temper, Major. If you were even in your normal condition of torpid sulkiness you'd be rather pleased to hear what I'm going to tell you."

"If you're going to tell me that you've dropped that statue folly, I shall be extremely pleased."

"The news I have," said Dr. O'Grady, "is far better than that. We've decided to ask the Lord-Lieutenant down to unveil the statue."

"He won't come," said the Major, "so that's all right."

"He will come when it's explained to him that——"

"Oh, if you offer him one of your explanations———"

"Look here, Major. I don't think you quite grasp the significance of what I'm telling you. Ever since I've known you you've been deploring the disloyalty of the Irish people. I don't blame you for that. You're by way of being a Unionist, so of course you have to. But if you were the least bit sincere in what you say, you'd be delighted to hear that Doyle and Thady Gallagher—Thady hasn't actually been told yet, but when he is he'll be as pleased as everyone else—you ought to be simply overjoyed to find that men like Doyle are inviting the Lord-Lieutenant down to unveil their statue. It shows that they're getting steadily loyaler and loyaler. Instead of exulting in the fact you start sneering in a cynical and altogether disgusting way."

"I don't believe much in Doyle's loyalty," said the Major.

"Fortunately," said Dr. O'Grady, "Doyle thoroughly believes in yours. He agrees with me that you are the first man who ought to be asked to join the reception committee. You can't possibly refuse."

"I would refuse if I thought there was the slightest chance of the Lord-Lieutenant coming. Do you think I want to stand about in a tall hat along with half the blackguards in town?"

"Mrs. Gregg is going to present a bouquet," said Dr. O'Grady.

"Looking like a fool in the middle of the street, while you play silly tricks with a statue?"

"You won't be asked to do all that," said Dr. O'Grady.

"I am being asked. You're asking me this minute, and if I thought it would come off——"

"As you think it won't you may as well join the committee."

"I won't be secretary," said the Major, "and I won't have hand, act, or part, in asking the Lord-Lieutenant to come here. We don't want him, for one thing."

"You'll not be asked so much as to sign a paper," said Dr. O'Grady. "If your name is required at the bottom of any document I'll write it for you myself."

"I wish to goodness," said the Major, "that Billing—if that's the man's name—had stayed in America attending to his own business, whatever it is, instead of coming here and starting all this fuss. There'll be trouble before you've done, O'Grady, more trouble than you care for. I wish to God it was all well over."

Nothing is more gratifying to the prophet of evil than the fulfilment of his own prediction. When the fulfilment follows hard on the prophecy, when not more than half an hour separates them, the prophet ought to be a very happy man. This was Major Kent's case. He foretold trouble of the most exasperating kind for Dr. O'Grady, and he was immediately justified by the event. Unfortunately he did not expect an immediate fulfilment of his words. Therefore he turned round in his chair and went to sleep again when the doctor left him. If he had been sanguine enough to expect that the doctor would be entangled in embarrassments at once, he would probably have roused himself. He would have followed Dr. O'Grady back to Ballymoy and would have had the satisfaction of gloating over the first of a long series of annoying difficulties. But the Major, though confident that trouble would come, had no hope that it would begin as soon as it did.

Dr. O'Grady was riding back to Ballymoy on his bicycle when he met Mrs. Ford, the wife of the stipendiary magistrate. She was walking briskly along the road which led out of the town. This fact at once aroused a feeling of vague uneasiness in the doctor's mind. Mrs. Ford was a stout lady of more than fifty years of age. She always wore clothes which seemed, and probably were, much too tight for her. Her husband's position and income entitled him to keep a pony trap, therefore Mrs. Ford very seldom walked at all. Dr. O'Grady had never before seen her walk quickly. It was plain, too, that on this occasion Mrs. Ford was walking for the mere sake of walking, a most unnatural thing for her to do. The road she was on led nowhere except to Major Kent's house, several miles away, and it was quite impossible to suppose that she meant to call on him. She had, as Dr. O'Grady knew, quarrelled seriously with Major Kent two days earlier.

Dr. O'Grady, slightly anxious and very curious, got off his bicycle and approached Mrs. Ford on foot. He noticed at once that her face was purple in colour. It was generally red, and the unaccustomed exercise she was taking might account for the darker shade. Dr. O'Grady, arriving within a few yards of her, took off his hat very politely. The purple of Mrs. Ford's face darkened ominously.

"Nice day," said Dr. O'Grady. "How's Mr. Ford?"

Mrs. Ford acknowledged this greeting with a stiff, scarcely perceptible bow. Dr. O'Grady realised at once that she was angry, very seriously angry about something. Under ordinary circumstances Mrs. Ford's anger would not have caused Dr. O'Grady any uneasiness. She was nearly always angry with someone, and however angry she might be she would be obliged to call on Dr. O'Grady for assistance if either she or her husband fell ill. There was no other doctor in the neighbourhood. The simplest and easiest thing, under the circumstances, would have been to pass on without comment, and to wait patiently until Mrs. Ford either caught influenza or was so deeply offended with someone else as to forget her anger against him. Society in small country towns is held together very largely by the fact that it is highly inconvenient, if not actually impossible, to keep two quarrels burning briskly at the same time. When, a week or two before, Mrs. Ford had been seriously angry with Mrs. Gregg, she confided her grievances to Dr. O'Grady. Now that she was annoyed with him she would be compelled to condone Mrs. Gregg's offence in order to tell her what Dr. O'Grady had done. In due time, so Dr. O'Grady knew, he would be forgiven in order that he might listen to the story of the quarrel, which by that time she would have picked with Major Kent. Therefore the doctor's first impulse was to imitate the Levite in the parable, and, having looked at Mrs. Ford with sympathy, to pass by on the other side.

But Dr. O'Grady was engaged in a great enterprise. He did not see how Mrs. Ford's anger could make or mar the success of the Lord-Lieutenant's visit to Ballymoy, but he could not afford to take risks. No wise general likes to leave even a small wood on the flank of his line of march without discovering whether there is anything in it or not. Dr. O'Grady determined to find out, if he could, what Mrs. Ford was sulking about.

"I daresay you have heard," he said, "about the Lord-Lieutenant's visit to Ballymoy. The date isn't fixed yet, but— —"

Mrs. Ford sniffed and walked on without speaking. Dr. O'Grady was not the kind of man who is easily baffled. He turned round and walked beside her.

"I needn't tell you," he said, "that the visit may mean a good deal to Mr. Ford. We've all felt for a long time that his services and ability entitle him to some recognition from the Government."

Mrs. Ford was quite unmollified. She walked on without looking round. She even walked a little quicker than she had been walking before. This was a foolish thing to do. She was a fat and elderly lady. Some of her clothes, if not all of them, were certainly too tight for her. The doctor was young and in good condition. She could not possibly hope to outstrip him in a race.

"My idea is," said Dr. O'Grady, "that when the Lord-Lieutenant meets Mr. Ford and becomes personally acquainted with him—there's to be a lunch, you know, in the hotel. A pretty good lunch, the best Doyle can do. Well, I confidently expect that when the Lord-Lieutenant finds out for himself what an able and energetic man Mr. Ford is— — After all, there are much nicer places than Ballymoy, besides all the jobs there are going under the Insurance Act, jolly well paid some of them, and you'd like living in Dublin, wouldn't you, Mrs. Ford?"

Mrs. Ford stood still suddenly. She was evidently going to say something. Dr. O'Grady waited. He had to wait for some time, because the lady was very-much out of breath. At last she spoke.

"Dr. O'Grady," she said, "I believe in plain speaking."

Neither Dr. O'Grady nor anyone else in Ballymoy doubted the truth of this. Nearly everybody had been spoken to plainly by Mrs. Ford at one time or another. Kerrigan, the butcher, was spoken to with uncompromising plainness once a week, on Saturday mornings.

"Quite right," said Dr. O'Grady, "there's nothing like it."

"Then I may as well tell you," said Mrs. Ford, "that I think it was due to my position—however much you may dislike me personally——"

"I don't. On the contrary——"

"——Due to my position as the wife of the resident magistrate that I, and not that Mrs. Gregg, should have been invited to present the bouquet to Lady Chesterton."

Dr. O'Grady gasped. Then he realised that he had made a fearful blunder.

"Half an hour ago," said Mrs. Ford, "that woman, who isn't even a lady, bounced into my house, giggling, and told me to my face that you had asked her——"

"Silly little thing, isn't she?" said Dr. O'Grady. "But of course, you have far too much sense to be annoyed by anything she said."

"Don't imagine for a moment," said Mrs. Ford, "that I am vexed. The slight, although it was evidently intentional, does not affect me in the least. If you knew me a little better than you do, Dr. O'Grady, you would understand that I am not at all the sort of person who cares about presenting bouquets."

"Of course not," said Dr. O'Grady. "We quite realised that. We understood that in your position, as wife of the resident magistrate of the district, the presentation of a bouquet would have been *infra dig*. After all, what's a bouquet? Poor little Mrs. Gregg! Of course it's a great promotion for her and she's naturally a bit above herself. But no one would dream of asking you to present a bouquet. We have far too high a respect for Mr. Ford's position."

"I think," said Mrs. Ford, "that I ought to have been consulted."

"Didn't you get my letter?"

"I got no letter whatever. The first news I had of his Excellency's intention of visiting Ballymoy came to me from that Mrs. Gregg half an hour ago, when she rushed into my drawing-room with her hair tumbling about her ears——"

"That's the worst of Doyle. He means well, but he's frightfully careless."

"What has Mr. Doyle to do with it?"

"I gave him the letter to post. Did you really not get it?"

"I got no letter whatever."

"I don't know what you must have thought of us. I don't know what Mr. Ford must have thought. I don't know how to apologise. But the first thing we did, the very first——Mrs. Gregg and the bouquet were a mere afterthought, we just tacked her on to the programme so that the poor little woman wouldn't feel out of it. She is a silly little thing, you know. Not more than a child after all. It was better to humour her."

"What was in the letter which you say you posted?" said Mrs. Ford.

"I didn't say I posted it. I said Doyle forgot to. It's in his pocket at this moment, I expect."

"What was in it?"

"Can you ask? There is only one thing which could possibly be in it. It expresses the unanimous wish of the committee—the reception committee, you know—Major Kent's on it—that you should present an illuminated address of welcome to His Excellency."

"If such a letter were really written——"

"My dear Mrs. Ford! But I don't ask you to take my word for it. Just walk straight into Ballymoy yourself. I'll stay here till you come back. Go into the hotel. You'll find Doyle in his own room drinking whisky and water with Thady Gallagher. Don't say a word to him. Don't ask him whether he was given a letter or not. Simply put your hand into his breast pocket and take it out."

"Thank you," said Mrs. Ford. "I do not care to have anything to do with Mr. Doyle when he is drunk."

"He won't be. Not at this hour. It takes a lot to make Doyle drunk."

"When the letter arrives, if it ever does, I shall consult Mr. Ford as to what answer I shall give."

"I can tell you what he'll say beforehand," said Dr. O'Grady. "He'll realise the importance of the illuminated address. He'll understand that it's *the* thing and that the bouquet——"

"Good-bye, Dr. O'Grady," said Mrs. Ford.

The doctor mounted his bicycle. His face was very nearly as purple as Mrs. Ford's. He had, with the greatest difficulty survived a crisis. He rode at top speed into Ballymoy, and dismounted, very hot, at the door of the hotel. It was shut. He ran round to the back of the house and entered the yard. Constable Moriarty and Mary Ellen were sitting side by side on the wall of the pig-stye. They were sitting very close together. Moriarty was whistling "Eileen Allan-nah" softly in Mary Ellen's ear.

"Where's Mr. Doyle?" said Dr. O'Grady.

"As regards the visit of the Lord-Lieutenant," said Constable Moriarty rousing himself and moving a little bit away from Mary Ellen, "what I was saying this minute to Mary Ellen was——"

"Where's Mr. Doyle?" said Dr. O'Grady.

"He's within," said Mary Ellen. "Where else would he be?"

"As regards the Lord-Lieutenant," said Constable Moriarty, "and seeing that Mary Ellen might be a near friend of the gentleman that the statue's for——"

Dr. O'Grady hurried through the back door. He found Doyle sitting over account books in his private-room. That was his way of spending Sunday afternoon.

"A sheet of notepaper," said Dr. O'Grady. "Quick now, Doyle. I have my fountain pen, so don't bother about ink."

"Where's the hurry?" said Doyle.

"There's every hurry."

He wrote rapidly, folded the letter, addressed it to Mrs. Ford, and handed it to Doyle.

"Put that in your trousers' pocket," he said, "and roll it round a few times. I want it to look as if it had been there for two or three days."

"What's the meaning of this at all?" said Doyle.

"Now get your hat. Go off as fast as you can pelt to Mr. Ford's house. Give that letter to the servant and tell her that you only found out this afternoon that you'd forgotten to post it."

"Will you tell me——?"

"I'll tell you nothing till you're back. Go on now, Doyle. Go at once. If you hurry you'll get to the house before she does. She was two miles out of the town when I left her and too exhausted to walk fast. But if you do meet her remember that you haven't seen me since yesterday. Have you got that clear in your head? Very well. Off with you. And, I say, I expect the letter will be looking all right when you take it out again, but if it isn't just rub it up and down the front of your trousers for a while. I want it to be brownish and a good deal crumpled. It won't do any harm if you blow a few puffs of tobacco over it."

CHAPTER IX

An hour later Doyle entered the doctor's consulting room.

"I have it done," he said. "I done what you bid me; but devil such a job ever I had as what it was." Doyle had evidently suffered from some strong emotion, anger perhaps, or terror. He felt in his pocket as he spoke, and, finding that he had no handkerchief, he wiped his forehead with the back of his hand. He looked at his hand afterwards and sighed. The hairs on the back of it were pasted down with sweat "Have you such a thing as a drop of anything to drink in the house?"

"I have not," said Dr. O'Grady, "how could I? Do you think I've lost all my self-respect? Is it likely I'd order another bottle of whisky out of your shop when you're dunning me every day of my life for the price of the last I got? Tell me what happened about the letter?"

Doyle passed a parched tongue across his lips. The inside of his mouth was quite dry. Extreme nervous excitement often produces this effect.

"If it was even a cup of tea," he said, "it would be better than nothing. I've a terrible thirst on me."

"Sorry," said Dr. O'Grady, "but I've no tea either. Not a grain in the house since last Friday. I hope this will be a lesson to you, Doyle, and will teach you not to ballyrag your customers in future. But I don't want to rub it in. Get on with your story."

"It could be," said Doyle, "that there'd be water in your pump. I'm not sure will I be able to speak much without I drink something."

"The pump's all right," said Dr. O'Grady. "Just sit where you are for a moment and I'll fetch you some water. It may give you typhoid. I wouldn't drink it myself without boiling it, but that's your look out."

He left the moor and returned a few minutes later with a large tumbler of cold water. Doyle looked at it mournfully. He knew perfectly well that the doctor had both whisky and tea in the house, but he recognised the impossibility of getting either the one or the other. He raised the glass to his mouth.

"Glory be to God," he said, "but it's the first time I've wetted my lips with the same this twenty years!"

"It will do you a lot of good if it doesn't give you typhoid," said Dr. O'Grady. "How did you get so frightfully thirsty?"

The question was natural. Doyle drank the whole tumbler of water at a draught. There was no doubt that he had been very thirsty.

"Will you tell me now," he said, "what had that one in the temper she was in?"

"Mrs. Ford," said Dr. O'Grady, "was annoyed because she thought she wasn't going to be given a chance of making herself agreeable to the Lord-Lieutenant."

"If she speaks to the Lord-Lieutenant," said Doyle, "after the fashion she was speaking to me, it's likely that she'll not get the chance of making herself agreeable to him a second time. Devil such a temper I ever saw any woman in, and I've seen some in my day."

"I know she'd be a bit savage. I hoped you wouldn't have met her."

"I did meet her. Wasn't she turning in at the gate at the same time that I was myself? 'There's a letter here, ma'am,' says I, 'that the doctor told me I was to give to you,' 'I suppose it was half an hour ago,' said she, 'that he told you that,' Well, I pulled the letter out of my pocket, and I gave it a rub along the side of my pants the same as you told me. 'I suppose you're doing that,' said she, 'to put some dirt on it, to make it look,' said she, 'as if it had been in your pocket a week.'"

"You wouldn't think to look at her that she was so cute," said Dr. O'Grady. "What did you say?"

"I said nothing either good or bad," said Doyle, "only that it was to get the dirt off the letter, and not to be putting it on that I was giving it a bit of a rub. Well, she took the letter and she opened it. Then she looked me straight in the face. 'When did you get this letter from the doctor?' says she. So I told her it was last Friday you give it to me, and that I hadn't seen you since, and didn't care a great deal if I never seen you again. 'You impudent blackguard,' says she, 'the letter's not an hour written. The ink's not more than just dry on it yet,' 'I'm surprised,' said I, 'that it's that much itself. It's dripping wet I'd expect it to be with the sweat I'm in this minute on account of the way I've run to give it to you.'"

"Good," said Dr. O'Grady. "If there was a drop of whisky in the house I'd give it to you. I'll look in a minute. There might be some left in the bottom of the bottle. A man who can tell a lie like that on the spur of the moment——"

"It was true enough about the sweat," said Doyle. "You could have wrung my shirt into a bucket, though it wasn't running did it, for I didn't run. It was the way she was looking at me. I'm not overly fond of

Mr. Ford, and never was; but I don't know did ever I feel as sorry for any man as I did for him when she was looking at me."

The doctor rose and took a bottle of whisky from the cupboard in the corner of the room. There was enough in it to give Doyle a satisfactory drink and still to leave some for the doctor himself. He got another tumbler and two bottles of soda water.

"You needn't be opening one of them for me," said Doyle, "I have as much water drunk already as would drown all the whisky you have in the bottle. What I take now I'll take plain."

"She may be a bit sceptical about the letter," said Dr. O'Grady, "but I expect when she's talked it over with Ford she'll see the sense of presenting the illuminated address."

"Is it that one present the address? Believe you me, doctor, if she does the Lord-Lieutenant won't be inclined for giving us the pier. The look of her would turn a barrel of porter sour."

"She'll look quite different," said Dr. O'Grady, "when the time comes. After all, Ford has to make the best of his opportunities like the rest of us. He can't afford to allow his wife to scowl at the Lord-Lieutenant."

"Was there no one else about the place, only her?" said Doyle.

"There were others, of course; but—the fact is, Doyle, if we got her back up at the start her husband would have written letters to Dublin Castle crabbing the whole show. Those fellows up there place extraordinary confidence in resident magistrates. They'd have been much more inclined to believe him than either you or me. If Ford was to set to work to spoil our show we'd probably not have got the Lord-Lieutenant down here at all. That's why I was so keen on your getting the letter to her at once, and leaving her under the impression that you'd had it in your pocket for two days."

"Devil the sign of believing any such thing there was about her when I left."

"She may come to believe it later on," said Dr. O'Grady, "when she and Ford have had time to talk the whole thing over together."

The doctor's servant came into the room while he spoke.

"Constable Moriarty is outside at the door," she said, "and he's wishing to speak with you. There's a young woman along with him."

"Mary Ellen, I expect," said Dr. O'Grady.

"He's upset in his mind about that same Mary Ellen," said Doyle, "ever since he heard she was the niece of the General. It's day and night he's round the hotel whistling all sorts and——"

"You told me all about that before," said Dr. O'Grady. "Bring him in, Bridgy, bring in the pair of them, and let's hear what it is they want."

Constable Moriarty entered the room, followed at a little distance by Mary Ellen. He led her forward, and set her in front of Dr. O'Grady. He looked very much as Touchstone must have looked when he presented the rustic Audrey to the exiled Duke as "a poor virgin, sir, an ill-favoured thing, sir, but mine own."

"If you want a marriage license," said Dr. O'Grady, "you've come to the wrong man. Go up to Father McCormack."

"I do not want a marriage license," said Constable Moriarty, "for I'm not long enough in the force to get leave to marry. And to do it without leave is what I wouldn't care to risk."

"If you don't want to marry her," said Doyle, "I'd be glad if you'd let her alone the way she'd be able to do her work. It's upsetting her mind you are with the way you're going on."

"Is it true what they tell me," said Moriarty, "that the Lord-Lieutenant's coming to the town?"

"I think we may say it is true," said Dr. O'Grady.

"To open the statue you're putting up to the General?"

"'Open' isn't the word used about statues," said Dr. O'Grady, "but you've got the general idea right enough."

"What I was saying to Mary Ellen," said Moriarty, "is that seeing as she's the niece of the General——"

"She's no such thing," said Doyle, "and well you know it."

"The doctor has it put out about her that she is," said Moriarty, "and Mary Ellen's well enough content. Aren't you, Mary Ellen?"

"I am surely," said Mary Ellen. "Why wouldn't I?"

"Look here, Moriarty," said Dr. O'Grady, "if you've got any idea into your head that there's a fortune either large or small coming to Mary Ellen out of this business you're making a big mistake."

"I wasn't thinking any such thing," said Moriarty. "Don't I know well enough it's only talk?"

"It will be as much as we can possibly do," said Dr. O'Grady, "to pay for the statue and the incidental expenses. Pensioning off Mary Ellen afterwards is simply out of the question."

"Let alone that she doesn't deserve a pension," said Doyle, "and wouldn't get one if we were wading up to our knees in sovereigns."

"So you may put it out of your head that Mary Ellen will make a penny by it," said Dr. O'Grady.

"It wasn't that I was thinking of at all," said Moriarty, "for I know you couldn't do it. My notion—what I was saying to Mary Ellen a minute ago—is that if the Lord-Lieutenant was to be told—at the time that he'd be looking at the statue—whenever that might be—that Mary Ellen was the niece of the General——"

"If you're planning out a regular court presentation for Mary Ellen," said Dr. O'Grady, "the thing can't be done. No one here is in a position to present anyone else because we have none of us been presented ourselves. Besides, it wouldn't be the least use to her if she was presented. The Lord-Lieutenant wouldn't take her on as an upper housemaid or anything of that sort merely because she'd been presented to him as General John Regan's niece."

"It wasn't a situation for Mary Ellen I was thinking of," said Moriarty.

"In the name of God," said Doyle, "will you tell us what it is you have in your mind?"

"What I was thinking," said Moriarty, "was that if the matter was represented to the Lord-Lieutenant in a proper manner—-about Mary Ellen being the General's niece and all to that—he might, maybe, see his way to making me a sergeant. It was that I was saying to you, Mary Ellen, wasn't it, now?"

"It was," said Mary Ellen.

"The idea of trotting out Mary Ellen on the occasion isn't at all a bad one," said Dr. O'Grady. "I'll see what can be done about it."

"I'm obliged to you," said Moriarty.

"But I don't promise that you'll be made a sergeant, mind that now."

"Sure I know you couldn't promise that," said Moriarty. "But you'll do the best you can. Come along now, Mary Ellen. It's pretty near time for me to be going on patrol, and the sergeant will check me if I'm late."

"There's something in that idea of Moriarty's," said Dr. O'Grady, when he and Doyle were alone again.

"I don't see what good will come of it," said Doyle, "and I'm doubting whether Thady Gallagher will be pleased. Mary Ellen's mother was a cousin of his own."

"She's a good-looking girl," said Dr. O'Grady. "If we had her cleaned up a bit and a nice dress put on her she'd look rather well standing at the foot of the statue. I expect the Lord-Lieutenant would be pleased to see her."

"And who'd be getting the lunch for the Lord-Lieutenant," said Doyle, "when Mary Ellen would be playing herself?"

"We'll get someone to manage the lunch all right. The great thing for us is to be sure of making a good general impression on the Lord-Lieutenant, and I think Mary Ellen would help. I daresay you've never noticed it, Doyle—it would be hard for you when she will not wash her face—but she really is a good-looking girl. The Lord-Lieutenant will want something of the sort to look at after he's faced Mrs. Ford and her illuminated address. She's not exactly—-"

"The man that would run away with that one," said Doyle vindictively, "would do it in the dark if he did it at all."

"Besides," said Dr. O'Grady, "we ought to think of poor little Mary Ellen herself. It'll be a great day for her, and she'll enjoy having a new dress."

"Who's to pay for the dress?" said Doyle.

"The dress will be paid for out of the general funds. I'll ask Mrs. Gregg to see about having it made. She has remarkably good taste. I'll tell her not to get anything very expensive, so you need not worry about that. And now, Doyle, unless there's anything else you want to settle with me at once, I think I'll write our invitation to the Lord-Lieutenant."

"It would be well if you did," said Doyle, "so as we'd know whether he's coming or not."

"Oh, he'll come. If he boggles at it at all I'll go up to Dublin and see him myself. A short verbal explanation—— We'll let him choose his own date."

Doyle lit his pipe and walked back to the hotel. He found Thady Gallagher waiting for him in his private room.

"What's this I'm after hearing," said Gallagher, "about the Lord-Lieutenant?"

"He's coming down here," said Doyle, "to open the new statue."

He spoke firmly, for he detected a note of displeasure in the tone in which Thady Gallagher asked this question.

"I don't know," said Gallagher, "would I be altogether in favour of that."

"And why not? Mustn't there be someone to open it? And mightn't it as well be him as another?"

"It might not as well be him."

"Speak out, Thady, what have you against the man?"

"I'm a good Nationalist," said Gallagher, "and I always was, and my father before me was the same."

"I'm that myself," said Doyle.

"And I'm opposed to flunkeyism, whether it's the flunkeyism of the rent office or— — —"

"Well and if you are, isn't it the same with all of us?"

"What I say is this," said Gallagher, "as long as the people of Ireland is denied the inalienable right of managing their own affairs I'd be opposed to welcoming into our midst the emissaries of Dublin Castle, and I'd like to know, so I would, what the people of this locality will be saying to the man that's false to his principles and goes back on the dearest aspirations of our hearts?"

He glared quite fiercely while he spoke, but Doyle remained serenely unimpressed.

"Talk sense now, Thady," he said. "Nobody'll say a word without it'd be yourself and you making a speech at the time. It's for the good of the town that we're getting him down here."

"What good?" said Gallagher, "tell me that now. What good will come of the like?"

Doyle was unwilling to confide the whole pier scheme to Gallagher. He contented himself with a vague reply.

"There's many a thing," he said, "that would be for the good of the town that might be got if it was represented properly to the Lord-Lieutenant."

"If I thought that," said Gallagher, "I might— —"

He was in a difficult position. He did not want to quarrel with Doyle, who provided him with a good deal of bottled porter, but he did not want to identify himself with a public welcome to the Lord-Lieutenant, because he had hopes of becoming a Member of Parliament. The idea of conferring a benefit on the town attracted him as offering a way out of his difficulty.

"I might— — —" he repeated slowly. "I wouldn't say but it's possible that I might."

"And you will," said Doyle soothingly, "you will."

"I'll not be a party to any address of welcome from the Urban District Council," said Gallagher.

"We wouldn't ask it of you. Doesn't everybody know that you wouldn't consent to it?"

"It's the Major put you up to it," said Gallagher.

"It was not then."

"If it wasn't him it was Mr. Ford, the R.M."

"If you'd seen Mrs. Ford when she heard of it," said Doyle, "you wouldn't be saying that. Tell me this now, Thady. Have you your speech ready for the meeting on Tuesday? Everybody's saying you'll be making a grand one."

"I haven't it what you'd call rightly ready," said Gallagher, "but I have it so as it will be ready when the time comes."

"It's you the people will be wanting to hear," said Doyle. "It's you they'd rather be listening to than any other one even if he was a member of Parliament: It's my opinion, Thady, and there's more than me that says it—it's my opinion there's better men that isn't in Parliament than some that is. I'll say no more presently; but some day I'll be doing more than say it."

CHAPTER X

The public meeting was a very great success, in spite of the absence of the Members of Parliament, who certainly gave poor value for their salaries. The town band, headed by young Kerrigan, who played the cornet, paraded the streets for half-an-hour before the meeting. It played "The Bonnie, Bonnie Banks of Loch Lomond" three times over, "The Boys of Wexford" twice, and "God Save Ireland" four times. This served to remind the people that something of an interesting and patriotic kind was going to happen. A band is much more effective in attracting public attention than a town crier, and it ought, one may suppose, to arrange a kind of code of tunes by means of which people would be able to tell at once without verbal inquiry what sort of event was intended. For an auction of household furniture, for instance, a thing which takes place when a family leaves the locality, the band might play "The Harp that Once Through Tara's Halls." Everybody would recognise the appropriateness of the words about the banquet hall deserted, and the departure of the people who had used it. For the other kind of auction, that at which the cows of men who refuse to pay their rents are sold, "God Save Ireland," would be suitable, and anyone who heard it would know that though he might attend the auction he had better not bid. An ingenious musician would have no difficulty in finding tunes which would suggest the presentation of illuminated addresses to curates or bank managers. Meetings convened for the purpose of expressing confidence in the Members of Parliament, of either the Nationalist or the Unionist parties, would naturally be announced by a performance of Handel's fine song "Angels ever Bright and Fair." There might be a difficulty about unusual events like the erection of statues, but a tune might be kept for them which would at all events warn people not to expect an auction, a presentation or a political meeting.

Nearly half the people who were doing business in the fair assembled at three o'clock in the square outside Doyle's hotel. According to the estimate printed afterwards in the *Connacht Eagle* there were more than two thousand persons present. Of these at least twenty listened to all the speeches that were made. The number of those who heard parts of some of the speeches was much larger, amounting probably to sixty, for there was a good deal of coming and going, of moving in and out of the group round the speakers. The rest of the audience stood about in various parts of the square. Men talked to each other on the interesting questions of the price of cattle and the prospects of a change in the weather. Women stood together with parcels in their hands and looked at each other without talking at all. But everyone was so far interested in the speeches as to join in the cheers when anything which ought to be cheered was said. The twenty stalwart listeners who stood out all the speeches attended to what was said and started the cheers at the proper moments. The stragglers who, hearing only a sentence or two now and then, were liable to miss points, took up the cheers which were started. The mass of the men, those who were talking about cattle, very courteously stopped their conversations and joined in whenever they heard a cheer beginning. There was, so Gallagher said in the next issue of the *Connacht Eagle,* an unmistakable and most impressive popular enthusiasm for General John Regan.

Father McCormack, standing on a chair borrowed from Doyle's Hotel, opened the proceedings. He said that Ireland had always been famed for its hospitality to strangers and its courtesy to women. He hoped that it always would be. Looking round on the faces of the men gathered in front of him, he felt quite certain that it always would be. Mr. Billing, who was to address the meeting that day, was a stranger, a very distinguished stranger, one whose name was a household word wherever the deeds of General John Regan were remembered, one whose name would be still better known when his forthcoming life of the General appeared. He was proud and pleased to extend to Mr. Billing on behalf of the audience a hearty *Caed Mille Failthe.* He hoped that Mr. Billing would carry back with him a pleasant recollection of Irish hospitality when he returned to—

Here Father McCormack hesitated and looked round. Dr. O'Grady, who was standing behind him whispered the word "Bolivia." Father McCormack repeated the word "Bolivia" aloud and everybody cheered. Father McCormack moistened his lips and went on to say that Mr. Billing was not a woman, but Irish courtesy, though always extended to women, was not confined to women. In the name of the audience he promised Mr. Billing some Irish courtesy.

A further reference to Mr. Billing's literary work gave Father McCormack an opportunity of warning his audience against Sunday newspapers published in England, which, he said, reeked of the gutter and were horribly subversive of faith and morals. Ireland, he added, had newspapers of her own which no one need be ashamed or afraid to read. As an evidence of the confidence he felt in the elevating character of Irish newspapers he called upon Mr. Thaddeus Gallagher, the distinguished editor of the *Connacht Eagle,* to address the meeting. Then with the assistance of Dr. O'Grady, he stepped off the chair. Having reached the ground safely he sat down on the chair. He had a perfect right to do this because he was chairman of the meeting; but a slight delay followed. Another chair had to be brought from the hotel for Gallagher to stand on.

Gallagher's speech was an eloquent paraphrase of the leading article which Dr. O'Grady had written for him the previous week. Once or twice he broke away from his original and said some very good things about the land question and Home Rule. But he always got back to Emmet, O'Connell, or one of the other patriots mentioned by Dr. O'Grady. Now and then, in a very loud tone, he said the name of General John Regan. Whenever he did so the audience was greatly pleased. He ended by announcing the names of the gentlemen who were to form "The Statue Committee." Father McCormack came first on the list. Mr. Billing was second. Major Kent, Dr. O'Grady, Doyle and Gallagher himself made up the number. He said that it was unnecessary for him to say anything about the fitness of these gentlemen for the high and responsible position to which they were being elected by the unanimous voice of their fellow countrymen.

Gallagher descended from his perch, but he was not allowed to sit down. He wanted to, because sitting down is a far more dignified way of ending a speech than slouching into the background. It was Doyle who interfered with him.

"Get up out of that, Thady," he said. "Don't you know the chair's wanted for the American gentleman? How is he to make a speech if you don't give him something to stand on?"

Gallagher, who had not actually succeeded in sitting down, left his chair with a protest.

"It would suit you better to be getting another chair," he said.

"It would not," said Doyle. "Would you have all the chairs that's in it brought out to the street?"

Mr. Billing stood up and smiled pleasantly. Father McCormack's exhortation had its effect. More than forty people gathered to hear what the stranger had to say. This was courtesy. The hospitality, it was presumed, had already been shown by Doyle. Gallagher, who still had hopes of finding out something about General John Regan, and Dr. O'Grady, who was equally anxious to hear the speech, leaned forward eagerly. Father McCormack crossed his legs and settled himself as comfortably as possible in his chair.

Mr. Billing proved a disappointment as a speaker. The substance of what he said was quite admirable, but he only spoke for five minutes. Now an audience, even if it is not listening and does not want to listen, is apt to complain that it is treated with a want of respect if a speaker gives it no more than five minutes.

"I reckon," said Mr. Billing, "that what's required of me is not oratory but dollars."

This was true but nude. In Ireland we have a sure instinct in such matters, and we know that the nude is never decent. We like everything, especially Truth, to have clothes on.

"Five hundred dollars is the amount that I'm prepared to hand over to your treasurer. As I understand, gentlemen, your doctor has secured the services of the Lord-Lieutenant of Ireland to unveil the statue. We don't figure much on fancy titles on our side, but I guess it's different here, and your doctor is a smart man. I may not see that Lord-Lieutenant, gentlemen, and I may not see the statue. I shall be researching in the principal libraries of the continent of Europe for documents bearing on the life of the great general. Whether I am here or not will depend on the date which that Lord-Lieutenant and your doctor fix up between them. But I'll be along for the occasion if I can."

The first sentence of Mr. Billing's speech was indecently nude. The remainder of it was offensively bald. There was once an elderly and cantankerous farm labourer who complained that he could not hear the curate when he preached. He was on the next occasion set in the forefront of the congregation and the curate spoke directly into his ear. The old man was unable to say that he did not hear, but he maintained an aggrieved attitude. "I heard him," he complained afterwards, "but what good was it to me? What I want is to have the Gospel druv well home to my soul." The feeling of most audiences is very much the same as his was. Unadorned statements of fact, or what is meant to be taken as fact, do not satisfy them. They like to have something, fact or fiction, driven thunderously home into their souls. The only one of Mr. Billing's hearers who was thoroughly well satisfied with his speech was Doyle. The statement that five hundred dollars were to be handed over to him was, in his judgment, of more value than many resonant periods.

But the Irish courtesy, praised by Father McCormack, prevailed against the general feeling of disappointment. When Mr. Billing ceased speaking there was a moment of doubtful silence. No one quite realised that he had really stopped. He had indeed descended from his chair, and, except for the top of his head, was invisible to most of the audience. But everyone expected him to get up again and start fresh. It seemed quite incredible that a public speaker, with an audience ready found for him, could possibly throw away a valuable opportunity and content himself with a simple five minutes of plain talk. It was not until Father McCormack rose from his chair with a sigh and began to make his way towards his presbytery that the people understood that the meeting was really at an end. Then they cheered quite heartily. Mr. Billing crossed the square and walked over towards the hotel. He smiled and nodded right and left as he went. An outburst of cheering pursued him through the door.

Sergeant Colgan and Constable Moriarty had stood during the speeches in a quiet corner near their barrack. When Father McCormack went home and Mr. Billing entered the hotel, they marched with great dignity up and down through the people. They looked as if they expected someone to start a riot It is the duty of the police in Ireland on all occasions of public meetings to look as if there might be a riot, and as if they are quite prepared to quell it when it breaks out. It is in this way that they justify their existence as a large armed force.

Occasionally Sergeant Colgan spoke a word of kindly advice to anyone who looked as if he had drunk more than two bottles of porter.

"It would be as well for you, Patsy," he would say, "to be getting along home."

Or, "I'm thinking, Timothy John, that you'd be better this minute if you were at home."

There are no stronger believers in the value of the domestic hearth than the police. They always want everyone to go home.

No one, least of all the individuals who received the advice personally, was inclined to leave the square. The meeting might be over, but there was still hope that young Kerrigan would muster the town band again and play "The Bonnie, Bonnie Banks of Loch Lomond" once or twice more. He did not do so, but the waiting people were rewarded for their patience by two events of some interest. Mr. Gregg came out of the barrack and crossed the square rapidly. He caught Dr. O'Grady and Major Kent just as they were turning to follow Mr. Billing into the hotel. Mr. Gregg was in uniform, and the determined way in which he took Dr. O'Grady by the arm would have made most people uncomfortable. It is not pleasant, even if your conscience is quite clear, to be grabbed suddenly by a police officer in the middle of the street. But Dr. O'Grady did not seem to mind. He went, though not very willingly, with Mr. Gregg into the police barrack. Major Kent followed them. Several men, perhaps a dozen, drifted across the square towards the barrack door. They had some hope of finding out what Mr. Gregg wanted with the doctor. They were not, however, given the opportunity of peering through the barrack windows. Sergeant Colgan saw them in good time and dispersed them at once.

"Get along home now out of that," he said, "every one of yez."

Then another event of great interest occurred. Mr. Billing backed his large motor-car along the lane which led from Doyle's back yard, and emerged into the square. There the car growled angrily while he shifted the levers and twisted the steering wheel. The people scattered this way and that while the machine, darting backwards and forwards, was gradually turned round. A splendid burst of cheering pursued him when he finally sped down the street and disappeared. It was understood by those who heard his speech that he had gone off at more than twenty miles an hour to ransack the great European libraries for information about General John Regan. Everyone felt that the splendid eagerness of his departure reflected a glory on Ballymoy.

Mr. Gregg led Dr. O'Grady and Major Kent into his office. He shut the door, offered his two guests chairs, and then lit a cigarette.

"It's rather an awkward business," he said, "and perhaps I oughtn't to say anything about it."

"If it hasn't anything to do with me personally," said the Major, "I think I'll leave you and the doctor to settle it together. I want to get home as soon as I can."

"Well, it does affect you more or less," said Mr. Gregg. "But of course you'll regard anything I say to you now as strictly confidential."

"Out with it, Gregg," said Dr. O'Grady. "I know by the look in your eye that you can't possibly keep it to yourself, whatever it is. You're simply bursting to tell it, whatever it is, whether we promise to keep it secret or not."

"All the same," said Gregg, "it wouldn't suit my book to have it generally known that I told you. It wouldn't suit at all. That fellow Ford is a vindictive sort of beast."

"Oh, it's Ford, is it?" said Dr. O'Grady. "I was afraid he might turn nasty. What an ass he is! Why can't he see that we're giving him the chance of his life?"

"He's doing his best to put a spoke in your wheel, O'Grady."

"Has he got anything against the statue?"

"Not exactly the statue."

"Or found out anything discreditable about the General?"

The doctor asked this question a little anxiously.

"No," said Gregg, "I don't think he knows a thing about the General. He asked me this morning who he was."

"Look here, O'Grady," said the Major. "You'd far better drop this whole business. What's the good of going on with it? A joke's a joke all right, but there's no use pushing things too far."

"What Ford's trying to do," said Gregg, "is to crab the Lord-Lieutenant part of the business. I thought I'd better tell you, so that you'd know exactly how things stand."

"You've not told me much, so far," said Dr. O'Grady. "What's Ford's particular line?"

"I expect he has more than one card up his sleeve," said Gregg, "but what he said to me this morning was that you couldn't possibly have the Lord-Lieutenant down here for any kind of public function unless— —"

"Can't I?" said Dr. O'Grady. "As it just happens I have a letter in my pocket this minute— —. It came by the midday post, just before the meeting, and I haven't shown it to anyone yet. He's coming this day fortnight, and will unveil the statue with the greatest pleasure."

"That settles it," said the Major, "you'll have to drop it now, whether you want to or not. You can't possibly have a statue ready by this day fortnight."

"Ford's point," said Gregg—"and there's something in it, you know—is that the Lord-Lieutenant can't attend a public function unless 'God Save the King' is played when he arrives. He simply must have that tune on account of his position. That's what Ford says, anyhow. And I'm inclined to think he's right. It always is played, I know."

"Well," said Dr. O'Grady, "we'll play it."

"You can't," said the Major. "If you attempt to get the town band to play 'God Save the King'— —"

"I don't think you can really," said Gregg. "I know you have a lot of influence with these fellows, but that blackguard Gallagher would get their backs up and— —"

"There'll be a riot," said the Major.

"There'll be no riot whatever," said Dr. O'Grady, "if the thing's managed properly."

"It's your affair, of course," said Gregg, "but I don't particularly want to have you going about under police protection, and that's what you'll be doing if Thady Gallagher catches you corrupting the nationalist principles of the people of Ballymoy by teaching the town band to play 'God Save the King.'"

This threat seemed to produce a certain effect on Dr. O'Grady. He sat silent for nearly a minute. Then he asked Gregg for a cigarette, lit it, and smoked thoughtfully.

"I say, Gregg," he said at last. "How many people are there in Ballymoy, do you think, who would recognise 'God Save the King' if it was played suddenly when they weren't expecting it?"

"Oh, lots," said Gregg, "lots."

"You would, I suppose," said Dr. O'Grady, "and the Major would. Ford would, I suppose. Father McCormack might. What about your police?"

"The sergeant might think it was 'Auld Lang Syne,'" said Gregg, "he has no ear whatever. But Moriarty would know it the minute he heard it."

"Moriarty might be made to keep his mouth shut," said Dr. O'Grady. "You could threaten him."

"Your idea," said Gregg, "is to spring it on the town band under some other name and have it played as if——"

"I'd tell them that it was one of Moore's Melodies."

"No good," said Gregg. "Far too many people know it. Even if you shut up Moriarty in a cell between this and then——"

"The thing for you to do, O'Grady," said the Major bitterly, "is to get a version of 'God Save the King 'with variations. I once heard 'Home, Sweet Home,' done that way and it was all I could do to make out what tune it was meant to be."

"That's probably meant to be sarcastic," said Dr. O'Grady, "but it's not at all a bad idea. I've heard 'Home Sweet Home' done that way and I know exactly how it goes. 'Tum—tum——tiddle—adle—diddle—tum—tum—twee— Mid pleasures and palaces—Tiddle—tiddle—tum—tiddle—rat—a ti—tee— too—though we may roam.' Just as you think that you're going to recognise the tune it kind of fades away and you're left with the impression that small dogs are chasing each other up and down the piano. I don't see why something of the same kind mightn't be done with 'God Save the King,' The Lord-Lieutenant would be quite satisfied, because he'd think we were always just going to begin and probably come to the conclusion in the end it was the fault of the band that the tune never quite came off. On the other hand Gallagher, whatever suspicions he might have, couldn't possibly swear that we were playing anything objectionable. I wonder if there's a version of 'God Save the King' with variations to be got anywhere?"

"Never heard of one," said Gregg.

"I'll write to-night," said Dr. O'Grady. "If there isn't such a thing I might work one up myself. It can't be very difficult."

"That will be just what's wanted," said the Major, "to ensure the success of the day. A musical composition of yours, O'Grady, played by our own town band, will be quite likely to distract the Lord-Lieutenant's attention from the fact that here's no statue here for him to unveil."

"You won't mind my using your piano, Major," said Dr. O'Grady. "I haven't got one of my own, and I'll have to strum it out for a bit before I get it into shape for the band."

"It'll be a score off Ford," said Gregg, "if you succeed. But I don't expect you will."

CHAPTER XI

Inflexible determination is one of the qualities which the truly great leader of men shares with the domestic pig; though in the case of the pig it is generally spoken of as obstinacy. But the leader—General, Prime Minister or Captain of Industry—is distinguished from the pig by a certain intellectual suppleness which makes his obstinacy a more effective though less showy thing. The pig, being determined to go his own way, has no better idea than to tug desperately against the rope which is tied round his ankle. He tugs unwaveringly up to the very last moment, but in the end he is beaten because his master, having at command stout sticks and other instruments of torture, is stronger than he is. It is noble and heroic of the pig to persist in refusing to recognise that merely tugging the opposite way is no use to him. The great commander is wiser and in reality no less noble. He realises very early that destiny, armed with whips and goads, has a rope round his leg. He tugs, but when he finds that the rope will not break and that the whip cuts cruelly, he stops tugging and goes about to outwit destiny. Pretending to yield to the pull of the rope, he succeeds at last in getting his own way. Thus a general, faced by a hostile army, securely entrenched on the opposite bank of a deep river, does not make more than one attempt to swim his men across in the face of a concentrated rifle fire. The pig would make several attempts, would go on trying until he had no soldiers left, because he would feel that the only thing really worth doing was to assert himself against the confident foe. But the general, when he has lost enough men to convince him of the impossibility of a frontal attack by swimming, stops trying it and adopts another plan. He sees not only the insolent flags which wave upon the opposite bank, but the far off end of the campaign. He is not less determined than the pig would be to chastise the foe which is thwarting him, but he sees that this can be done quite as effectually by occupying the enemy's capital as by the mere winning of a battle. He understands that it is good to sacrifice the immediate for the sake of the ultimate object. He gives up the idea of fighting his way across and sends out scouts to discover the source of the river. When he finds it he leaves part of his army to watch the enemy while the other part marches round the end of the river and enters the enemy's chief stronghold from the back.

Thus he gains his object and establishes his character for determination without losing half his army.

Dr. Lucius O'Grady was a born leader of men. He discovered very soon that in the matter of the performance of "God Save the King" by the town band, fate had a rope round his leg and was likely to scourge him uncomfortably if he pulled against it. The introduction of variations into the tune proved to be a much more difficult matter than he had supposed. He worked hard for six hours on Major Kent's piano, and produced two versions of which he thought well, though neither of them completely satisfied him. He sent for Constable Moriarty and played them over to him. Moriarty sat and listened to the first.

"Would you know what that tune was, Moriarty?" said Dr. O'Grady.

"I would, of course. Anybody would. I don't say but there's bits in it that isn't right, but you have the tune safe enough."

"Would Thady Gallagher know it?"

"He would," said Moriarty, "and what's more he'd be lepping mad when he heard it. And you couldn't wonder. You wouldn't like it yourself, doctor, if somebody was to play a tune at you that you hated worse nor you hate the devil."

Dr. O'Grady was disappointed.

"Are you sure now," he said, "that he wouldn't be taken in by the variations? I don't know whether you quite realise the number of variations there are? Just listen to me again."

He played his composition through once more, touching the notes which gave the tune very softly, hammering hard at the long runs and fiery groups of semi-quavers which he had sandwiched in between the scraps of tune.

"I wouldn't say," said Moriarty, "that you've destroyed it altogether; though it's my opinion that it's better the way it was before you set your hand to it. But anyhow you needn't be uneasy. There isn't a man, woman or child that ever heard the tune but would know what you're aiming at."

Dr. O'Grady felt that Moriarty's judgment in the matter was too decisive and confident to be ignored.

"Very well," he said. "Now listen to this."

He played through the second of his two compositions.

"Now," he said, "what tune is that, Moriarty?"

Moriarty scratched his head and looked inquiringly at the doctor.

"Is it what tune is that that you're asking me?" he said.

"Exactly. What tune is it?"

"It's no tune at all," said Moriarty.

"Do you mean to say you don't recognise it?"

"I do not, and what's more nobody could. For there's no tune in it, only noise."

The doctor hesitated. Moriarty's opinion was in one respect quite satisfactory. Neither Gallagher nor anyone else in Ballymoy was likely to recognise the tune. It might, of course, fail to impress the Lord-Lieutenant as being quite the proper thing. But that was a difficulty which could be got over. The Lord-Lieutenant was not likely to listen very attentively, and if he were told definitely that the band was playing "God Save the King" he might possibly believe it.

"I'm thinking," said Dr. O'Grady, "of teaching that piece of music to the town band."

"It'll fail you to do that," said Moriarty.

"I don't see why."

"You can try it," said Moriarty, "but you'll not be able. Anything those fellows could play, I'd be able to whistle, and if it's what I couldn't whistle they'll not be able to play it."

"You could whistle that all right if you tried."

"I could not. Nor I couldn't play it on an ivy leaf, nor yet on a comb, and if I couldn't there's nobody else could. I'm not saying it isn't good music, doctor, for it may be. But there's neither beginning nor end of it, nor there isn't anything in the middle that a man would be able to catch hold of."

Dr. O'Grady shut the piano with a bang. Constable Moriarty rose from his seat.

"If there's nothing more you'll be wanting with me, doctor," he said, "it might be as well if I was getting back to the barrack. The sergeant's terrible particular these times. Mr. Gregg, the D.I., has him annoyed with finding fault here and there and everywhere. Not that I blame Mr. Gregg, for everybody knows he's a nice quiet kind of a man who'd ask for nothing only to be let alone. But that's what he can't get on account of Mr. Ford."

"Mr. Ford's a public nuisance," said Dr. O'Grady; "but I think we'll be able to get rid of him."

"It would be no great harm if he was dead," said Moriarty.

"The Lord-Lieutenant," said Dr. O'Grady, "is almost sure to promote him. That kind of man who never can let other people's business alone, is just suited to Dublin Castle."

Moriarty got as far as the door of the room and then stopped.

"Will it be all right," he said, "about Mary Ellen? You'll remember, doctor, that I was speaking to you about her, the way she'd be given the chance of speaking to the Lord-Lieutenant."

"I'll settle about her at once," said Dr. O'Grady. "Did you say you were going straight back to the barrack?"

"I am," said Moriarty. "It'll be better for me if I do on account of the way Mr. Ford does be talking to— —"

"Are you going so straight that you won't see Mary Ellen on the way?"

"It could be," said Moriarty, "that I might see her."

"Very well, then, do. And tell her to meet me at Mrs. Gregg's house at— —" He glanced at his watch.

"Let me see, it's nearly half past two, and I'll have to spend a few minutes pacifying the Major. Suppose you tell her to meet me at Mrs. Gregg's at a quarter past three. Will you be sure to give her that message?"

"I will," said Moriarty.

"And don't you keep the girl late now, Moriarty, with love making in the pig-stye or any nonsense of that kind."

"Is it likely I would?"

"It is very likely. But don't do it."

"It is not likely then, seeing as how I ought to be back in the barrack this minute on account of the way Mr. Gregg has the sergeant annoyed— —"

"There's only one thing worse than keeping Mary Ellen late," said Dr. O'Grady, "and that is delaying me. Be off with you at once."

Constable Moriarty marched off towards the barrack, fully determined to call on Mary Ellen on the way. Dr. O'Grady went into the stable yard to look for Major Kent. He found him smoking a pipe and reading the last number of the *Connacht Eagle* in an empty loose box.

"I thought you'd like to know," said Dr. O'Grady, "that I've finished with the piano, so you can go back into the house again."

"Quite sure you're finished?" said the Major.

"Quite."

"Because if there are any final touches to put to your oratorio, you'd better do them to-day. The piano won't be there to-morrow. I've made up my mind to sell it at once."

"Silly thing to do," said Dr. O'Grady. "You won't get half what it's worth if you sell it in a hurry like that."

"Even if I have to pay someone to take it away," said the Major, "I shall make a good bargain. It's better to lose a little money than to spend the rest of my life in a lunatic asylum."

"You know your own business best, of course, and if you think you can preserve what little intelligence you have by giving Thady Gallagher or some other fellow a present of your piano—"

"I think I can save myself from being turned into a gibbering maniac," said the Major, "by making sure that you'll never have the chance of composing music in my house again. Since eight o'clock this morning you've been at it. I could hear you whenever I went, mixing up hymns and waltzes and things with 'God Save the King.' I tried to get a bit of lunch at half past one, but I had to fly from the house."

"It's over now anyhow," said Dr. O'Grady. "And you needn't sell the piano. I've given up the idea of producing a new version of that tune for the Lord-Lieutenant. I find that the thing can't be done in the time. I'm going to give him 'Rule Britannia' instead."

"With variations?"

"No. Quite plain. It'll do him just as well as the other. In fact from his point of view it's rather the more patriotic tune of the two, and there won't be any local objection to it because nobody can possibly recognise it."

It was in this way that Dr. O'Grady showed the true greatness of his mind. A weaker man, daunted by the difficulty of arranging "God Save the King" in such a way as to suit all tastes, might have given up the attempt to provide a musical welcome for the Lord-Lieutenant. A man of narrow obstinacy, the kind of man who is really like a pig, would have persevered, in spite of Constable Moriarty's warning, in trying to teach his variations to the town band. Dr. O'Grady, knowing that the main thing was the success of his general scheme, turned from a tune which presented insuperable difficulties, and fixed upon another, which would, he hoped, be comparatively easy to manage. The Major ought to have admired him; but did not He was in a condition of extreme nervous exasperation which rendered him unfit to admire anything.

"You'll get us all into an infernal mess with your foolery," he said sulkily, "and when you do, you needn't come to me to help you out."

"I won't. But don't forget the committee meeting to-morrow morning. Half past eleven, in Doyle's Hotel."

"What committee?"

"Strictly speaking," said Dr. O'Grady, "it's two committees—the Statue Erection Committee and the Lord-Lieutenant Reception

Committee—but the same people are on both, so we may as well make one meeting do."

"I'll go," said the Major, "in the hope, utterly vain of course, of keeping you from further excesses."

"Good," said Dr. O'Grady. "And now I must hurry off. I've a lot to do between this and then."

Major Kent was a kind-hearted man. He had suffered intensely during the earlier part of the day and for some hours had been seriously angry with Dr. O'Grady. But his sense of hospitality was stronger than his resentment.

"Stop for half an hour," he said, "and have something to eat Now that you've given up punishing my poor old piano we might have lunch in peace."

"Can't possibly waste time in eating. I've far too much to do. To tell you the truth, Major, I don't expect to sit down to a square meal until I join the Lord-Lieutenant's luncheon party. Till then I must snatch a crust as I can while running from one thing to another."

Dr. O'Grady mounted his bicycle and hurried off. He reached the Greggs' house at twenty minutes past three, Mary Ellen was standing on the step outside the door, smiling in a good-humoured way. Mrs. Gregg, who looked hot and puzzled, was just inside the door.

"Oh, Dr. O'Grady," she said, "I'm so glad you've come. This girl won't go away and I can't make out what she wants."

"It was Constable Moriarty bid me come," said Mary Ellen.

"It's all right," said Dr. O'Grady. "I arranged for her to be here. I'll explain everything in one moment. Is that the only frock you own, Mary Ellen?"

"It is not; but I have another along with it."

"I don't expect the other is much better," said Dr. O'Grady. "Just look at that dress, will you, Mrs. Gregg?"

Mrs. Gregg looked at Mary Ellen's clothes carefully. She did not appear to admire them much.

"There's a long tear in the skirt," she said. "It might be mended, of course, but—and she has only one button on her blouse, and her boots are pretty well worn out, and she's horribly dirty all over."

"In fact," said Dr. O'Grady, "you couldn't very well present her to the Lord-Lieutenant as she is at present."

"The Lord-Lieutenant!" said Mrs. Gregg.

"Perhaps I forgot to mention," said Dr. O'Grady, "that Mary Ellen must be presented. She's the grand niece of General John Regan."

"Are you really?" said Mrs. Gregg.

"It's what the doctor has put out about me," said Mary Ellen.

"It isn't a matter of what I've put out or haven't put out," said Dr. O'Grady. "Mr. Billing has publicly acknowledged her as the grand niece of the General. Didn't he, Mary Ellen?"

"He did," said Mary Ellen.

"And Mr. Billing is the greatest living authority on everything connected with the General. So that settles it. Under those circumstances she must, of course, be presented to the Lord-Lieutenant when he comes down to unveil the statue."

"I wonder what Mrs. Ford will say?" said Mrs. Gregg.

"We'll talk about that afterwards. What I want to get at now is this: Will you undertake to see that Mary Ellen is properly dressed for the ceremony?"

"Oh, I couldn't possibly."

Mrs. Gregg looked at Mary Ellen again as she spoke, looked at her very carefully and then smiled.

Mary Ellen was also smiling. The proper dressing of Mary Ellen was plainly a very difficult task. Mrs. Gregg's smile was at first contemptuous. Mary Ellen's, on the other hand, was purely good-natured, and therefore very attractive, Mrs. Gregg began to relent.

"Won't you come in?" she said to Dr. O'Grady.

"Certainly," he replied. "Mary Ellen, you sit down on that chair in the hall and wait till we call you."

"I don't know can I wait," said Mary Ellen.

"If Moriarty's lurking about for you," said Dr. O'Grady, "let him wait. It'll do him good. It's a great mistake for you to make yourself too cheap. No girl ought to. Moriarty will think a great deal more of you in the end if you keep him waiting every day for half an hour or so."

"It's not him I'm thinking of," said Mary Ellen, "but it's Mr. Doyle."

Dr. O'Grady took no notice of this remark. He did not believe that Mary Ellen was very much afraid of Mr. Doyle. He followed Mrs. Gregg into the dining-room. Mary Ellen sat down.

"She really is rather a pretty girl," said Mrs. Gregg.

"Then you'll undertake the job," said Dr. O'Grady. "You won't have to pay for anything, you know. We'll charge whatever you like to buy against the statue fund."

Mrs. Gregg did not appear to be listening. She was thinking deeply.

"I have an old silk slip," she said, "which might be made down."

"Capital! A silk slip will be the very thing."

Dr. O'Grady had no idea what a silk slip might be. But his enthusiastic welcome of the suggestion passed unnoticed. Mrs. Gregg was still thinking.

"I could get a white muslin," she said, "with an embroidered yoke and a wide collar. It wouldn't cost very much."

"We'd like the thing done well," said Dr. O'Grady, "not extravagantly, of course, but well."

"Shell look quite sweet," said Mrs. Gregg; "but what will Mrs. Ford say?"

"She'll have to be kept in a good temper."

"Kept!" said Mrs. Gregg, giggling delightedly.

She was very much afraid of Mrs. Ford, but she found a fearful joy in entering into a conspiracy against her with Dr. O'Grady for ally.

"Kept!" she repeated, "but she never is."

"My idea," said Dr. O'Grady, "is that you should dress Mary Ellen yourself, according to your own ideas, and at the same time consult with Mrs. Ford, giving her the impression that she's doing the whole thing herself. I should think you ought to be able to manage that."

This did not seem to Mrs. Gregg a very easy thing to do. She hesitated.

"I'm afraid I couldn't," she said at last. "I don't see how I could."

"All that's required," said Dr. O'Grady, "is a little tact. You are always good at tact, Mrs. Gregg. I'm perfectly certain that you'll be able to manage. You must suggest each garment you intend to put on the girl in such a way that Mrs. Ford will think that she suggested it. That ought to be easy enough." Everybody likes being credited with the possession of tact. This is curious, because hardly anyone likes being called a liar; and yet tact is simply a delicate form of lying. So, of course, is politeness of every kind, and nobody considers it wrong to aim at being polite. Mrs. Gregg, who would certainly have resented an accusation of habitual untruthfulness, felt flattered when Dr. O'Grady said she was tactful. She even believed him and allowed herself to be persuaded to undertake the management of Mrs. Ford.

"Good," said Dr. O'Grady. "Then I'll leave the whole business in your hands. I have to be off. But you've no time to lose. You'll have to set about your work at once. I'll send Mary Ellen to you as I go through the hall. You can measure her, and then take her over to see Mrs. Ford. After that you'd better order the new dress. If there's any hitch in the proceedings you can send for me, but I don't see why there should be."

He shook hands with Mrs. Gregg and hurried from the room, without giving her the chance of making any kind of protest or asking any more questions.

He found Mary Ellen seated on an uncomfortable oak chair in the hall.

"Mary Ellen," he said, "would you like a new dress?"

"I would."

"Then go into the dining-room—the room I've just come out of. You'll find Mrs. Gregg there. Do exactly what she tells you without making any objections or asking questions. If she insists on your washing your face, wash it, without grumbling. If Moriarty is waiting for you anywhere between this and the town—— Is Moriarty waiting for you?"

"He might."

"Well, if he is, I'll clear him out of the way. You'll be going into the town in a few minutes with Mrs. Ford and Mrs. Gregg. It wouldn't do at all to have him making eyes at you from the side of the road when you're walking with those two ladies. Mrs. Gregg mightn't mind; but Mrs. Ford would be certain to object. She's not the kind of lady who likes to see other people enjoying themselves."

"He wouldn't do the like," said Mary Ellen.

"I wouldn't trust him," said Dr. O'Grady.

Moriarty was, in fact, waiting for Mary Ellen about a hundred yards from the gate of the Greggs' house. Dr. O'Grady rebuked him sharply. Moriarty asserted that he was engaged in patrolling that particular road in simple obedience to the call of duty.

"That may possibly be true," said Dr. O'Grady, "though it doesn't sound likely."

"It was the sergeant gave me my orders," said Moriarty.

"Patrol some other road, then," said Dr. O'Grady. "You're not wanted here."

"What the sergeant said was that it would be better for me to patrol along between Mr. Gregg's house and Mr. Ford's, so that if either the one or the other of them was to see me he'd know that I *was* patrolling. I wouldn't say a word against Mr. Gregg, who's a nice gentleman enough, and easy pleased. But it's hard to pacify Mr. Ford, and the sergeant thought——"

"I can tell you this," said Dr. O'Grady, "that if Mrs. Ford catches you lying in wait for Mary Ellen on the road outside her house, it will be a jolly sight harder to pacify Mr. Ford than it was before. Surely you can understand that."

Moriarty understood it thoroughly. He was not very well pleased, but he was a young man of considerable prudence, and was filled with a sincere desire to rise in his profession. He spent the rest of the afternoon in patrolling a road at the other end of Ballymoy.

Dr. O'Grady hurried on. His next stop was at the door of Kerrigan's shop. The elder Kerrigan was leaning against the wooden slab on which he was accustomed to cut up joints. He was smoking a pipe.

"Where's your son?" said Dr. O'Grady.

"He's within in the back yard," said Kerrigan.

"Tell him I want to see him."

"I'm not sure can he come to you; for he's taking the skin off a sheep that he's just after slaughtering."

"Let him wash his hands," said Dr. O'Grady. "The sheep can wait."

"I'm not sure will he come," said Kerrigan. "He's not overly much pleased with you this minute, doctor, and that's the truth."

"What's the matter with him?"

"It's on account of your saying that he was thinking of getting married to Mary Ellen."

"It was Gallagher said that. I'd nothing to do with it one way or the other."

"I wouldn't be minding myself what you said," said Kerrigan, "knowing well that you wouldn't be meaning any harm, whatever it was; though the girl's no match for him, and I wouldn't care for him to be carrying on with her, when it's a girl with a fortune he ought to get, and what's more, can get, whenever I choose to ask for her. But I wouldn't pay any attention to what was put out about him and Mary Ellen. I'm only telling you so as you'd know why it is that the boy's mind is riz against you."

"What nonsense! Everybody in the place knows that it's Constable Moriarty who's after the girl."

"It's just that that's troubling the boy. On account of Constable Moriarty being a comrade of his; so that he wouldn't like him to be thinking—— But sure, I'll fetch him for you, if you like."

Young Kerrigan appeared a few minutes later. His father did not come back with him. He may have felt it necessary, in the interests of his business, to go on skinning the sheep. It was evident at once that the young man was in a bad temper, but Dr. O'Grady did not mean to waste time in explanations if he could possibly help it.

"Listen to me, Kerrigan," he said, "do you know this tune?"

He whistled "Rule Britannia" slowly and distinctly.

"I do not know it," said young Kerrigan, "nor I don't want to."

Dr. O'Grady whistled it through again.

"It's a good tune," he said. "It would be a nice one for the band to learn."

"It would not."

"What's the matter with you?" said Dr. O'Grady. "To look at the expression of your face anybody'd think that the sheep in the back yard had been skinning you."

"You know well what's the matter with me."

"If you're nursing a grievance," said Dr. O'Grady, "because Thady Gallagher told the American gentleman that you were married to Mary Ellen and had twins, you ought to have more sense."

It is always very difficult to remain in a bad temper with anyone who insists on being pleasant and cheerful. Young Kerrigan began to give way. He grinned unwillingly.

"That's the first I heard of twins," he said.

"And he only said it to please the American gentleman," said Dr. O'Grady. "Nobody believed him."

"Sure I know well enough," said young Kerrigan, "that there has to be lies told to the likes of that one. How else would you content them? I wouldn't mind myself what was said, knowing it was meant for the best, only that Constable Moriarty——"

"Moriarty doesn't mind a bit," said Dr. O'Grady; "so if it's only his feelings you're thinking of, you may just as well listen to this tune."

He whistled "Rule Britannia" through once more. He threw great spirit into the last few bars.

"It's a good tune enough," said young Kerrigan.

"Could the band learn it?"

"It could, of course, if so be that I had the tune right on the cornet. It would be a queer thing if I couldn't incense the rest of them into doing what had to be done with the other instruments."

"I can't play the cornet myself," said Dr. O'Grady, "but I'll whistle the tune to you as often as you like, or if you prefer it we might get the loan of a piano somewhere, and I'll play it for you. I can't borrow the Major's again for reasons which I'm not in a position to explain to you, but we can easily get the use of another if you think it would help you."

"The whistling will do," said young Kerrigan. "Will you come inside with me now and I'll try can I get it. But, doctor——"

He hesitated and looked doubtfully at Dr. O'Grady. It was plain that he had a favour to ask and was a little afraid of asking it.

"Well," said Dr. O'Grady encouragingly.

"If so be that you were to see Moriarty— —" said young Kerrigan.

Then he hesitated again.

"I see far too much of him," said Dr. O'Grady.

"I'd be obliged to you if you'd tell him that I never looked next nor nigh Mary Ellen, nor wouldn't. Even if I wanted the girl I wouldn't go behind Moriarty's back to get her; and I don't want her."

"I'll make that perfectly plain to him. Come along now and learn the tune."

CHAPTER XII

The cornet is of all instruments in an ordinary band the one which produces the most penetrating sounds. While young Kerrigan was practising a new tune on it all the inhabitants of the town of Ballymoy were able to hear him. He was aware of this and sorry for it. He did not, indeed, pity his fellow-citizens. He would not have understood a complaint made by a nervous person who found himself tortured by a long series of efforts to get a note in the middle of a tune right. It would have struck him as mere affectation if anyone had objected to hearing the same tune with the same gasping wheeze in the middle of it played over a hundred or a hundred and fifty times in one evening. Young Kerrigan's dislike of the necessary publicity of his practising was similar to that which other artists feel when members of the public break in and see their work in an incomplete condition. He liked his music to be appreciated. He felt that acknowledgment of the stages by which it came to its ultimate perfection was likely to diminish its glory. But he had no place in which he could practise except the back yard of his father's house, and that, unfortunately, was in the very middle of the town.

In order to get out of his difficulty young Kerrigan adopted the plan of learning new tunes only in autumn and winter, when strong gales were blowing. On a calm summer evening every note of the cornet, whether right or wrong, was heard. Even the sounds which were not quite notes but only painful grunts penetrated open windows and doors. But when a storm was raging most of the notes were blown away, and only occasionally, when there happened to be a lull, did anybody except young Kerrigan himself hear anything. The plan worked out very satisfactorily. Amid the rush and clatter of a tempest people took no notice of such stray wailings of the cornet as reached their ears. But, like many excellent plans, this one was liable to break down in emergencies. It broke down badly when Dr. O'Grady insisted that the band should learn "Rule Britannia" in the middle of August.

Young Kerrigan readily got a grip on the tune. He could whistle it and hum it quite correctly after he had heard it six or seven times. But to reproduce it on the cornet required practise, and the weather was remarkably calm and fine. Kerrigan, in spite of his dislike of being heard, was obliged to devote the evening to it after the doctor left him. Next morning he went at it again, beginning at about eleven o'clock. He got on very well up to the point at which the words declare that "Britons never, never, never shall be slaves." The notes which went to the "nevers" were particularly troublesome. He tried them slowly, one by one, leaving a short interval between them. He tried them fast, running them into each other. He tried beginning the tune again after each mistake, in hope of getting over his difficulty, as a bicyclist sometimes gets up a hill, by running. He was a man of patient disposition, and he was still working hard at one o'clock.

Mr. Thaddeus Gallagher spent the morning transcribing shorthand notes in his office. There had been a singularly interesting meeting of the County Council the day before in the neighbouring town of Dunbeg. Gallagher had written down every word of an acrimonious debate. He wanted to publish a verbatim report of it. As a rule noise of any kind affected him very little, and at first he took no notice whatever of young Kerrigan's cornet. But the continual repetition of the tune gradually beat it into his brain. He found his pencil moving across the paper in a series of short staccato bounds every time young Kerrigan got to "Never, never, never." He became by degrees vaguely uneasy. The tune was one which he had certainly heard before. He could not remember where he had heard it. He could not remember what it was. But he became more and more sure that it was connected in his mind with some unpleasant associations. At last he found it impossible to go on with his work. The most passionate invective of the most furious of the County Councillors failed to move him to any interest. He glanced at his watch. It was just one o'clock. The meeting of the Reception Committee was to take place at half-past one. Gallagher felt that he had just time to investigate thoroughly the disagreeable tune. He got up and left his office.

Constable Moriarty was standing at the door of the barrack listening to young Kerrigan. Being himself a musician, he appreciated the difficulty of playing "Rule Britannia" on a cornet, and enjoyed hearing young Kerrigan's efforts. When he saw Gallagher come out of his office he was greatly pleased, and showed his feeling by grinning broadly. Gallagher saw the grin, and his suspicion that the tune was an offensive one deepened at once. He crossed the road.

"What's that," he said, "that young Kerrigan's playing?"

"It's a new tune," said Moriarty, "and it's hoped that the town band will learn it."

"Where did he get it?"

"I'm after hearing," said Moriarty, "that it was the doctor taught it to him. But I don't know is that true. You can't believe the half of what you hear in this town."

"What tune is it?"

"I don't know that I could put a name to it this minute; but there's no need for you to be uneasy, Mr. Gallagher. It's not what you think it is."

"I'm not thinking about it at all," said Gallagher, very untruthfully.

"I'm glad of that," said Moriarty. "I was afraid from the look of you as you came out of the office that you might be thinking it was 'God Save the King.' But it's not."

"I was thinking no such thing, for young Kerrigan knows and the doctor knows, and you know yourself, Constable Moriarty, that the people of this town is all good Nationalists, and that if the tune you're after naming was to be played in the streets— —"

"It's not it, anyway," said Moriarty, "so you may make your mind easy."

Gallagher's mind was very far from being easy, but he saw that he was not likely to get any more information out of Constable Moriarty. He crossed the road and entered the hotel. Doyle was in the commercial room trying to induce Mary Ellen to sweep the floor. It was in the commercial room that the meeting of the Committee was to be held that afternoon. Doyle wanted some, if not all, of the dirt removed from the floor beforehand.

"What tune's that young Kerrigan's playing?" said Gallagher.

"I don't know," said Doyle. "I've more to do than to be listening to tunes. Mary Ellen, can you not see that there's three corks out of porter bottles underneath the table? Will you take them out of it now, like a good girl?"

"I'm not satisfied in my mind about that tune," said Gallagher.

"What harm is there in it?"

"I don't know yet is there any harm, but I don't like it, and I'd be glad if I knew what tune it is. I have it in my mind that it's a tune that ought not to be played."

"Mary Ellen," said Doyle, "what tune is it that young Kerrigan's playing?"

"How would I know?" said Mary Ellen.

"Well, put down that sweeping brush," said Doyle. "For all the good you're doing with it you might as well never have taken it up. I never seen such a girl. Put it down now and run across to Constable Moriarty, who's standing at the door of the barrack— —"

"I'd be ashamed," said Mary Ellen, "so I would."

"If you're not ashamed of the state this room's in," said Doyle, "it would take more than Moriarty to shame you. Run along now, when you're bid, and ask him what tune it is that Kerrigan's playing."

Mary Ellen, who hoped that the interruption might put an end to the sweeping once for all, left the room.

"If there's one in the town that knows the tune," said Doyle, "it'll be Moriarty. I'd say myself that he must know pretty near every tune there is in the world."

"He might tell her," said Gallagher, "or he might not. I was talking to him this minute and he wouldn't tell me."

"He'll tell Mary Ellen," said Doyle. "He's always after that girl, and it's my belief he'll tell her anything that she'd ask him. There's some that's took that way. Foolishness I call it."

"It's the way he wouldn't tell me when I asked him," said Gallagher, "that and the grin on his face when he saw me that has me sure that there's some insult intended to the people of this town with that tune. It's what I wouldn't stand, and the doctor and the rest of them may make their minds up to it. It's what I won't stand is to have tunes played here that is against the political convictions of the people."

"Who'd do the like?" said Doyle soothingly.

"What I say is this," said Gallagher, "if there's no reason to be ashamed of the tune, let them say out boldly what tune it is. I have it in the back of my mind that I've heard that tune before now, and it's not the kind of tune that decent men would be listening to."

"Have sense, can't you, Thady. There's nobody wanting to annoy you."

"There may not be," said Gallagher, "but there's more than one in this town that's the enemies of the Irish people and would be glad to see the cup of freedom dashed from the lips of the men that have spent their lives in the struggle for Home Rule and that has it now as good as got."

"Have sense," said Doyle, but he spoke without real energy or much purpose. He had little hope that Gallagher, once embarked on a peroration, would stop until he had used up all the words at his command. He was quite right in his reading of his friend's character. Gallagher went on:

"It isn't the declared enemies of the people that we'd be afraid of," he said. "We'll meet them in the open field as we've always met them and they'll fly before the spectacle of a united people as they've always fled, the tyrants of other days, the blood-sucking landlords——"

"God help the poor Major," said Doyle.

"But the traitors within the camp," said Gallagher, "the men that is occupying positions in the gift of the people of Ireland, that's taking our pay, and at the same time plotting contrivances for the heaping of insults on the dearest convictions of our hearts——"

Mary Ellen entered the room while Gallagher was speaking. Bewildered by the splendour of his eloquence she stopped short just inside the door and gazed at him with her mouth open. Doyle took advantage of a slight hesitation in Gallagher's oration to speak to her.

"What tune is it, Mary Ellen?" he said.

"I couldn't rightly say," said Mary Ellen.

"Didn't I tell you," said Gallagher, "that there was underhand work going on?"

"What tune did Moriarty say it was?" said Doyle.

"He said it was a tune the doctor is after teaching young Kerrigan," said Mary Ellen.

"What did I tell you?" said Gallagher. "Maybe you'll believe me now."

"The best thing for you to do, Thady." said Doyle, "if you're dead set on finding out about that tune is to go and ask young Kerrigan what it is. The boy's a decent boy, and he'll tell you if you speak civil to him."

"I'll do that same," said Gallagher, "and if I discover——"

"You'd better be quick about it then," said Doyle, "for the committee is to meet at half after one and I wouldn't like you'd miss the proceedings."

"Come along with me," said Gallagher. "I wish you to hear the way I mean to talk to young Kerrigan."

Doyle did not want to listen to Gallagher browbeating young Kerrigan, but he realised that he would save time and a long argument if he went at once. He made a last appeal to Mary Ellen to collect at least the corks which were on the floor. Then he went out with Gallagher. In the porch of the hotel they met Major Kent who was a scrupulously punctual man, on his way to the committee meeting.

"You're a bit early, Major," said Doyle. "But if you'll step into the commercial room you won't have long to wait. Thady and I have to cross the street on a matter of business but we'll be back in less than five minutes. The doctor might be here any time and I see Father McCormack coming along from the presbytery."

Doyle was unduly optimistic. He was not back in five minutes. He did not, indeed, get back for nearly half an hour.

Kerrigan, very red in the face, and rather exhausted, was still blowing vigorously into his cornet when Gallagher and Doyle entered the back-yard. Gallagher went straight to business without wasting any time on preliminary politeness.

"Will you stop that blasted noise," he said.

Kerrigan took the cornet from his lips and gazed at Gallagher in extreme surprise.

"Speak civil to the boy," said Doyle.

"What tune is that?" said Gallagher.

"What Mr. Gallagher's meaning to say," said Doyle, "is that party tunes is unsuitable to this locality where the people has always lived in peace and harmony, Protestant and Catholic together, and respected one another. That's what Mr. Gallagher means, and if Constable Moriarty didn't annoy him it's what he'd say."

"It's a tune the doctor taught me," said young Kerrigan, "and it's a fine tune, so it is."

"What's the name of it?" said Gallagher.

"That," said young Kerrigan, "is what I was meaning to ask the doctor next time he happened to be passing but if you're in a hurry to know, Mr. Gallagher, you can ask him yourself. It's likely you'll be seeing him before I do."

Young Kerrigan's words were perfectly civil; but there was a look in his eyes which Gallagher did not like and the tone in which he spoke suggested that he meant to be impudent.

"I'll take no back talk from you," said Gallagher. "What tune is it?"

"I don't know what tune it is," said Kerrigan.

"You're a liar," said Gallagher. "You know well what tune it is."

"Speak civil now, Thady," said Doyle, "speak civil to the boy."

"I may be a liar," said Kerrigan, "but it's the truth I told you this minute. And liar or no liar it's the truth I'll speak now, when I tell you that I'm not near as damned a liar as yourself, Mr. Gallagher. So there's for you. What do you mean by telling the American gentleman that I was married to Mary Ellen and her with twins? Was that a lie now or was it not? Twins! Cock the like of that one up with twins! If I'm a liar I'd tell more sensible lies than that."

"Whisht, now, whisht," said Doyle. "Sure if Mr. Gallagher said that, isn't the girl a cousin of his own, and hadn't he the best right to say it?"

"Come along out of this," said Gallagher.

"The sooner you're gone the better I'll be pleased," said Kerrigan.

"And let me tell you this, Mr. Kerrigan, junior. You'll be sorry for this day's work for the longest day ever you live. When the League boys hear, and they will hear, about the tune that you mean to play——"

"Come along now, Thady," said Doyle. "Come along. You've enough said. We're late for the meeting of the committee already, and we'll be later yet if you don't come on. You wouldn't like to keep Father McCormack waiting on you."

"I've had enough of your committee," said Gallagher. "What's your statue only foolishness?"

"Sure everybody knows that," said Doyle.

"And what's your Lord-Lieutenant only——"

"Come on, now," said Doyle, "isn't it for the benefit of the town we're doing it? And it's yourself that's always to the fore when there's good work to be done."

"I will not go with you," said Gallagher.

They had passed through Kerrigan's shop and reached the street, when Gallagher delivered this ultimatum. Doyle hesitated. He was already late for the committee meeting. If he waited to coax Gallagher out of his bad temper he might miss the meeting altogether. He looked at the door of the hotel. Father McCormack was standing at it, waiting, perhaps, for him and Gallagher.

"Come now, Thady," he said, "have sense. Don't you see Father McCormack waiting for you?"

"I see him," said Gallagher.

"And don't you know well enough that you'll have no luck if you go against the clergy?"

The appeal was a strong one, and had he been in any ordinary temper Gallagher would have yielded to it at once. But he was very angry indeed, far too angry to be influenced by purely religious considerations. He walked straight across the square to his office, entered it, and slammed the door behind him. Doyle followed him as far as the threshold. There he stopped and looked round. He saw Father McCormack go into the hotel. A minute later Mrs. Gregg hurried down the street and went into the hotel. Doyle sighed heavily and entered Gallagher's office. Difficult and unpleasant as his task was likely to be, he felt that he must propitiate Thady Gallagher.

"Thady," he said, "is there a drop of anything to drink in the place?"

"There is not," said Gallagher, "nor I wouldn't drink it if there was."

This confirmed Doyle's view of the extreme seriousness of the situation. That Gallagher should be prepared to defy the clergy was bad enough. That he should adopt an ascetic's attitude towards drink was worse. But Doyle did not quite believe that Gallagher meant what he said. He opened a door at the far end of the office and whistled loudly. A small boy who had been cleaning type in the printing-room, appeared, rubbing his inky hands on his trousers.

"Michael Antony," said Doyle, "will you step across to the hotel and tell Mary Ellen to give you the bottle of whisky that she'll find in the cupboard in my own room? If you can't find Mary Ellen—and it's hardly ever she is to be found when she's wanted—you can fetch the bottle yourself. If you don't know the way to my room you ought to."

Michael Antony, who was very well accustomed to errands of this kind, went off at once. Doyle glanced at Gallagher, who appeared to be absorbed in completing the transcription of his shorthand notes, the task at which he had been interrupted in the morning by young Kerrigan's cornet playing. He seemed to be very busy. Doyle got up and left the room, went into the kitchen which lay beyond the printing-room, and returned with two tumblers and a jug of water. Gallagher looked up from his writing for an instant. Doyle noticed with pleasure the expression of violent anger was fading from his eyes. Michael Antony, who was a brisk and willing boy, returned with a bottle rather more than half full of whisky.

"Mary Ellen was upstairs along with a lady," he said. "But I found the bottle."

"If you were three years older," said Doyle, "I'd give you a drop for your trouble. But it wouldn't be good for you, Michael Antony, and your mother wouldn't be pleased if she heard you were taking it."

"I have the pledge since Christmas, anyway," said Michael Antony.

"Thady," said Doyle, when the boy had left the room, "it's a drink you want to quench the rage that's in you."

Gallagher looked up from his papers. He did not say anything, but Doyle understood exactly what he would have said if his pride had not prevented him from speaking.

"The width of two fingers in the bottom of the tumbler," said Doyle, "with as much water on top of that as would leave you free to say that you weren't drinking it plain."

The amount of water necessary to soothe Gallagher's conscience was very small. Doyle added it from the jug in driblets of about a teaspoonful at a time. At the sound of the third splash Gallagher raised his hand. Doyle laid down the jug at once. Gallagher, without looking up from his papers, stretched out his left hand and felt about until he grasped the tumbler. He raised it to his lips and took a mouthful of whisky.

"Thady," said Doyle, "you've no great liking for Mr. Ford."

"I have not," said Gallagher. "Isn't he always going against me at the Petty Sessions, he and the old Major together, and treating me as if I wasn't a magistrate the same as the best of them?"

"He does that, and it's a crying shame, so it is, that he's allowed to; but sure that's the way things are in this country."

Gallagher took another gulp of whisky and waited. Doyle said nothing more. He appeared to have nothing more to say and to have mentioned Mr. Ford's name merely for the sake of making conversation. But Gallagher wished to develop the subject.

"What about Mr. Ford?" he said, after a long silence.

"He's terrible down on the erection of the statue to General John Regan."

"I'm that myself," said Gallagher.

"Mr. Ford will be pleased when he hears it; for there'll be no statue if you set your face against it. It'll be then that Mr. Ford will be proud of himself. He'll be saying all round the Country that it was him put a stop to it."

"It will not be him that put a stop to it."

"It's what he'll say, anyway," said Doyle.

Gallagher finished his whisky in two large gulps.

"Let him," he said.

"Have another drop," said Doyle. "It's doing you good."

Gallagher pushed his tumbler across the table. Doyle replenished it.

"I'd be sorry," said Doyle, "if Mr. Ford was to be able to say he'd got the better of you, Thady, in a matter of the kind."

"It'll not be me he'll get the better of."

"He'll say it," said Doyle, "and what's more there's them that will believe it. For they'll say, recollecting the speech you made on Tuesday, that you were in favour of the statue, and that only for Mr. Ford you'd have had it."

"If I thought that——" said Gallagher.

"Come along over now to the committee," said Doyle, "and we'll have the statue just in derision of him."

"It isn't the statue that I'm objecting to," said Gallagher, "nor it isn't the notion of a new pier. You know that, Doyle."

"I do, of course."

"And if it's the wish of the people of this locality that there should be a statue——"

"It is the wish," said Doyle. "Didn't you say yourself that the people was unanimous about it after the meeting in the market square?"

Gallagher rose from his chair and pushed his papers back on the table. He crushed his soft hat down on the back of his head and turned to the door.

"Come on," he said.

"I knew well," said Doyle, "that you'd do whatever was right in the latter end. And as for the tune that was troubling you, it's even money that the band will never play it. Father McCormack was telling me yesterday that the big drum's broke on them on account of one of the boys giving it a kind of a slit with the point of a knife. The band will hardly ever be able to play that tune or any other tune when they haven't got a big drum."

CHAPTER XIII

Major Kent passed through the narrow hall of the hotel, went up a flight of stairs and entered the commercial room. Mary Ellen was on her hands and knees under the table which stood in the middle of the room. She was collecting the corks which had offended Doyle's eye. There were more than three of them. She had four in her left hand, and was stretching out to grasp two more when the Major entered the room. As soon as she saw him she abandoned the pursuit of the corks, crept out from underneath the table, and stood looking at the Major. She expected him to order a drink of some sort. Most people who entered Doyle's commercial room ordered drinks. The Major was slightly embarrassed. Mary Ellen evidently expected him to say something to her, and he did not know what to say. He did not want a drink, and he could not think of any subject of conversation likely to interest a tousled girl who had just been crawling about the floor on her hands and knees. At last he said "Good morning." Mary Ellen gaped at him and then smiled. The Major, recollecting that it was half-past one o'clock, and therefore no longer morning, said that it was a fine evening. Mary Ellen's smile broadened. The Major expressed a polite hope that she was quite well. He thought of shaking hands with her, and wished that he had brought a pair of gloves with him, Mary Ellen's hands were certainly dirty and they looked hot. But he was not obliged to shake hands. Mary Ellen realised that he was a kind of man new to her, one who did not want a drink. She left the room, came back again almost at once for the broom which she had forgotten, and then left decisively, slamming the door.

The Major crossed the room and looked out of the window. He saw Doyle and Gallagher go into Kerrigan's shop, and wondered vaguely what they wanted there. He saw Constable Moriarty telling a story, evidently of a humorous kind, to Sergeant Colgan, at the door of the police barrack. The story—he judged from Moriarty's gestures—had something to do with Doyle and Gallagher. He wondered, without much real interest, what the story was. There was nothing else of an exciting kind to be seen from the window. The Major turned and walked to the opposite corner of the room. He stood in front of a small square mahogany table. On it was a stuffed fox in a glass case. The Major looked at it carefully from several points of view. It was a very ordinary fox, and appeared to have been stuffed a long time. Moths had eaten the fur off its back in several places, and one of its eyes, which were made of bright brown beads, was hanging from the socket by a thread. The glass of the case was exceedingly dusty. The Major, finding the fox dull and rather disgusting, left it and went over to the fireplace. Over the chimney piece hung a portrait of a very self-satisfied priest who looked as if he had just dined well. A gold Latin cross, attached to a black ribbon watch guard, rested gracefully on the large stomach of the man. The stomach struck the Major as one which was usually distended to its utmost capacity. The portrait was remarkable for that fuzziness of outline which seems to be inevitable in enlarged photographs. The frame was a very handsome one, elaborately carved and gilt.

Next the picture of the priest, unframed and attached to the wall with tacks, was a large coloured supplement, taken from an American paper. It presented a famous boxer stripped to the waist in the act of shaking hands with a dejected-looking opponent. Underneath his large picture was a list of the boxer's most famous conflicts, with date and a note of the number of rounds which each victim had survived. Round the central picture were twelve small ones, in which the hero appeared in the act of felling other fighters, not so heroic or less muscular. The Major, who had done some boxing in his day, looked at the picture with critical interest. Then Father McCormack entered the room.

"I'm in good time after all," he said. "I was afraid, maybe, the meeting might be over when I saw Doyle and Thady Gallagher going into the office of the *Connacht Eagle* after leaving Kerrigan's shop."

"You're time enough," said the Major. "If you're not more than half-an-hour late it's time enough for any meeting that's held in this town."

"That's true too," said Father McCormack. "As a general rule that's true enough. But I've known meetings that was over and done with before the time when they ought to be beginning. That would be when there might be something to be done at them that some of the members would be objecting to if they were there. I've known that happen, and I shouldn't wonder if you'd been caught that way yourself before now."

"So far as I know," said the Major, "nothing of the sort has happened this time. There's no reason why it should. When anything as silly as this statue business is on hand everybody is sure to be unanimously in favour of it."

"That's true enough. But where's the rest of the committee?"

"Nobody has turned up so far, except myself," said the Major.

"Well," said Father McCormack, "I'm as well pleased. To tell you the truth, Major, I'm glad of the chance of a few minutes quiet talk with you while we have the place to ourselves. I thought it my duty, and you'll understand me that I'm not casting reflections on you nor yet on the doctor, and I'd be sorry to say a word against Doyle, or for the matter of that against Thady Gallagher, though it would be better if he had more sense. But anyway, I thought it my duty to acquaint the bishop with what was going on."

"The statue idea?" said the Major. "Well, what did he say? I don't know your bishop personally, but I suppose a man could hardly be in his position if he was altogether a fool."

"Believe me or not as you like," said Father McCormack, "but when I got the bishop's answer to my letter, it turned out that he knew no more than myself about General John Regan."

"That doesn't surprise me in the least. I don't believe any one knows who he was."

"What the bishop said was that it might look queer if I was to take no part in the proceedings when the Lord-Lieutenant was coming to unveil the statue."

"That puts you in a safe position anyhow," said the Major. "If it turns out afterwards that there is anything fishy about the General, the bishop and the Lord-Lieutenant will have to share the blame between them."

"What I want to know from you," said Father McCormack, "is this: Is the Lord-Lieutenant coming or is he not?"

"I've only got the doctor's word for it. He says he is."

"The doctor's a fine man, and there's not many things he'd set his hand to but he'd carry them through at the latter end. But the Lord-Lieutenant! The Lord-Lieutenant is—well now, do you think it likely that the Lord-Lieutenant is coming down here?"

"It's not the least likely," said the Major, "but there's nothing about this whole business that is. It isn't likely in my opinion that there was such a person as General John Regan. It wasn't likely beforehand that we'd subscribe to put up a statue to him. I don't see that the Lord-Lieutenant is any more unlikely than lots of other things that have happened."

"I'm glad to hear you say that," said Father McCormack.

He and Major Kent were standing together at the window while they talked. Neither of them noticed that Mary Ellen had come into the room. She stood for some time near the door, hoping that either the Major or Father McCormack would look round. Neither of them did, so she sidled slowly into the room and stood beside the stuffed fox. She was a very well mannered girl, and most unwilling to interrupt an earnest, possibly an important conversation. When Father McCormack made his last remark she felt that her chance had come. It was evident from the tone in which he spoke, that he and the Major had reached a more or less satisfactory conclusion of their business, She coughed, and then tapped lightly with her knuckles on the glass case of the stuffed fox. Both Father McCormack and the Major looked round.

"There's a lady below," said Mary Ellen.

"A lady!" said Major Kent. "Surely to goodness we're not going to have women on this committee. Things are bad enough without that."

"Who is she?" said Father Mctormack.

"It's Mrs. Gregg," said Mary Ellen, "and it's the doctor she's asking for."

"The doctor's not here," said Father McCormack. "Can't you see that for yourself?"

"If it's Mrs. Gregg," said the Major, "you'd better show her up. You can't leave her standing by herself in the hall till the doctor chooses to come. I wish to goodness he would come. I can't think why he isn't here. This is his show entirely."

Mrs. Gregg came into the room while the Major was speaking. She looked agitated and, in spite of the fact that she had been waiting downstairs for nearly ten minutes, was almost breathless.

"Oh, Major Kent," she said, "where's Dr. O'Grady? Such a dreadful thing has happened. I don't know what to do. Just fancy—Mrs. Ford has written to me——"

"There's no use appealing to me," said the Major. "I can't do anything with Mrs. Ford. She and I are hardly on speaking terms. It's not my fault—at least I don't think it is—but you must see Mrs. Gregg, that I can't interfere about any letter she may have written to you."

Mrs. Gregg shook hands with Father McCormack, but her head was turned away from him as she did so. She had little hope that he could interfere effectually to settle the difficulty created by Mrs. Ford.

"Dr. O'Grady said that I——"

The Major interrupted her.

"You'd far better wait till the doctor comes," he said. "He'll be here in a minute."

"But I can't wait. Mrs. Ford is down at the dressmaker's now. It'll be too late if I wait. What am I to do? It will spoil the whole thing if Mrs. Ford insists——"

Dr. O'Grady came in. He was whistling cheerfully, not "Rule, Britannia," but a harmless Irish jig.

"Hullo!" he said. "You here, Major. Good. And Father McCormack. There's nothing like punctuality. And Mrs. Gregg. How do you do, Mrs. Gregg? Everything going on all right about Mary Ellen's costume?"

"Oh, no, it isn't. But I'm so glad you've come. Mrs. Ford— —"

"Excuse me one moment, Mrs. Gregg," said Dr. O'Grady. "I just want to ask Father McCormack one question. Listen now, Father McCormack. Do you know this tune?"

He began to whistle "Rule, Britannia." When he was about half way through Mrs. Gregg interrupted him.

"I can't wait," said Mrs. Gregg. "I really can't. Mrs. Ford is at the dressmaker's and— —"

"I'll attend to that in one minute, Mrs. Gregg. But I must get Father McCormack's opinion on this tune first. Doyle and Gallagher may arrive at any moment, and then I shan't be able to go into the question. Now Father McCormack, do you recognise the tune I whistled you?"

"I've heard it," said Father McCormack, "and to the best of my belief it was at a military tournament up in Dublin last year."

"It's 'Rule, Britannia,'" said the Major. "And if it's played in this town there'll be a row."

"There might be," said Father McCormack, "if Thady Gallagher knows what tune it is."

"He won't," said Dr. O'Grady. "You didn't know yourself, Father McCormack, and if you didn't I'm quite satisfied that Thady Gallagher won't. We can count on your keeping your mouth shut, Major, I suppose. Now, Mrs. Gregg, what has Mrs. Ford been doing?"

"She says," said Mrs. Gregg, "that Mary Ellen is to wear a plain dark grey tweed dress, and I had it all planned out— —"

"White muslin," said Dr. O'Grady, "with a silk slip. I remember."

"It'd look perfectly sweet," said Mrs. Gregg, "and I took her to the dressmaker yesterday evening just as you told me. I had the whole thing arranged. She was to have a blue sash."

"I was," said Mary Ellen, who was still standing beside the stuffed fox.

"And Mrs. Ford agreed at the time," said Mrs. Gregg, "and now I've just got a note from her saying that a dark grey tweed would be much more suitable because it would be useful afterwards."

"It seems to me," said Dr. O'Grady, "that you haven't managed this business quite as tactfully as I expected you would."

"Mrs. Ford said she was going straight to the dressmaker to order the grey tweed. She's there now, most likely."

Mrs. Gregg's voice had a break in it. It seemed to Dr. O'Grady that she was on the verge of tears. He turned to Mary Ellen.

"Which would you rather have, Mary Ellen, a white muslin frock, or a grey tweed, one that would be useful to you afterwards? Don't be in a hurry to decide. Think it well over."

Mary Ellen seemed very well inclined to take this advice. She stood quite silent with one of her fingers pressed against the corner of her mouth. She was thinking deeply.

"I can't bear to have everything I settled upset by that woman," said Mrs. Gregg. "I wish you'd never made me ask her to help. I wish I'd never— —"

"We had to keep her in a good temper," said Dr. O'Grady.

"You'll not be able to do that," said the Major, "nobody could."

"It's nothing but spite makes her do it," said Mrs. Gregg. "It's just because I'm presenting a bouquet and she's not."

"Hang it all!" said Dr. O'Grady. "It can't be that. I told her distinctly that she'd be allowed to hand over the illuminated address. What more can she want?"

"It's all spite and jealousy," said Mrs. Gregg, "and Mary Ellen will look perfectly hideous."

"Mary Ellen," said Dr. O'Grady, "have you made up your mind yet which of those two dresses you'd like?"

"I have," said Mary Ellen.

"She'd like the white muslin, of course," said Mrs. Gregg. "No girl would choose— —"

"I'd like the both of them," said Mary Ellen.

"You shall have them," said Dr. O'Grady. "That's the best way I see out of the difficulty. Mrs. Gregg, you get the dress you want for her, privately, without saying a word about it. Agree with everything Mrs. Ford says, and let her order a red flannel petticoat if she likes."

"But which will she wear?" said Mrs. Gregg, "for if she's to be dressed in a ridiculous stuffy grey tweed— —"

"She'll wear your one, of course," said Dr. O'Grady. "She'll put it on and stand in the middle of the square just underneath the statue. There'll be a large crowd of people, and it will be too late for Mrs. Ford to do anything. She can't change the girl's clothes in the street."

"Don't count on any delicacy of feeling in Mrs. Ford," said the Major.

"And will I have the both of the dresses after?" said Mary Ellen.

"You will," said Dr. O'Grady, "unless Mrs. Ford manages to drag the grey tweed one away from you."

"She'll be furious," said Mrs. Gregg.

"She may be as furious as she likes then," said Dr. O'Grady. "She won't be able to show it while the Lord-Lieutenant's wife is shaking hands with her out of the motor-car, and it won't matter to us what she does afterwards. The only thing we have to be careful about is to keep her in a good temper— —"

"You can't do that," said the Major.

"In as good a temper as possible between this and then. And now, Mrs. Gregg, if you'll excuse my saying so, I think you and Mary Ellen had better trot off to the dressmaker. If any further difficulty arises refer to me at once. But I don't see how anything can. All you've got to do is to let Mrs. Ford have her own way, and give your orders when she's gone home."

Mrs. Gregg did not seem entirely satisfied with this settlement of her difficulty, but she and Mary Ellen went off together to meet Mrs. Ford at the dressmaker's.

"Women," said Dr. O'Grady, "are the devil."

He was not much better satisfied than Mrs. Gregg was with his new plan. He foresaw very serious difficulties in carrying it out.

"You've no one but yourself to thank for all this bother!" said the Major. "There wasn't the slightest necessity to have Mary Ellen in the affair at all, dressed or undressed."

Dr. O'Grady was not listening to a word the Major said. He was thinking deeply. His face lightened suddenly and he rushed across the room to the door.

"Mrs. Gregg!" he shouted. "Mrs. Gregg! Just one moment. I've got a capital suggestion to make, one to which there can be no possible objection from any point of view."

He ran downstairs. Father McCormack went to the door and looked after him. Then he turned and addressed the Major.

"You might go a long journey," he said, "before you'd meet the equal of the doctor."

The Major received this remark in silence. He was of opinion that a man who went a long journey in order to discover a second Dr. O'Grady would be a fool.

"Tell me this," said Father McCormack. "What relation is Mary Ellen to the General?"

"I've never been able to make that out for certain. Sometimes I'm told she's his niece, and sometimes his grand-niece."

Father McCormack looked round him cautiously and sank his voice to a whisper.

"Is she any relation at all?" he said slowly.

"No more than you are to the Sultan of Turkey."

"I was thinking as much myself," said Father McCormack.

Dr. O'Grady, having finished his talk with Mrs. Gregg, entered the room again.

"I've settled that matter satisfactorily anyhow," he said. "It occurred to me just after Mrs. Gregg had left the room, that some sort of fancy dress for the girl would be likely to please the Lord-Lieutenant, and would be a compromise which both ladies could accept without loss of dignity. Mary Ellen is to be rigged out as a traditional Irish colleen, the sort you see on the picture postcards they sell to tourists in Dublin. Mrs. Gregg is delighted, and Mrs. Ford can't possibly say that a crimson flannel skirt won't be useful to her afterwards. She'll look uncommonly well, and the Lord-Lieutenant will be all the more inclined to believe that the General was an Irishman when he sees his niece——"

"Tell me this," said Father McCormack, "is she a niece of the General or is she not?"

"The grand-niece," said Dr. O'Grady.

"She's neither the one nor the other," said the Major.

Dr. O'Grady glanced at Father McCormack. He saw by the look on the priest's face that there was no use trying to prove Mary Ellen's relationship. He laughed good-naturedly, and at once offered a satisfactory explanation of the position.

"Mr. Billing," he said, "insisted on our producing some sort of relative for the dead General. He wouldn't have given that £100 if we hadn't. Now what I say is this——"

"You'd say anything," said the Major.

"I'm not talking to you now, Major. I'm talking to Father McCormack, who's a man of sense, with some knowledge of the world. The way I'm putting it to him is this: Supposing there was a job going a begging, a nice comfortable job under the Government, with no particular duties attached to it, except just to look pleasant and be generally agreeable—there are such jobs."

"Plenty, plenty," said Father McCormack.

"And they're well paid," said the Major.

"And supposing that you were asked to nominate a man for the post——" Dr. O'Grady still addressed himself only to Father McCormack. "You might be, you know. In fact you, and other people in your position often are, though there's always supposed to be a competitive examination."

"Nobody believes in examinations," said the Major.

"That's exactly what I'm saying," said Dr. O'Grady. "Now what would you do in a case of the kind? As a matter of fact what do you do? What did you do when they were appointing a secretary to the Old-Age Pension Committee?"

"I'd look out for some decent poor fellow," said Father McCormack. "One that might be wanting something of the kind, a man that nobody would have anything particular to say against."

"You wouldn't spend a lot of time arguing about whether there ought to be such a secretary or not?"

"I would not, of course," said Father McCormack. "What would be the use? If the job's there and a man's wanted I'd have no business talking about the rights or wrongs of it beyond saying that the salary ought to be a bit larger."

"Exactly," said Dr. O'Grady. "Now that's just what's happened in this case. It isn't exactly a job, under the Government, not under our Government, though it may lead on to something in Bolivia. Here's a dead General that has to be fitted out with a niece——"

"You said a grand-niece a minute ago," said the Major.

"The principle's the same," said Dr. O'Grady. "What I'm trying to get you to see is that Mary Ellen may just as well step into the position as anyone else."

"When you put it that way," said Father McCormack, "there's no more to be said. The girl's a decent girl, and I wouldn't stand in the way of her bettering herself."

"She'll be the better by a new dress, anyway!" said the Major. "I don't know that she'll benefit in any other way. But that's something."

"I rather think," said Dr. O'Grady, "that I hear Doyle downstairs. We'll be able to get on with the business of the committee now, whether he has Thady with him or not. We've wasted time enough."

"We'll waste a lot more before we've done," said the Major. "The whole thing's waste of time. There'll never be a statue in Ballymoy either to General John Regan or to anyone else."

Dr. O'Grady had drawn a bundle of papers from his pocket and laid them on the table before him.

"Our first business, gentlemen," he said, "is to settle about the illuminated address which Mrs. Ford has kindly consented to present to the Lord-Lieutenant."

Thady Gallagher glared at Dr. O'Grady savagely. He did not like being interrupted in the middle of a speech.

"Order, gentlemen, order," said Father McCormack, nervously tapping the table with his pencil.

"With regard to the illuminated address," said Doyle, "I'm of opinion that the carrying out of it should be given into the hands of a Dublin firm. It's our duty to support Irish manufacture. There's too much money sent over to England that might be far better kept at home. You'll agree with me there, Thady."

"What are you going to say in the address?" said the Major.

"Oh, the usual things," said Dr. O'Grady. "I don't think we need go into that in detail. All addresses are pretty much the same."

"I won't sign my name to anything political," said the Major.

"I'm with you there," said Father McCormack. "It's one of the curses of this country the way politics are dragged into business."

"Nobody wants politics," said Dr. O'Grady. "The address will contain nothing but nice little compliments to the Lord-Lieutenant with a word or two about the value of piers put in at the end."

"If the matter's left in the hands of the firm I have in mind," said Doyle, "it'll be done right. They've illuminated three-quarters of the addresses that have been presented in the country, and whether it's a bank manager or a priest going on a new mission, or a Lord-Lieutenant that the address is for, the firm I mean will know what to put into it. They've had the experience, and experience is what is wanted."

"We'll give him names and dates," said Dr. O'Grady, "and tell him that this is a seaport town with no proper pier. With that information any fool could draw up the text of an illuminated address. I propose that the matter be left in the hands of a subcommittee consisting of Mr. Doyle."

"Are you all agreed on that, gentlemen?" said Father McCormack.

Thady Gallagher rose slowly to his feet.

"With regard to what Mr. Doyle has just laid before the meeting," he said, "and speaking of the duty of supporting Irish manufacture, I'm of opinion that his words do him credit. I'm an out and out supporter of the Industrial Revival, and when I look round about me on the ruined mills that once were hives of industry, and the stream of emigration which is flowing from our shores year after year———"

"I don't think we need spend much time discussing the bouquet," said Dr. O'Grady. "It'll have to be ordered from Dublin too."

"There's no flowers here to make a bouquet of," said Doyle, "unless, maybe, the Major— —"

"I've a few Sweet-Williams," said the Major, "and a bed of mixed stocks. If you think they'd be any use to you you're welcome to them."

"We might do worse," said Father McCormack.

"We'll have to do better," said Dr. O'Grady. "You can't offer a lady in the position of a Lord-Lieutenant's wife a bundle of ordinary stocks! What we have to get is lilies and roses."

"It's only right that we should," said Father McCormack, "but I think the thanks of the meeting ought to be given to Major Kent for his generous offer."

"I second that," said Doyle. "The Major was always a good friend to anything that might be for the benefit of the town or the locality."

"The ordering of the bouquet," said Dr. O'Grady, "to be left to the same subcommittee which has charge of the address."

"And it to be sent to the hotel here," said Father McCormack, "on the morning of the ceremony, so as it will be fresh. Are you all agreed on that, gentlemen? What's the next business, doctor?"

"The next business is the statue."

"What's the date of the Lord-Lieutenant's visit?" said the Major.

"Thursday week," said Dr. O'Grady.

"That's ten days from to-day," said the Major. "We may just as well go home at once as sit here talking to each other. There's no time to get a statue."

"We'll do our business before we stir," said Dr. O'Grady.

"What's the use of saying things like that?" said the Major. "You know jolly well, O'Grady, that you can't get a statue in ten days. The thing's impossible. It takes a year at least to make a statue of any size. You can't go into a shop and buy a statue, as if it were a hat or an umbrella."

"There's a good deal in what the Major says," said Father McCormack. "I'm inclined to agree with him. I remember well when they were putting up the monument to Parnell in Dublin it took them years before they had it finished."

"It's a good job for everybody concerned," said the Major, "that we're brought up short. We'd simply have made ourselves publicly ridiculous if we'd gone on with this business."

The Major, Dr. O'Grady, and Doyle, spoke when they did speak, in an easy conversational tone without rising from their chairs. But this was not Gallagher's idea of the proper way of conducting public business. He believed that important discussions ought to be carried on with dignity. When he spoke he stood up and addressed the committee as if he were taking part in a political demonstration, using appropriate gestures to emphasize his words. The difficulty about the statue gave him a great opportunity.

"I stand here to-day," he said, "as the representative of the people of this locality, and what I'm going to say now I'd say if the police spies of Dublin Castle was standing round me taking down the words I utter."

Young Kerrigan had been obliged to stop practising "Rule, Britannia" on the cornet in order to eat his dinner. When he had satisfied his appetite and soothed his nerves with a pipe of tobacco he set to work at the tune again. The hour's rest had not helped him in any way. He made exactly the same mistake as he had been making all the morning. It happened that he took up his cornet again shortly before Gallagher began his speech in which he declared himself a representative of the people of the locality. The noise of the music floated through the open window of the committee room. It had a slightly exasperating effect on Gallagher, but he went on speaking.

"What I say is this," he said, "and it's what I always will say. If it is the unanimous wish of the people of this locality to erect a statue to the memory of the great patriot, who is gone, then a statue ought to be erected. If the Major is right—and he may be right—in saying that it takes a year to make a statue, then we'll take a year. We'll take ten years if necessary. Please God the most of us has years enough before us yet to spare that many for a good work."

Young Kerrigan continued to break down at the "never, never, never," part of the tune. Dr. O'Grady began to fidget nervously in his chair.

"Sit down, Thady," said Doyle. "Don't you know that if we postpone the statue we'll never get the Lord-Lieutenant to open it? Didn't he say in his letter that Thursday week was the only day he could come?"

"As for the so-called Lord-Lieutenant of Ireland," said Gallagher, waving his arm in the air, "we've done without him and the likes of him up to this, and we're well able to do without him for the future."

He brought his fist down with tremendous force as he spoke, striking the table with the pad of flesh underneath his little finger. Dr. O'Grady jumped up.

"Excuse me one moment, gentlemen," he said. "That young fool, Kerrigan, is getting the tune wrong every time, and if I don't stop him he'll never get it right at all."

He walked across to the window as he spoke and looked out. Then he turned round.

"Don't let me interfere with your speech, Thady," he said. "I'm listening all right, and I'm sure Father McCormack and the rest of the committee want to hear every word of it."

But Gallagher, in spite of this encouragement, did not seem inclined to go on. He sat down and scowled ferociously at Doyle. Dr. O'Grady put his head out of the window and shouted.

"Moriarty," he called, "Constable Moriarty, come over here for a minute and stop grinning."

Then he drew in his head and turned round.

"Major," he said, "you're a magistrate. I wish to goodness you'd give orders that Moriarty isn't to grin in that offensive way. It's a danger to the public peace."

"I shan't do anything of the sort," said the Major. "In the first place I can't. I've no authority over the police. They are Gregg's business. In the second place— —"

He stopped at this point because Dr. O'Grady was not listening to him. He had stretched his head and shoulders out of the window and was talking in a very loud tone to Moriarty.

"Run over," he said, "and tell young Kerrigan to come here to me for a minute. When you've done that go to bed or dig potatoes or do any other mortal thing except stand at the door of the barrack grinning."

"What tune's that young Kerrigan's after playing?" said Gallagher solemnly.

Father McCormack looked anxiously at Major Kent. The Major fixed his eyes on the stuffed fox in the glass case. It was Doyle who answered Gallagher.

"It's no tune at all the way he's playing it," he said. "Didn't you hear the doctor saying he had it wrong?"

"What tune would it be," said Gallagher, "if so be he had it right?"

"I told you before," said Doyle. "I told you till I'm tired telling you that I don't know the name of it. It's not a tune that ever I heard before."

"I'll find out what tune it is," said Gallagher savagely. "I'll drag it out of you if I have to drag the black liver of you along with it."

"Order, gentlemen, order," said Father McCormack. "That's no language to be using here."

"I was meaning no disrespect to you, Father," said Gallagher. "I'd be the last man in Ireland to raise my hand against the clergy."

"It's the doctor's liver you'll have to drag, Thady, if you drag any liver at all," said Doyle, "for he's the only one that knows what the tune is."

Moriarty appeared to have conveyed the message to young Kerrigan. Dr. O'Grady, still leaning out of the window, spoke again, this time evidently to Kerrigan.

"Don'ts you know you're getting it wrong every time?" he said.

Young Kerrigan's voice, faint and apologetic, reached the members of the committee through the window.

"Sure I know that well enough; but the devil's in it that I can't get it right."

"Listen to me now," said Dr. O'Grady.

He whistled the tune shrilly, beating time with his hand.

"Now, Kerrigan," he said, "try it after me."

He whistled it again slowly. Kerrigan followed him note by note on the cornet. After a very short hesitation he got over the difficult passage. Dr. O'Grady drew in his head and returned to the table with a sigh of relief.

"I think he has it now," he said, "but it's a tough job teaching that fellow anything."

"What tune is it?" said Gallagher.

"It's not a tune that ever you heard before," said Dr. O'Grady.

"I'm of opinion that I did hear it," said Gallagher. "But let you speak out now if you're not ashamed of it, and tell me what tune it is."

"It's the 'Battle March of King Malachi the Brave,'" said Dr. O'Grady, "the same that he played when he was driving the English out of Ireland. And you can't possibly have heard it before because the manuscript of it was only dug up the other day at Tara, and this is the first time it's ever been played publicly in the west of Ireland."

"There now, Thady," said Doyle, "didn't I tell you all along that you'd nothing to do only to ask the doctor?"

"I'm of opinion that I did hear it," said Gallagher. "You may say what you like about the Hill of Tara, but I've heard that tune."

"It's just possible," said Dr. O'Grady, "that Mr. Billing may have whistled it while he was here. I believe the people of Bolivia are fond of it. They learned it, of course, from General John Regan. He may have heard it from his grandmother. It's wonderful how long music survives among the people long after the regular professional musicians have forgotten all about it. But I mustn't interrupt you any more, Thady. You were just making a speech about the Lord-Lieutenant. Perhaps you have finished what you were saying. As well as I recollect we were just settling about the statue."

"Major Kent was after saying," said Father McCormack, "that we couldn't get a statue in the time."

"My friend Mr. Doyle," said Dr. O'Grady, "has a proposal to lay before the meeting. Where's that card, Doyle, that you showed me last week?"

Doyle drew a bundle of grimy papers from his breast pocket and went through them slowly. One, which appeared to be a letter written on business paper, he laid on the table in front of him. At the bottom of the bundle he came on a large card. He handed this to Father McCormack. The printing on it was done in Curiously shaped letters, evidently artistic in intention, with a tendency towards the ecclesiastical. Round the outside of the card was a deep border of black, as if the owner of it were in mourning for a near relative.

Father McCormack looked at it dubiously.

"Read it out," said Dr. O'Grady. "I'd like the Major to hear exactly what's on it."

"'Mr. Aloysius Doyle,'" read Father McCormack.

"He's a nephew of my own," said Doyle.

"He would be," said Gallagher. "If he wasn't we'd hear nothing about him."

He was still feeling sore about the "Battle March of King Malachi the Brave," and was anxious to make himself disagreeable to someone. It struck him that it would be easy to annoy Doyle by suggesting that he was trying to do a good turn to his nephew at the expense of the statue fund.

"I needn't tell you, gentlemen," said Doyle, with great dignity, "that it's not on account of his being a nephew of my own that I'm recommending him to the notice of this committee. If he was fifty times my nephew I wouldn't mention his name without I was sure that he was as good a man as any other for the job we have on hand."

No one, of course, believed this, but no one wanted to argue with Doyle about it. Father McCormack went on reading from the black-edged card which he held in his hand.

"'Mortuary Sculptor,'"

"Sculptor!" said Dr. O'Grady. "You hear that, Major, don't you? Sculptors are people who make statues."

"Mortuary sculptors, I suppose," said the Major viciously, "make statues of dead men."

"The General's dead anyway," said Doyle, "so that's suitable enough."

"'Address—The Monumental Studio, Michael Angelo House, Great Brunswick. Street, Dublin,'" read Father McCormack. "That'll be where your nephew lives, Mr. Doyle?"

"It's where he has his works," said Doyle. "He lives down near Sandymount."

"'Celtic Crosses, Obelisks and every kind of Monument supplied at the shortest notice,'" said Father McCormack, still reading from the card. "'Family Vaults decorated. Inscriptions Cut. Estimates Free. Low Prices'."

"I don't see that we could possibly do better than that," said Dr. O'Grady.

"Even Doyle's nephew can't make a statue in ten days," said the Major.

"He says 'shortest notice' on his card. You ought to believe the man, Major, until you've some evidence that he's a liar."

"I don't care what he says," said the Major. "He can't make a statue in ten days."

"We'll get to that point in a minute," said Dr. O'Grady. "The first thing we have to decide is whether Mr. Aloysius Doyle is a suitable man to be entrusted with the work."

"There's no other tenders before us," said Father McCormack, "so I suppose we may as well——"

"Excuse my interrupting you, Father," said Doyle, "but before you take the opinion of the meeting on this point, I'd like to say that I'm offering no opinion one way or the other; and what's more I won't give a vote either for or against. I wouldn't like to do it in a case where my own nephew is a candidate."

"You needn't tell us that, Mr. Doyle," said Father McCormack. "We all know that you're not the kind of man who'd be using his public position to further the interests of his relatives. What do you say now, gentlemen? Is Mr. Aloysius Doyle to be given the contract for the statue or not? What do you say, Major?"

"If he can make a full-sized statue of a General in ten days," said the Major, "he's a man who deserves every encouragement we can give him."

"Now, doctor," said Father McCormack, "what's your opinion?"

"I'm for giving him the job," said the Doctor.

"Mr. Doyle won't vote," said Father McCormack.

"I will not," said Doyle firmly.

"So we'd be glad of your opinion, Mr. Gallagher."

"If his price is satisfactory," said Gallagher, "we may as well give him the preference. I'd be in favour of supporting local talent when possible, and although Mr. Aloysius Doyle isn't a resident among us at present, his family belongs to Ballymoy."

"Carried unanimously," said Father McCormack. "And now about the price. What will that nephew of yours do us a statue for, Doyle? And mind you, it must be done well."

"Before we go into that," said Dr. O'Grady, "I'd like the committee to hear a letter which Mr. Doyle has received from his nephew. I thought it well, considering how short the time at our disposal is——"

"Ten days," said the Major. "Ten days to make a statue——"

"The letter which we are just going to read," said Dr. O'Grady, "will meet the Major's difficulty. I thought it well to get into communication with Mr. Aloysius Doyle at once so as to have everything ready for the committee."

"I wonder you haven't the statue ready," said the Major.

"I wrote to him, or rather I got Doyle to write to him, the day before yesterday, and the letter you are now going to hear is his reply. I may say that we laid the circumstances full before him; especially the shortness of the time. You're not the only person who thought of that difficulty, Major. Just read the letter, will you, Doyle?"

Doyle took up the letter which lay on the table in front of him and unfolded it. He glanced at it and then put it down and began to fumble in his pocket.

"Go ahead," said Dr. O'Grady.

"I can't," said Doyle. "This isn't that letter, but another one altogether."

He drew his packet of papers from his pocket again and began to go through them rapidly. There was a light tap at the door.

"Who on earth's that?" said Dr. O'Grady. "I said specially that this meeting was not to be disturbed."

"Possibly Doyle's nephew," said the Major, "with a sample statue. He ought to submit samples to us."

"Come in whoever you are," said Dr. O'Grady.

Mary Ellen half opened the door and put her head into the room. Dr. O'Grady realised the moment he saw her that something must have gone wrong in the dressmaker's shop. He assumed, without enquiry, that Mrs. Ford had been making herself objectionable.

"What has Mrs. Ford done now?" said Dr. O'Grady. "I can't go to her till this meeting is over."

"Mrs. Ford's off home this half hour," said Mary Ellen. "She said she wouldn't put up with the nonsense that was going on."

This was a relief to Dr. O'Grady. If Mrs. Ford had gone home the difficulty, whatever it was, must be capable of adjustment.

"Then what on earth do you want? Surely you and Mrs. Gregg haven't been quarrelling with each other."

"Mrs. Gregg says— —" said Mary Ellen.

Then she paused, looked at Dr. O'Grady, looked at Doyle, and finally took courage after a glance at Father McCormack.

"She says, is there to be white stockings?"

"Certainly not," said Dr. O'Grady. "White stockings would be entirely out of place. If we're dressing you as an Irish colleen, Mary Ellen, we'll do it properly. Go and tell Mrs. Gregg that your stockings are to be green, bright green. Did you ever hear such a silly question?" he added turning to the other members of the committee. "Who ever saw an Irish colleen in white stockings?"

"While you're at it, O'Grady," said the Major, "you'd better settle the colour of her garters."

Mary Ellen, grinning broadly, withdrew her head and shut the door.

"What's that about green stockings for Mary Ellen?" said Father McCormack.

"Oh, it's all right," said Dr. O'Grady. "The stockings will scarcely show at all. Her dress will be right down to her ankles, longer by far than the ones she usually wears. I needn't tell you, Father McCormack, that I wouldn't consent to dressing the girl in any way that wasn't strictly proper. You mustn't think— —"

"I wasn't thinking anything of the sort," said Father McCormack.

"You very well might be," said Dr. O'Grady, "Anyone would think we intended her to appear in a ballet skirt after that remark of the Major's about her garters."

"All I was thinking," said Father McCormack, "was that if you dressed the girl up in that style she'll never be contented again with ordinary clothes."

"I'd be opposed, so I would," said Gallagher, "to anything that wouldn't be respectable in the case of Mary Ellen. Her mother was a cousin of my own, and I've a feeling for the girl. So if you or any other one, Doctor, is planning contrivances——"

"Oh, don't be ridiculous, Thady," said Dr. O'Grady.

"I tell you she'll be all right. Now, Doyle, will you read us that letter from your nephew? If we don't get on with our business we'll be here all night."

CHAPTER XV

"I can't find the letter high or low," said Doyle.

"Maybe now," said Father McCormack, "it's not in your pocket at all."

"It should be," said Doyle, "for it was there I put it after showing it to the doctor here yesterday."

"It doesn't matter," said Dr. O'Grady, "you can tell us what he said in your own words."

"What I told my nephew," said Doyle, "when I was writing to him, was that the committee was a bit pressed in the matter of time, owing to next Thursday week being the only day that it was convenient for the Lord-Lieutenant to attend for the opening of the statue. Well, gentlemen, by the height of good luck it just happens that my nephew has a statue on hand which he thinks would do us."

"He has what?" said the Major.

"A statue that has been left on his hands," said Doyle. "The way of it was this. It was ordered by the relatives of a deceased gentleman, and it was to have been put up in St. Patrick's Cathedral in Dublin."

"That shows," said Dr. O'Grady, "that it's a first rate statue. They wouldn't let you put up anything second rate in a cathedral like that."

"It must be a good one, surely," said Father McCormack.

"But when the relatives of the deceased party went into his affairs," said Doyle, "they found he hadn't died near as well off as they thought he was going to; so they told my nephew that they wouldn't take the statue and couldn't pay for it. It was pretty near finished at the time, and what my nephew says is that he could make sure of having it ready for us by the end of this week at the latest."

"Look here, O'Grady," said the Major, "I'm as fond of a joke as any man; but I must draw the line somewhere. I'm hanged if I'll be mixed up in any way with a second-hand statue."

"It's not second-hand," said Dr. O'Grady, "it's perfectly new. At this moment it isn't even finished; I wouldn't ask this committee to buy anything second hand. But you can surely see, Major—you do see, for you raised the point yourself, that with the very short time at our disposal we must, if we are to have a statue at all, get one that's more or less ready made."

"But—Good Heavens! O'Grady," said the Major. "How can you possibly put up a statue of somebody else and call it General John Regan? It won't be the least like him. How can you—the thing's too absurd even for you. Who was this man that the statue was made for?"

"Who was he, Doyle?" said Dr. O'Grady. "It doesn't really matter to us who he was; but you may as well tell the Major so as to satisfy him."

"I disremember his name," said Doyle, "and I can't lay my hand on the letter; but he was a Deputy-Lieutenant of whatever county he belonged to."

"There you are now, Major," said Dr. O'Grady. "A Deputy-Lieutenant! Nothing could be more respectable than that. You're only a J.P. yourself, and I don't believe you'll ever be anything more. You can't afford to turn up your nose at a Deputy-Lieutenant. We shan't be doing any injury to the General's reputation by allowing him to be represented by a man of high position, most likely of good family, who was at all events supposed to be well off before he died."

"I wasn't thinking of the General's reputation," said the Major. "I don't care a hang——"

"I don't see that we are bound to consider the feelings of the Deputy-Lieutenant," said Dr. O'Grady. "After all, if a man deliberately leads his relatives to suppose that he is rich enough to afford a statue in a cathedral and then turns out to be too poor to pay for it, he doesn't deserve much consideration."

"I wouldn't cross the road," said Doyle, "to do a good turn to a man that let my nephew in the way that fellow did. For let me tell you, gentlemen, that statue would have been a serious loss to him if——"

"I'm not thinking of him or Doyle's nephew either," said the Major. "I don't know who that Deputy-Lieutenant was, and I don't care if his statue was stuck up in every market town in Ireland."

"If you're not thinking of the General," said the doctor, "and if you're not thinking of the Deputy-Lieutenant, what on earth are you grumbling about?"

"I'm grumbling, as you call it," said the Major, "about the utterly intolerable absurdity of the whole thing. Can't you see it? You can of course, but you won't. Look here, Father McCormack, you're a man of some sense and decency of feeling. Can we possibly ask the Lord-Lieutenant to come here and unveil a statue of General John Regan—whoever he was—when all we've got is a statue of some other man? Quite possibly the Lord-Lieutenant may have known that Deputy-

Lieutenant personally, and if he recognises the statue where shall we be?"

"There's something in what the Major says," said Father McCormack. "I'll not deny there's something in what he says."

"There isn't," said Dr. O'Grady. "Excuse my contradicting you flatly, Father McCormack, but there really isn't. We all know Doyle, and we respect him; but I put it to you now, Father McCormack, I put it to any member of the committee: Is Doyle likely to have a nephew who'd be able to make a statue that anybody would recognise?"

"There's something in that," said Father McCormack. "I'm not well up in statues, but I've seen a few in my time, and all I can say is that unless Doyle's nephew is a great deal better at the job than most of the fellows that makes them, nobody would know, unless they were told, who their statue's meant to be like."

"My nephew's a good sculptor," said Doyle. "If he wasn't I wouldn't have brought his name forward to-day; but what the doctor says is true enough. I've seen heads he's done, for mural tablets and the like, and so far as anybody recognising them for portraits of the deceased goes, you might have changed the tablets and, barring the inscriptions, nobody would have known to the differ. Not but what they were well done, every one of them."

"There now, Major," said Dr. O'Grady. "That pretty well disposes of your last objection."

"That's only a side issue," said the Major, speaking with a calm which was evidently forced. "My point is that we can't, in ordinary decency, put up a statue of one man to represent another."

"I don't know that I altogether agree with the Major there," said Father McCormack, "but there's something in what he says."

"I can't see that there's anything," said Dr. O'Grady. "Deputy-Lieutenants have uniforms, haven't they? So have Generals. Nobody can possibly know what the uniform of a Bolivian General was fifty or a hundred years ago. All we could do, even if we were having the statue entirely made to order, would be to guess at the uniform. It's just as likely to be that of a modern Deputy-Lieutenant as anything else."

"That's true of course," said Father McCormack.

"Anyway," said Doyle, "if we're to have a statue at all it'll have to be this one. There's no other for us to get, so what's the use of talking?"

The Major shrugged his shoulders helplessly.

"There's evidently no use my talking," he said.

"Is it your wish then, gentlemen," said Father McCormack, "that the offer of Mr. Aloysius Doyle to supply a statue of General John Regan be accepted by the committee?"

"It is," said Dr. O'Grady.

"Subject to the price being satisfactory," said Gallagher. "We haven't heard the price yet."

"I have the letter about the price which my nephew sent me," said Doyle, "and I think you'll all agree with me that he's giving it cheap."

"He ought to," said Gallagher, "considering that if he doesn't sell it to us it's not likely he'll sell it at all."

"The demand for second-hand statues must be small," said the Major.

"What he says is," said Doyle, "that considering he's dealing with a member of his own family he'll let the statue go at no more than the price of the raw material, not making any charge for the work he's putting into it. I don't know that we can expect more than that from him."

"You cannot, of course," said Father McCormack.

"Let's hear the figure," said Gallagher.

"I should say," said the Major, "that £10 would be a liberal offer on our part."

"Shut up, Major," said Dr. O'Grady. "What do you know about the price of statues? You wouldn't get a plaster cast of a pet dog for £10."

Doyle smiled amiably.

"There's not a man in Ballymoy," he said, "fonder of a joke than the Major."

"Let's hear the figure," said Gallagher.

"What he says," said Doyle, "is £81."

Major Kent whistled.

"But I wouldn't wonder," said Doyle, "but you could get him to knock 10s. off that and say £80 10s."

Dr. O'Grady pulled a sheet of paper towards him and began to write rapidly.

"Statue £80 10s.," he said. "Carriage, say £1 10s. The railway companies are robbers. Expenses of erection, say £2. You'll let us have any mortar and cement that are needed for nothing, Doyle; so we'll only have to pay for labour. I'll superintend the erection without charging a fee. Illuminated Address, £4. Bouquet £1 is. That's a good deal to give for a bouquet, but I don't think we'll get a decent one for less. Dresses, etc., for Mary Ellen—the green stockings will have to be ordered specially, and so will come to a little money. And we may have to get that grey tweed dress which Mrs. Ford wants, just to prevent her kicking up a row. Two dresses, stockings, etc., for Mary Ellen, say £4. That will include shoes with buckles. She'll have to wear an Irish brooch of some sort, but we'll probably be able to borrow that. Lunch for the Vice Regal party on the day of the unveiling—there'll be at least four of them, say five in case of accidents. That will allow for two aides de camp and a private secretary. They can't want more. The five of us and Mr. Billing, who said he'd be back for the ceremony. That makes eleven. I suppose you could do us really well, Doyle, at 7s. 6d. a head, including drinks, and there'll have to be three or four bottles of champagne on the sideboard, just for the look of the thing. We may not have to open more than one. Eleven times 7s. 6d. makes £4 2s. 6d. What do you mean to charge us for the printing of the posters, Gallagher?"

"I'll say £3," said Gallagher, "to include posters and advertisements in the paper. I'll be losing money on it."

"You'll not be losing much," said Dr. O'Grady, "but we'll say £3. That will make—let me see——"

He added up his column of figures and then checked the result by adding them downwards.

"That comes to £100 3s. 6d.," he said, "and we've not put down anything for postage. You'll have to get your nephew to knock another 10s. off the price of the statue. After all, when he said £81, he must have been prepared to take £80, and he'll have to cut the inscription for us without extra charge."

"He might," said Doyle, "if we approached him on the subject."

"He'll have to," said Dr. O'Grady, "for £100 is all we've got, and we can't run into debt."

"He did say," said Doyle, "that 3d. a letter was the regular charge for cutting inscriptions."

"We'll make it short," said Dr. O'Grady. "We won't stick him for more than about 10s. over the inscription. After all long inscriptions are vulgar. I propose that Mr. Thaddeus Gallagher, as the only representative of the press among us, be commissioned to write the inscription."

"We couldn't have a better man," said Father McCormack.

"I'll not do it," said Gallagher. He had a solid reason for refusing the honour offered to him. The writer of an inscription at the base of a statue is almost bound to make some statement about the person whom the statue represents.

"You will now, Thady," said Doyle, "and you'll do it well."

"I will not," said Gallagher. "Let the doctor do it himself."

"There's no man in Connacht better fit to draw up an inscription of the kind," said Father McCormack, "than Mr. Gallagher."

Thady Gallagher was susceptible to flattery. He would have liked very well to draw up an inscription for the statue, modelling it on the resolutions which he was accustomed to propose at political meetings in favour of' Home Rule. But he was faced with what seemed to him an insuperable difficulty. He did not know who General John Regan was.

"Let the doctor do it," he said reluctantly.

"Whoever does it," said Doyle, "it'll have to be done at once. My nephew said that on account of the way we are pressed for time he'd be glad if the words of the inscription was wired to him to-day."

"It would, maybe, be better," said Father McCormack, "if you were to do it, doctor. We'll all be sorry that the words don't come from the accomplished pen of our respected fellow citizen, Mr. Gallagher— —"

"I'll not do it," said Gallagher, "for I wouldn't know what to say."

"Write it out and have done with it, O'Grady," said the Major. "What's the good of keeping us sitting here all day?"

"Very well," said Dr. O'Grady. "After all, it's not much trouble. How would this do? 'General John Regan—Patriot—Soldier—Statesman—Vivat Bolivia'."

"We couldn't do better," said Father McCormack.

"What's the meaning of the poetry at the end of it?" asked Gallagher.

"It's not poetry," said Dr. O'Grady, "and it doesn't mean much. It's the Latin for 'Long live Bolivia.'"

Gallagher rose to his feet. He had been obliged to confess himself unable to write an inscription; but he was thoroughly well able to make a speech.

"Considering," he said, "that the town of Ballymoy is in the Province of Connacht which is one of the provinces of Ireland, and considering the unswerving attachment through long centuries of alien oppression which the Irish people have shown to the cause of national independence, it's my opinion that there should be something in the inscription, be the same more or less, about Home Rule. What I say, and what I've always said— —"

"Very well," said Dr. O'Grady, "I'll put 'Esto Perpetua,' if you like. It's the same number of letters, and it's what Grattan said about the last

Home Rule Parliament. That ought to satisfy you, and I'm sure the Major won't mind."

"I'm pretty well past minding anything now," said the Major.

"There's no example in history," said Gallagher, "of determined devotion to a great cause equal to that of the Irish people who have been returning Members of Parliament pledged to the demand which has been made with unfaltering tongue on the floor of the House at Westminster——"

"Get a telegraph form, Doyle," said Dr. O'Grady, "and copy out that inscription while Thady is finishing his speech."

"There's one other point that I'd like to mention," said Doyle, "and it's this——"

"Wait a minute, Thady," said Dr. O'Grady. "We'll just deal with this point of Doyle's and then you'll be able to go on without interruption. What is it, Doyle?"

"My nephew says," said Doyle, "that he'd be glad of a cheque on account for the statue; he having been put to a good deal of out-of-pocket expense."

"Very well," said Dr. O'Grady, "send him £25. Now go on, Thady."

"Is it me send him £25?" said Doyle doubtfully.

"Of course it's you. You're the treasurer."

"But it's you has Mr. Billing's cheque," said Doyle.

"I haven't got Mr. Billing's cheque," said Dr. O'Grady.

"If you haven't," said Doyle, helplessly, "who has?"

"It's my belief," said Gallagher, in a tone of extreme satisfaction, "that there's no cheque in it."

"Do you mean to say, Doyle," said Dr. O'Grady, "that you've been such a besotted idiot as to let that American escape out of this without paying over his subscription for the statue?"

"You'll never see *him* again," said Gallagher. "He's not the first man that skipped the country after letting everybody in."

"Gentlemen, gentlemen," said Father McCormack, "order, please, order."

"We'll have to drop the whole thing now," said the Major, "and I must say I'm extremely glad."

"I'm no more an idiot than you are yourself, doctor," said Doyle, "and I won't have language of the kind used to me. How was I to know he hadn't given you the cheque?"

"You were the treasurer," said Dr. O'Grady. "What on earth is a treasurer for if he doesn't get in the subscriptions?"

"That nephew of yours will have his statue on his hands a bit longer," said Gallagher.

He still spoke in a tone of satisfaction; but even as he contemplated the extreme disappointment of Doyle's nephew it occurred to him that there might be a difficulty about paying his own bill for £3. The same thought struck Father McCormack.

"Gentlemen," he said, "there's been an unfortunate mistake, but it might be worse."

"That American fellow has us robbed," said Gallagher.

"We'll prosecute him when we catch him," said Doyle.

"It might be worse," said Father McCormack. "We haven't spent very much yet. The dresses for Mary Ellen can hardly have been put in hand yet, so we won't have to pay for them."

"There's my bill," said Gallagher.

"So there's only Mr. Gallagher's little account," said Father McCormack.

"We'll have a house-to-house collection," said Doyle, "till we get the money raised."

"Don't be a blithering idiot, Doyle," said Dr. O'Grady. "How can you go round and ask people to subscribe to——"

"Gentlemen, gentlemen," said Father McCormack.

"We must fall back upon the subscription list that was published in the *Connacht Eagle*," said the Major, "as well as I recollect we all promised——"

"Nobody promised anything," said Doyle. "It was Dr. O'Grady that promised for us and before I pay a penny for a man that owes me more this minute than he can pay——"

"Oh, do shut up, Doyle," said Dr. O'Grady. "What's the good of raking up the past? What we've got to do now is to find a way out of the confounded hole we've been let into through your incompetence and carelessness."

"I'm down for £5," said the Major, "and I'll consider that I'm very well out of this business if I have to pay no more. I'd rather give five pounds any day than stand by watching Mary Ellen and the Lord-Lieutenant making faces at a second-hand statue."

"It's a handsome offer, so it is," said Father McCormack, "and the thanks of the meeting——"

"I'll not pay a penny," said Doyle, "and what's more, if the doctor doesn't pay me what he owes me I'll put him into the County Court."

"It's you that'll have to pay," said Gallagher, "whether you like it or not."

"I'm damned if I do," said Doyle.

"Gentlemen, gentlemen," said Father McCormack, "will you mind what you're saying? That's no language to be using, Mr. Doyle; and I don't think the doctor has any right—not that I mind myself what you say for I'm not particular; but if it was to get out to the ears of the general public that this meeting had been conducting itself in ways that's very far from being reputable— —"

"There's no general public here," said Dr. O'Grady, "and that's just as well."

"What I'm trying to tell you," said Father McCormack, "and what I would tell you if you'd listen to me, is that there's somebody knocking at the door of the room we're in and whoever it is must have heard every word that's been said this last five minutes."

Doyle and Gallagher stopped growling at each other when the priest spoke. Dr. O'Grady sat upright in his chair and bent his head towards the door. There was a moment's silence in the room and a very faint, as it were an apologetic, knock was heard at the door.

"Come in," said Dr. O'Grady.

Mary Ellen opened the door and looked in. She appeared to be rather frightened. If, as Father McCormack supposed she heard every word spoken during the previous five minutes, she had very good reason for feeling nervous. She had a still better reason a moment later when Doyle caught sight of her. Doyle had completely lost command of his temper.

"Get away out of that, Mary Ellen," he said, "and if I catch sight of you here again before I call for you I'll have the two ears cut off you and yourself sent home to your mother with them in a paper parcel in the well of the car."

Curiously enough this appalling threat seemed to cheer Mary Ellen a little. She smiled.

"Mrs. Gregg says— —" she said.

"If you're not outside the door and it shut after you before I've done speaking I'll do what I've said and worse on top of that," said Doyle.

"I won't have Mary Ellen bullied," said Dr. O'Grady. "It's all you're fit for, Doyle, to frighten helpless little girls. If you'd talked that way to Billing when he was trying to run away without paying— —"

"You're a nice one to talk about paying," said Doyle.

Dr. O'Grady left his seat and walked over lo the door.

"What is it now, Mary Ellen?" he said.

"Mrs. Gregg says," she said, "will I be wearing a hat or will I not?"

"Go back to Mrs. Gregg," said Dr. O'Grady, "and tell her that you will not wear a hat, but you'll have your hair tied up with a green silk ribbon to match your stockings. Would you like that?"

"I'd as soon have a hat," said Mary Ellen, "and Mr. Moriarty says——"

"Surely to goodness," said Dr. O'Grady, "he hasn't been helping to order your clothes!"

"He has not," said Mary Ellen, "but he was outside the barrack and me coming along the street——"

"He always is," said Dr. O'Grady.

"And he said to me that it wouldn't do for me to be dressed up any way foolish like."

"Let Constable Moriarty mind his own business," said Dr. O'Grady. "You go back and tell Mrs. Gregg what I say."

The other members of the committee sat listening with amazed interest to all Dr. O'Grady said to Mary Ellen. Even Doyle was too much astonished to attempt an interruption. He said nothing till the doctor, having dismissed Mary Ellen, returned to the table. Then he spoke.

"And who's going to pay for the green ribbon which is to go along with the stockings? Who's going to pay for it? That's what I'm asking you. You needn't be thinking that I will."

"Gentlemen," said Dr. O'Grady, "I owe you all an apology. I'm afraid I lost my temper for a minute or two. Father McCormack, I beg your pardon, and if I said—as I fear I did say—anything disrespectful to you as chairman——"

"Don't speak another word, Doctor," said Father McCormack, "you've said enough. Sure anyone might have been betrayed into a strong expression when he was provoked. Not that you said a word to me that you've any reason to be sorry for."

"Major Kent," said Dr. O'Grady, "if I've in any way insulted you——"

"Not worse than usual," said Major Kent. "I'm quite accustomed to it."

"Mr. Doyle," said the doctor, "I'm afraid that in the heat of the moment I may have—but I can do no more than ask your pardon———"

"I don't care a thraneen," said Doyle, "what you called me, and I'll give you leave to call me that and more every day of the week if you see your way to get the £100 out of the American gentleman."

"I can't do that," said Dr. O'Grady, "but I have a proposal to lay before the meeting which I think will get us out of our difficulty."

CHAPTER XVI

"Let you speak out," said Doyle, "and if so be that you're not asking us to pay up——"

"I think we may take it for granted, gentlemen," said Dr. O'Grady, "that if we produce a creditable statue for the Lord-Lieutenant to unveil and give him a really gratifying illuminated address——"

"The statue and the illuminated address would be all right," said Doyle, "if there was any way of paying for them."

"And a bouquet," said Dr. O'Grady; "and a good luncheon. If we do all that and make ourselves generally agreeable by means of Mary Ellen and in other ways the Lord-Lieutenant couldn't very well refuse to give us a grant of Government money to build a pier."

"It's likely he'd give it," said Father McCormack, "it's likely enough that he'd give it—if we——"

"He couldn't well not," said Doyle, "after us giving him a lunch and all."

"If so be," said Gallagher, "that he was to refuse at the latter end we'd have questions asked about him in Parliament; and believe you me that's what he wouldn't like. Them fellows is terrible afraid of the Irish Members. And they've a good right to be, for devil the finer set of men you'd see anywhere than what they are. There isn't a thing goes wrong in the country but they're ready to torment the life out of whoever might be responsible for the man that did it."

"Very well," said Dr. O'Grady. "Now do we want a pier?"

"We want the money," said Doyle.

"I don't know," said Father McCormack, "could we get the money without we'd build a pier when we'd got it."

"My point is," said Dr. O'Grady, "that the pier itself, the actual stone structure sticking out into the sea, being no particular use to any one once it's built——"

"It'd be a public nuisance," said the Major.

"We can do very well with an inferior kind of pier," said Dr. O'Grady. "What I mean to say is we might spend a little less than we're actually given."

"What about the inspector they'd send down?" said Doyle.

"Them inspectors," said Gallagher, "is as thick about the country as fleas on a dog. Hardly ever a man would turn round without he'd have one of them asking him what he was doing it for."

For once Gallagher had spoken in a way that was acceptable to the other members of the committee. There was a general murmur of assent. Everyone present was more or less conscious of the enormous numbers of inspectors in Ireland. Even Major Kent, who had been in a bad temper all along, brightened up a little.

"I was reading a paper the other day," he said, "that 80 per cent, of the adult population of Leinster, Munster and Connacht, were paid by the Government to teach the other people how to get their livings, and to see that they did what they were told. That included schoolmasters."

"I shouldn't wonder now," said Father McCormack, "that those figures would be about right."

"It was only the week before last," said Doyle, "that there was a man stopping in my hotel, a man that looked as if he was earning a comfortable salary, and he——"

Doyle spoke in the tone of a man who is going to tell a long and leisurely story. Dr. O'Grady, who had heard the story before, interrupted him.

"Of course we'd have to talk to the inspector when he comes," he said.

"You'd do that, O'Grady," said the Major. "You'd talk to a bench of bishops."

"I'm not sure," said Father McCormack, "that I quite see what the doctor's getting at."

"It's simple enough," said Dr. O'Grady, "Suppose he offers us £500 for a pier—he can't well make it less——"

"It'll be more," said Doyle optimistically. "It'll be nearer a thousand pounds."

"Say £500," said Dr. O'Grady. "What I propose is that we spend £400 on a pier and use the other hundred to pay for the statue and the rest of the things we have to get."

"Bedamn," said Doyle, "but that's great. That's the best ever I heard."

Major Kent rose to his feet. He was very red in the face, and there was a look of rigid determination in his eyes.

"I may as well tell you at once," he said, "that I'll have nothing to do with any such plan."

"Why not?" said Dr. O'Grady.

"Because I'm an honest man. I raised no particular objection when you merely proposed to make a fool of me and everybody else concerned——"

"You've done very little else except raise objections," said Dr. O'Grady.

"—But when it comes to a deliberate act of dishonesty———"

"That's a hard word, so it is," said Doyle.

"It's not a bit too hard," said the Major, "and I say it again. Dishonesty. I won't have anything to do——"

"The Major's right," said Father McCormack, "there's no denying it, the Major's right."

"He would be right," said Dr. O'Grady, "he'd be perfectly right if there were any dishonesty about the matter. I hope it isn't necessary for me to say that if I thought the plan a dishonest one I'd be the last man in Ireland to propose it."

"Of course, of course," said Father McCormack.

"The doctor wouldn't do the like," said Doyle.

"Sure we all know that," said Father McCormack, "but the objection that the Major has raised——"

"It's all very well talking," said the Major. "But talking won't alter facts. It is dishonest to get a grant of money for one purpose and use it for something totally different."

"I'm not quite sure," said Dr. O'Grady, "whether you quite understand the philosophy of modern charity, Major."

"I understand the ten commandments," said the Major, "and that's enough for me."

"Nobody's saying a word against the ten commandments," said Dr. O'Grady.

"You're going to do something against one of them," said the Major, "and that's worse. If you merely said things against them I shouldn't mind. We all know that you'd say anything."

"You're begging the question, Major, you really are. Now listen to me. What's the ordinary recognised way of raising large sums of money for charitable objects? Some kind of bazaar, isn't it?"

"It is," said Father McCormack. "There's hardly ever a winter but there's one or two of them up in Dublin for hospitals or the like."

"Very well," said Dr. O'Grady. "What happens when a bazaar is held?"

"It doesn't matter to us what happens," said the Major. "We're not holding one."

"Let the doctor speak," said Doyle.

"What happens is this," said Dr. O'Grady. "A large sum of money, very often an enormous sum, is spent on getting up switch-back railways, and Alpine panoramas, and underground rivers, and old English villages. Those things are absolutely necessary to the success of the show. They cost thousands of pounds sometimes. Now, who pays for them? The charity pays, and is jolly glad to. The price of them is deducted from the gross receipts and the balance is handed over to the hospital. Is there anything dishonest about that?"

"There is not, of course," said Father McCormack. "It's always done."

"Wouldn't a bishop do it? A bishop of any church?"

"Lots of them do," said Father McCormack.

"Well, if a bishop would do it, it can't be dishonest," said Dr. O'Grady. "You'll agree to that, I suppose, Major? You won't want to accuse the hierarchy of Ireland, Protestant and Roman Catholics, of flying in the face of the ten commandments."

The Major had sat down again. While Dr. O'Grady was speaking he turned his chair half round and stared out of the window. He wished to convey the impression that he was not listening to a word that was said. When Dr. O'Grady appealed to him directly he turned round again and answered:

"It's dishonest to take money given for one purpose and use it for another," he said.

"I'm with you there, Major," said Father McCormack. "I'm with you there."

"Are you prepared," said Dr. O'Grady, "to go back on the whole theory of necessary expenses? Would you refuse to allow the unfortunate secretary of a charitable society to refund himself for the postage stamps he uses in sending out his appeals?"

"Secretaries have nothing to do with us," said the Major. "This is a simple question of right and wrong."

"You haven't quite caught my point yet," said Dr. O'Grady patiently. "What I'm trying to explain to you is this: we're in exactly the same position as the charity that's getting up a bazaar. In order to make the money we want for the good of the town—the good of the town, mind you, Major—that's a worthy object."

"A pier wouldn't be any good if you had it," said the Major.

"A lot of money would be spent building it," said Dr. O'Grady, "and that would do us all good. But in order to get a pier we must incur some expense. We shan't get the pier unless we succeed in enticing a Lord-Lieutenant down here."

"You will not," said Doyle. "It's waste of time writing letters to those fellows, for they don't read them."

"And we can't get the Lord-Lieutenant down unless we have a statue for him to unveil," said Dr. O'Grady.

"He wouldn't come without he had something of the sort," said Father McCormack. "That's sure."

"Therefore," said Dr. O'Grady, "the statue is a necessary part of our expenses in getting the pier. So is the illuminated address. So is the bouquet. And we're just as well entitled to charge what they all cost us against the money we succeed in making, as the secretary of a charitable bazaar is to debit his gross earnings with the hire of the hall in which the show is held."

"Now that you put it in that way," said Father McCormack, "I can see well that there's something in what you say."

"Honesty and dishonesty are two different things," said the Major.

"Don't keep on making those bald and senseless assertions," said Dr. O'Grady. "Even an income tax collector, and he's the most sceptical kind of man there is with regard to assertions about money—but even he allows his victims to deduct the expenses necessarily incurred in making their incomes from the gross amount which they return to him. You can't want to go behind the income tax authorities, Major."

"It's all very well arguing," said the Major, "and I can't answer you when you confuse things in the way you do. But I know perfectly well that it isn't right——"

"Well do what the doctor says, anyway," said Doyle. "Doesn't the Government rob the whole of us every day more than ever we'll be able to rob it?"

"There's something in that, too," said Father McCormack.

Curiously enough Doyle's statement produced far more effect on Major Kent's mind than the elaborate arguments of Dr. O'Grady. He was accustomed to gnash his teeth over the burden of taxation laid upon him. He had often, in private conversation, described governments, especially Liberal Governments, as bandits and thieves.

"We are robbed," he said. "I admit that. What with the extra tax on unearned income and the insurance of servants against accidents, and this infernal new unemployment insurance, and the death duties, and——"

"There was a report of the Financial Relations Commission," said Gallagher, "which presented a case on behalf of Ireland that showed——"

"Don't drag in politics, Thady," said Dr. O'Grady. "The Major admits that he's robbed. That ought to be enough for you. Now, Major, if you were attacked by a highwayman——"

"I didn't say the Government was a highwayman," said the Major.

"You said it was a robber. Didn't he, Father McCormack?"

"He said it had him robbed," said Father McCormack, with the air of a man who is carefully making a fine distinction.

"That's exactly the same thing. Now, Major, if a robber stole your money, wouldn't you take the first chance you could of getting it back? You know you would. We all would. And would you call that dishonesty? You would not. Now we're offering you the chance of getting something back, a mere trifle, but still something, out of a Government which, as you admit, has robbed you. Why on earth do you start making a fuss?"

"I can't argue with you, O'Grady," said the Major, "but you're wrong."

"What's the good of talking?" said Doyle. "We'll do what the doctor says."

"Your nephew won't be able to get that advance he asked for," said Dr. O'Grady.

"Let him not," said Doyle. "I don't pity him. He'll get his money in the end."

"Gentlemen," said Father McCormack, "is it your will that the plan now laid before the meeting by Dr. O'Grady, be adopted?"

"It is," said Gallagher.

"What else is there for us to do?" said Doyle.

"You may take me as dissenting," said the Major.

"I'll make a note of that in the minutes," said Dr. O'Grady, "and then your conscience will be perfectly clear, no matter what happens."

"Well, gentlemen," said Father McCormack, "I suppose that completes our arrangements for to-day. When shall we have our next meeting?" He rose to his feet as he spoke. Everyone else rose too. Major Kent put on his hat and walked towards the door. When he reached it he turned.

"I shan't come to any more meetings," he said.

"I don't think there's any necessity to hold another meeting," said Dr. O'Grady, "until after the Lord-Lieutenant has left and the time comes for squaring up things. I shall be so busy between this and the day of his visit that I shan't have time to attend meetings."

"Very well," said Father McCormack. "I shall be all the better pleased."

He left the room and followed Major Kent down the stairs.

"Thady," said Doyle, "do you go down to the bar, and I'll be with you in a minute. I've a word to say to the doctor."

"I could do with a sup of porter after all that talk," said Gallagher, as he left the room.

"Doctor," said Doyle, "if things turn out the way we hope——".

"I suppose you're knocking a commission out of that nephew of yours for selling his statue for him?"

"Twenty-five per pent, is the amount agreed on. It isn't everyone I'd tell, but I've confidence in you, doctor."

"And if we get £500 for the pier?"

"A middling good pier," said Doyle, "as good a pier as anyone'd have a right to expect in a place like this, might be built for £300."

"That'll put £120 into your pocket, Doyle, not counting anything you may make on the luncheons!"

"What I was meaning to say, doctor, is, that it would be a satisfaction to me if there was something coming to yourself. You deserve it."

"Thank you, Doyle; but I'm not in this business to make money."

"It would be well," said Doyle with a sigh, "if you'd make a little more now and again."

"If you're going to start about that wretched bill I owe you——"

"I am not then. Nor I won't mention it to you until such time as you might be able to pay it. If so be that things turn out the way you say I shouldn't care——"

"If you keep Gallagher waiting too long for his drink," said Dr. O'Grady, "he'll start breaking things. He must be uncommonly thirsty after all the speeches he made this afternoon."

"That's true," said Doyle. "I'd maybe better go to him."

Constable Moriarty stood just outside the door of the hotel. He saluted Major Kent as he passed. He touched his hat respectfully to Father McCormack. He saw Gallagher come downstairs and enter the bar. A few minutes later he saw Dr. O'Grady. All traces of his usual smile vanished from his face. He drew himself up stiffly, and his eyes expressed something more than official severity. When Dr. O'Grady passed through the door into the street, Moriarty confronted him.

"I'm glad to see," said Dr. O'Grady, "that you've stopped grinning. It's quite time you did."

"It's not grins I'm talking about now," said Moriarty. "It's Mary Ellen."

"Nice little girl, isn't she?"

"It's a nice little girl you'll make of her before you've done! What's this I'm after hearing about the way you have in mind for dressing her up?"

"Do be reasonable, Moriarty! What's the good of asking me what you've heard? I can't possibly know, for I wasn't there when you heard it."

"You know well what I heard."

"Look here, Moriarty," said Dr. O'Grady. "If you think I'm going to stand here to be bullied by you in the public street you're greatly mistaken. Why don't you go and patrol somewhere?"

"I'll not have Mary Ellen play-acting before the Lord-Lieutenant, so now you know, doctor."

"There's no play-acting to be done," said Dr. O'Grady. "We haven't even had time to get up a pageant. I wish we had. You'd look splendid as a Roman Emperor trampling on a conquered people. I'm not sure that I wouldn't get you up as an Assyrian bull. The expression of your face is just right this minute."

"Mary Ellen's an orphan girl," said Moriarty, "with no father to look after her, and what's more I'm thinking of marrying her myself. So it's as well for you to understand, doctor, that I'll not have her character took from her. It's not the first time you've tried that same, but it had better be the last."

"I don't know what you're talking about, Moriarty. There's nobody injuring the girl's character except, maybe, yourself. Doyle tells me you're never out of the back-yard of the hotel."

"You put it out that she was married to young Kerrigan."

"That was Thady Gallagher," said Dr. O'Grady, "and it didn't do her a bit of harm. Nobody except Mr. Billing believed it."

"I don't mind that so much now," said Moriarty, "though I don't deny I was angry at the time, but what I won't have is Mary Ellen dressed up to be an ancient Irish colleen. It's not respectful to the girl."

"You told me the other day that you want the Lord-Lieutenant to make you a sergeant. Did you mean that when you said it, or did you not?"

"It's no way to make a sergeant of me to be dressing up Mary Ellen."

"It's far the best way. When the Lord-Lieutenant sees her and hears——"

"It's not going to be done, anyway," said Moriarty, "for I won't have it."

"Listen to me now," said Dr. O'Grady, "and you may take it that this is my last word, for I haven't time to waste talking to you. If I catch you interfering with Mary Ellen in any way or setting the girl's mind up against the costume that Mrs. Gregg has designed for her, I'll speak to Mr. Gregg, and have you transferred to some different county altogether, where you'll never see Mary Ellen either in fancy dress or any other way. What's more I'll represent your conduct to the Lord-Lieutenant, so that you'll never be made a sergeant as long as you live."

These threats affected Moriarty. He had no doubt in his mind that Dr. O'Grady could and would carry out the first of them. About the second he was not quite so sure, but it remained a horrible possibility.

He saw that there was nothing to be done by opposing his will to a powerful combination of private influence and official power. Without speaking another word he turned and walked across the street to the barrack. But his anger had by no means died away. He found Sergeant Colgan asleep in the living-room. He woke him at once.

"I'll be even with that doctor," he said, "before I've done with him."

"That's threatening language," said the sergeant, who was not pleased at being wakened, "and it's actionable; so you'd better mind yourself, Moriarty. There's many a better man than you has gone to jail for less than that. I knew a Member of Parliament one time that got three weeks for no more than saying that he'd like to see the people beating the life out of a land grabber. What has the doctor been doing to you?"

"It's about Mary Ellen."

"Get out," said the sergeant, "you and your Mary Ellen! It's too fond you are of running here and there after that same Mary Ellen."

It was plain that no sympathy was to be expected from Sergeant Colgan. Moriarty sat down on a chair in the corner and meditated on plans of vengeance. The sergeant dropped off to sleep again.

CHAPTER XVII

According to the official programme—so described by Dr. O'Grady—the Lord-Lieutenant and Lady Chesterton were to arrive in Ballymoy by motorcar at half-past twelve o'clock. There might be two motorcars. That depended on the number of aides-de-camp and of the suite which the Lord-Lieutenant brought. There would certainly be one, and Doyle had the coach-house in his back-yard emptied and carefully cleaned to serve for the garage. Everything in the town was ready before half-past ten. The statue had been erected on its pedestal the day before and excited general admiration. Even Major Kent admitted that it was a striking work of art which would be an ornament to the town. The deceased Deputy-Lieutenant was dressed in flowing robes which resembled those worn by judges. He held a large roll, intended to represent parchment, in his left hand. This, Dr. O'Grady said, might very well be taken for the original draft of the Bolivian Constitution. His right hand pointed upwards with extended forefinger. In the case of the Deputy-Lieutenant, who was almost certainly a strong Unionist, this may have symbolised an appeal to the higher powers—the House of Lords, or even the King—to refuse consent to a Home Rule Bill. When the statue ceased to be a Deputy-Lieutenant and became General John Regan the attitude was taken to express his confidence in the heavenly nature of the national liberty which he had won for Bolivia. This was the explanation of the uplifted forefinger which Dr. O'Grady offered to Thady Gallagher. But Gallagher was curiously sulky and suspicious. He seemed unimpressed.

Doyle's nephew came down to Ballymoy and personally superintended the fixing of the statue on its pedestal. He complained that the cement supplied for the purpose by his uncle was of very inferior quality, and expressed grave doubts about the stability of the structure. Dr. O'Grady did not seem very anxious. He hinted that the people of Ballymoy would be quite satisfied if the statue stood for twenty-four hours. The weather was exceptionally fine and calm. There was no reason—if the unveiling were carefully done—why Doyle's cement should be subjected to any strain whatever.

At nine o'clock on the morning of the Lord-Lieutenant's visit, Dr. O'Grady, with the help of Doyle and two labourers, who had three step-ladders, veiled the statue. They draped it from the head to the bottom of the pedestal in a large sheet of blay calico of a light yellowish colour. This was carefully done, and an elaborate arrangement of string was made, leading out from the statue to the place where the Lord-Lieutenant was to stand. Dr. O'Grady satisfied himself by a series of experiments that the apparatus would work. At a single pull at the end of the string the whole sheet fluttered to the ground and exposed the Deputy-Lieutenant to public view.

It was ten o'clock before these arrangements were completed and the step-ladders taken away. Dr. O'Grady went into the barrack and warned Sergeant Colgan that he would be held personally responsible if any curious wayfarer pulled the string before the proper time. Sergeant Colgan at once ordered Moriarty to mount guard over the statue. Dr. O'Grady went over to the hotel and inspected the luncheon table. He had laid it himself the night before, so he felt fairly confident that everything was as it should be; but he was not inclined to run any risks. It was just possible that Doyle, acting on advice from somebody else, might have altered the position of the spoons and forks during the night.

"It'll be after lunch," said Dr. O'Grady, "that we'll introduce the subject of a pier."

"Then or sooner," said Doyle.

"Hints will have been given before that," said Dr. O'Grady. "Father McCormack has promised to touch on the undeveloped condition of our fishing industry when he's making his introductory remarks previous to the unveiling of the statue. If I get half a chance, I mean to point out what excellent stones there are in that old mill of yours. The matter is distinctly alluded to at the end of the illuminated address, but I'm afraid they're not likely to read that till they get back to Dublin, if then. I suppose, by the way, the address has arrived all right?"

"It has," said Doyle, "but I haven't it unpacked yet. It's in a case."

"We'd better have it quite ready. Get a screwdriver, will you, and a hammer."

The address turned out to be very large indeed and most magnificently coloured. In the top left-hand corner was a small photograph of the market square of Ballymoy, without the statue. In the right-hand Corner was a picture, supplied by Mr. Aloysius Doyle, of the statue itself. In the bottom left-hand corner was a photograph of the Viceregal Lodge in the Phoenix Park, and opposite it a portrait of the Lord-Lieutenant in his state robes. The whole left-hand side of the address was occupied by an immensely complicated design made up of spirals, serpents, and trumpet pattern ornaments, which twisted in and out of each other in a way most bewildering to the eye. This was supposed to represent the manner in which ancient Irish artists made the letter "t," when they were not in a hurry. "T" is the first letter of the word "to" with which the actual address began. The words "Excellency," "Lord," and "Lieutenant" were similarly honoured with capital letters of Celtic design, but inferior size. "Ireland," which came on a line to itself, was blazoned in red and green, on a background of dull gold, laid on smoothly, and afterwards dinted here and there with some instrument which must have resembled a blunt pin. The rest of the letter-press was done in crooked, angular characters, very ornamental to look at, but most difficult to read.

"It's a good address, so it is," said Doyle, "and worth the money, though, mind you, it was a big lot we gave for it. A cheaper one would have done well enough."

"I call it cheap at the price," said Dr. O'Grady. "I'd no idea you could get so much for £4. Now what about the bouquet?"

"I have it in a jug of water," said Doyle, "under the counter of the bar. I thought it would be better in water the way it would be fresh."

"Quite right. But be sure you wipe the stalks before you give it to Mrs. Gregg. It doesn't so much matter about Lady Chesterton. She must be pretty well accustomed to handling damp bouquets. But I'd be sorry to spoil Mrs. Gregg's new gloves. She's sure to have new gloves. By the way, what's being done about getting Mary Ellen ready? That girl can't be trusted to dress herself."

"Mrs. Gregg is putting the clothes on her this minute," said Doyle, "above in the best bedroom. She said she'd do it early so as she'd have time after to go home and dress herself."

"There's been no trouble with Moriarty, I suppose? I told you about the way he threatened me, didn't I?"

"He hasn't said a word to me, but he's a fellow I wouldn't trust further than I can see him, and he's had an ugly look about him this three days, like as if he had some mischief in his mind."

"I wouldn't trust him either," said Dr. O'Grady; "but I don't see what he could do. He wouldn't venture to meddle with the statue, would he? Tangle up the strings we have tied to the sheet or anything of that sort?"

"He would not; for he knows well it would be the worse for him if he did. It's not likely Mr. Gregg would overlook it if Moriarty did anything that put a stop to Mrs. Gregg presenting the bouquet."

"We'll have to chance it anyway, and I don't see that he can do much except sulk, and that won't hurt us. I think I'll be getting home now, Doyle. I have to shave and generally clean up a bit before the Viceregal party arrives. You don't own a silk hat, I suppose?"

"I do not. What would I have the like for?"

"You might have worn it if you had," said Dr. O'Grady. "My own is so old that I'm ashamed to put it on. However, it doesn't really matter. Both the Major and Father McCormack are sure to have them, so the Lord-Lieutenant won't notice that you and I haven't and nobody would expect much from Thady Gallagher. After all, our hats will be in our hands most of the time, and we can keep them behind our backs."

At half-past eleven Mary Ellen and Mrs. Gregg came out of the hotel together. Mary Ellen's costume was beautifully complete. An English tourist accustomed to buy the coloured picture postcards with which the Germans obligingly supply our shops, would have recognised her at once as an Irish colleen. Her stockings were of the brightest shade of green. Her shoes, which were highly polished, had aggressively square toes and enormous steel buckles which flashed in the sunlight as she walked. Her skirt reached half way down the calves of her legs. It was of crimson flannel, made very wide. A green and black tartan shawl was fastened round her with a large Tara brooch which also held in its place a trail of shamrock. Underneath the shawl she had a green silk blouse. It showed very little but it exactly matched her stockings. Her hair was brushed smoothly back from her forehead, and covered with a black and white-checked kerchief tied beneath her chin and falling in a neat triangle at the nape of her neck. Mrs. Gregg, who was naturally very pleased, led Mary Ellen over to the statue, placed her beside it, and told her not to move or in any way disorder her dress. Then she herself hurried away.

Constable Moriarty, who was on guard beside the statue, scowled at Mary Ellen. He approached her slowly, walked round her, surveyed her from every point of view, and then snorted with intense disapproval.

"Your mother wouldn't know you," he said.

Mary Ellen smiled. She was greatly pleased at her own appearance and chose to take Moriarty's remark as a compliment.

"She might not," she said, in a tone of evident delight.

Moriarty intended to say more; but at that moment the town band began to play. Young Kerrigan had collected the members of it early in the day and kept them in a group outside his father's shop. The arrival of Mary Ellen seemed to him to be a suitable occasion for a tune. He gave a signal and the band struck up. "Rich and Rare Were the Gems She Wore" was the tune on which they chanced. It was remarkably appropriate. The band marched twice round the statue playing that tune. With the last note it came to rest again in its old position outside Kerrigan's shop. Then Thady Gallagher came out of his office. He walked over and looked at Mary Ellen.

"If you're not ashamed of yourself," he said, "you ought to be."

"I am not, then," said Mary Ellen.

Gallagher turned to Moriarty.

"You're sure now," he said, "that the tune the band is to play is the one you told me."

Moriarty grinned malevolently.

"I am sure," he said.

"For if you're playing any kind of a trick on me——"

"I am not. Amn't I wanting to get my knife into the doctor the same as yourself?"

"And why would you want that?"

"It's on account of the way he has Mary Ellen dressed up. Will you look at the girl?"

Gallagher looked at her again, long and carefully.

"Play acting!" said Moriarty, "and she's a respectable girl. It's not decent, so it's not."

"If the tune's what you say it is," said Gallagher, "it'll not be played in Ballymoy to-day nor any other day. I'll put the fear of God into young Kerrigan before he's an hour older."

Moriarty grinned again. It seemed that, with the aid of Gallagher, he was going to hit Dr. O'Grady on a vital spot. He understood that great importance was attached to the performance of "Rule, Brittania" by the band. Gallagher walked across to young Kerrigan.

"I know now," he said, "what the tune is you're meaning to play."

"If you know that," said Kerrigan, "you know more than I do."

"None of your lies now. Constable Moriarty is after telling me the name of the tune."

"If you know it," said Kerrigan, "maybe you'll tell me. Not that I care what the name of it is, for it's a good tune, name or no name."

"You will care," said Gallagher. "You will care before the day is out."

"Why don't you tell me the name of it, then? if so be you know it."

"You know well why I don't tell you. It's because I wouldn't defile my lips with the name of it, because I wouldn't say the words that would be a disgrace to any Irishman."

"You're mighty particular," said young Kerrigan. "It would have to be a pretty bad name that's on the tune if it's worse than what you said many a time."

Gallagher was not in a mood to submit calmly to taunts of this kind. He knew that he was perfectly right in refusing to pronounce the name of the tune. He was convinced that young Kerrigan knew and was able to talk as he did only because he was dead to all sense of decency or shame.

"Let me tell you this," he said, "and it's my last word. If that tune's played in Ballymoy to-day it'll be the worse for you, and the worse for your father, and the worse for all belonging to you. Let you not play that tune or the grass will be growing on the step outside your father's shop before any decent Nationalist will go into it to buy a bit of meat. Them that makes their living off the people will have to mind themselves that they don't outrage the convictions of the people."

This was an awful threat, and it cowed young Kerrigan a good deal. He did not believe that Gallagher was capable of having it carried out to the last extremity. The grass would not actually grow on his father's doorstep, because the people of the west of Ireland, though swift and passionate in resentment, find a difficulty in keeping up a personal quarrel long enough to permit of the growth of grass. But a great deal of temporary inconvenience might be caused by a boycott initiated by Gallagher and taken up by the local branch of the League. Young Kerrigan was shaken.

"You'd better speak to the doctor about it," he said. "It's his tune and not mine."

"I will speak to the doctor," said Gallagher. "I'll speak to him in a way he won't like. I was thinking all along he was up to some mischief with that tune; but I didn't know how bad it was till Moriarty was talking to me this morning. Where is the doctor?"

"He was over in Doyle's hotel a minute ago," said Kerrigan, "but I don't know is he there yet. He might not be, for I seen him going out of it and along the street."

"Wherever he is I'll make it hot for him," said Gallagher, as he turned away.

"Constable Moriarty be damned," said young Kerrigan softly but fervently as soon as Gallagher was safely out of earshot. Gallagher stopped on his way to the hotel to take another scornful look at Mary Ellen.

"If your father that's dead was alive this day," he said, "he'd turn you out of the house when he seen you in them clothes."

Mary Ellen had no recollection of her father, who had died before she was twelve months old, but she was more hopeful about him than Gallagher seemed to be.

"He might not," she said.

Then Father McCormack appeared, walking briskly up the street from the-presbytery. He was wearing, as Dr. O'Grady had anticipated, a silk hat. He had a very long and voluminous frock coat. He had even, and this marked his sense of the importance of the occasion, made creases down the fronts of his trousers. Gallagher went to meet him.

"Good morning, Thady," said Father McCormack cheerfully. "We're in great luck with the weather."

"Father," said Gallagher, "you were always one that was heart and soul with the people of Ireland, and it will make you sorry, so it will, sorry and angry, to hear what I have to tell you."

Father McCormack felt uneasy. He did not know what Gallagher meant to tell him, but he was uncomfortably conscious that the day of the Lord-Lieutenant's visit might be a highly inconvenient time for proving his devotion to the cause of the people. The worst of devotion to any cause is that it makes demands on the devotee at moments when it is most difficult to fulfil them. Father McCormack tried feebly to put off the evil hour.

"To-morrow, Thady, to-morrow," he said. "There isn't time now. It's half-past eleven, and the Lord-Lieutenant may be here any minute."

"Begging your reverence's pardon," said Gallagher firmly, "but to-morrow will be too late. The insult that is about to be offered to the people of this locality will be offered to-day if a stop's not put to it."

"Nonsense, Thady, nonsense, nobody is going to insult us."

"You wouldn't know about it," said Gallagher, "for you'd be the last man they'd dare to tell, knowing well that you'd be as angry as I am myself. Do you know what the tune is that the doctor has taught to the band?"

Father McCormack did know, but he was very unwilling to enter into a discussion of the subject with Gallagher.

"Constable Moriarty," said Gallagher, "is after telling me the name of the tune, and you'd be surprised, so you would, if you heard it."

"You may be mistaken, Thady, you may be mistaken. One tune's very like another when it's played on a band."

"I am not mistaken," said Gallagher, who was beginning to feel suspicious about the priest's evident desire to shelve the subject.

"And anyway," said Father McCormack, "it's Dr. O'Grady himself that you'd better be speaking to about the tune."

"I will speak to him; but he's not here presently."

"Try Doyle then," said Father McCormack. "There he is coming out of the hotel. I haven't time to go into the matter. I want to go over and look at Mary Ellen."

He slipped away as he spoke, leaving Gallagher standing, sulky and very suspicious, by himself. Doyle, who had no reason to think that anything had gone wrong, greeted him heartily. Gallagher replied angrily.

"Do you know what tune it is that the band's going to play?" he said.

"You and your old tune!" said Doyle. "You had the life plagued out of me about that tune. Can't you let it alone?"

"I will not let it alone, for——"

"Was it that you were talking to the priest about?"

"It was, and——"

"I thought it might have been," said Doyle, "by the look of him. Why can't you have sense, Thady, instead of tormenting the whole town about a tune?"

"It's my belief," said Gallagher, "that he knows more about the tune than he'd care to own up to. He and the doctor is in the conspiracy together."

"I'll not stand here listening to you talking disrespectfully about the clergy," said Doyle with a fine show of indignation.

He felt that he was on doubtful ground in discussing the tune, which might, for all he knew, be an objectionable one. It was a satisfaction to be able to put himself definitely in the right by protesting against Gallagher's tendency to anti-clericalism.

"I'd be the last man in Ireland," said Gallagher, "that would say a word against the clergy, but when we get Home Rule—and that won't be long now, please God——"

He paused impressively.

"Well," said Doyle, "what'll you do to the clergy when you get Home Rule?"

"There's some of them that will be put in their places mighty quick, them that's opposing the will of the people of Ireland behind their backs."

"If you mean Father McCormack, Thady, you'd better go home before you've said what you'll be sorry for."

"I'll not go home till I've told the doctor what I think of him."

"Well, go and see him," said Doyle. "He's in his house. When you come back you can tell me what he says to you. That'll be better worth hearing than anything you're likely to say to him."

Doyle looked round with an air of some satisfaction when Gallagher left him. He had no doubt that Dr. O'Grady would be able to deal satisfactorily with the difficulty about the tune. Everything else seemed to be going well. A considerable number of people had already gathered in the square. The band stood ready to play. Father McCormack was apparently very much pleased with the appearance of Mary Ellen. Constable Moriarty was on guard over the statue, looking unusually stern. Sergeant Colgan had come out of the barrack and was exerting all his authority to keep back a number of small children who wanted to investigate Mary Ellen's costume. Every time any of them approached her with the intention of pulling her shawl or testing by actual touch the material of her skirt, Sergeant Colgan spoke majestically.

"Get away out of that," he said. "Get along home out of that, the whole of yez."

The children did not, of course, obey him literally; but they always drew back from Mary Ellen when he spoke, and it was generally at least a minute before the boldest of them ventured to touch her again.

CHAPTER XVIII

Doyle's satisfaction did not last long. Major Kent drove into the town in his pony trap and pulled up opposite the statue. He called to Father McCormack, who had satisfied himself about Mary Ellen's appearance, and was prowling round the statue, making mild jokes about its ghostly appearance. Doyle detected a note of urgency in the Major's voice, and hurried across the square, reaching the pony trap just as Father McCormack did.

"So I hear," said the Major, "that the Lord-Lieutenant's not coming after all."

For a moment neither Father McCormack nor Doyle spoke at all. The rumour—it could be no more than a rumour—to which the Major referred was too terrible for immediate digestion.

"I shan't be sorry myself," said the Major, "if he doesn't come. I've always thought we were making fools of ourselves."

Then Doyle regained his power of speech.

"It's a lie," he said, "and whoever told it to you is a liar. The Lord-Lieutenant can't not come."

"It'll be a curious thing, so it will," said Father McCormack, "if he doesn't, but I can't believe it. Who was it told you, Major, if you don't mind my asking?"

"It was Mr. Ford," said the Major. "He was standing at his door as I drove past and he stopped me to say that he'd just had a telegram from Dublin Castle——"

"I don't believe it," said Doyle. "I don't believe a word of it. That fellow Ford was against us all the time, and he's just saying this now to annoy us."

"He seemed to believe it himself," said the Major.

"Where's the doctor?" said Father McCormack. "If there's any truth in it he'll be sure to know."

"If so be that such a telegram was sent," said Doyle, "it'll be on account of something that fellow Ford has been doing. He was always against us."

"Where's the doctor?" said Father McCormack helplessly.

"Probably bolted," said the Major. "If Ford's news is true that's the only thing for the doctor to do."

"He was with me half-an-hour ago," said Doyle, "taking a look round at the luncheon and the rest of it. He went away back to his house to clean himself. If he knew— —but he didn't."

"I'll go and see him at once," said Father McCormack.

"You'll find that he's cut and run," said the Major.

"You needn't go, Father," said Doyle, "for Thady Gallagher's just after going to him, and I see him coming back at the far end of the street this minute."

Thady Gallagher pushed his way through the crowd which had gathered thickly at the lower end of the square. It was plain from the way he elbowed the people who stood in his way that he was in a very bad temper indeed. He strode up to the Major's trap and began to speak at the top of his voice.

"Let me tell you this, gentlemen," he said: "if you deserve the name of gentlemen, which you don't, that the conspiracy which you're engaged in for insulting the people of this district by means of a tune— —"

He appeared to be addressing himself particularly to Major Kent, whom he evidently regarded as, next to the doctor, the chief conspirator. The Major disliked being abused. He also shrank from complicated situations. He foresaw that an argument with Gallagher about a tune which might be played if the Lord-Lieutenant did not fail to keep his appointment, was likely to be a confused and highly complex business. He touched his pony with the whip and drove away in the direction of Doyle's yard, where he usually put up his trap.

"Have sense, Thady," said Father McCormack appealingly.

"I will not have sense," said Gallagher. "Why would I have sense when— —"

"Did you speak to the doctor?" said Doyle.

"I did not, but if I had— —"

"The Lord save us and deliver us," said Doyle in despair. "He's gone, the way the Major said he would."

"What are you talking about?" said Gallagher. "The doctor's shaving himself."

"Are you sure of that?"

"I am sure. Didn't I go through the house till I found him? Didn't I open the door of the room he was in? Didn't I see him standing there with a razor in his hand?"

"And what did he say to you, Thady? Did he tell you— —"

"He told me to get along out of that," said Gallagher.

"It's likely he'd heard the news. He'd never have said the like of that to you, Thady, if he hadn't been upset about something."

"What'll we do at all?" said Doyle. "There's the statue to be paid for and the dress for Mary Ellen and the luncheon. It's ruined we'll be, for where will we get the money?"

"I had my mind made up," said Gallagher, "to speak out plain to the doctor about the tune the band's to play. I had my mind made up to tell him straight what I thought of him. And to tell him what I thought of the whole of you."

"Be quiet, Thady," said Father McCormack. "Don't you know——"

"There's more than you will want to speak plain to the doctor," said Doyle in sudden anger. "It's him that's got us into the trouble we're in. It's him that ought to be made to pay up what'll have to be paid; only he can't do it, for he owes more this minute than ever he'll pay. Tell me now, Thady, what you said to him. Tell me the language you used. It'll be some satisfaction to me to hear the words you said to the doctor."

"I said nothing," said Gallagher. "Is it likely I'd speak the way I meant to a man with an open razor in his hand? I'd have had my throat cut if I'd said a word."

Mrs. Gregg rode hurriedly into the market square on her bicycle, while Gallagher was making his confession. She wore a delicate and flimsy pink silk skirt, entirely unsuited for cycling. A very large hat, adorned with a wreath of pink roses, had been forced to the back of her head by the speed at which she rode, and was held there with much strain by two large pins. She had only one glove, and several hooks at the back of the upper part of her dress were unfastened. No one could doubt that Mrs. Gregg had left home before she was quite ready. No one could doubt that she had come into Ballymoy as fast as she could. She dismounted in front of Father McCormack and panted. She said "Oh" three times, and each time was prevented saying anything else by lack of breath. Then she caught sight of Major Kent, who was coming out of the hotel yard after stabling his pony. She let her bicycle fall at the feet of Father McCormack, and ran to the Major.

"Oh," she said. "Oh! my husband—just told me—a telegram—isn't it frightful? What are we to do?"

"I'm rather glad myself," said the Major, "but everybody else is making a fuss."

Doyle, Father McCormack and Gallagher followed Mrs. Gregg. Father McCormack, who was a chivalrous man even when agitated, picked up her bicycle and brought it with him.

"Is it true, ma'am," said Doyle, "what we're after hearing?"

"It's quite true," said Mrs. Gregg. "My husband had a telegram. So had Mr. Ford. And Mrs. Ford is so pleased. Oh, it's too much! But where's Dr. O'Grady?"

"Everybody is asking that," said the Major. "My own impression is that he's bolted."

"If only Dr. O'Grady were here," said Mrs. Gregg, "he might do something."

"There's one thing the doctor won't do," said Gallagher, "Lord-Lieutenant or no Lord-Lieutenant, he'll not have the town band playing the tune that he's after teaching young Kerrigan."

"Doyle," said Major Kent, "do you think you could get Thady Gallagher out of this? He's becoming a nuisance. Nobody's temper will stand a Home Rule speech at the present moment."

"Thady," said Doyle, persuasively, "a drop of something to drink is what will suit you. The inside of your throat is dried up the same as if you'd been eating lime on account of the rage that's in you."

Doyle was himself no less perplexed than everyone else. He was more acutely sensitive than anyone to the danger of financial disaster. But he was a man of cool judgment even in a crisis. He saw that Gallagher's presence was highly inconvenient.

"A bottle of porter, Thady," he said, "or maybe two, would do you good."

Gallagher made a strong effort to swallow, intending when he had done so to speak again. But the description Doyle gave of the inside of his throat and the thought of cool draughts of porter, had actually induced a very real dryness of his mouth. He turned doubtfully towards the hotel, walked a few steps and then stood still again.

Doyle caught a glimpse, through a momentary opening in the crowd, of Dr. O'Grady, shaved, and very carefully dressed in a new grey tweed suit. He became more than ever anxious to get Gallagher into the hotel.

"If you fancy a glass of whisky, Thady," he said, "it's in there for you and welcome. There'll be no tunes played here for the next half hour, anyway, so you needn't be afraid to go."

He took Gallagher by the arm as he spoke and led him towards the hotel. Gallagher went at first with apparent reluctance, but as he got near the door his steps quickened. Doyle did not leave him till he handed him over to the care of the young man who stood behind the bar while Doyle himself was absent.

Dr. O'Grady made his way through the crowd with gay confidence, smiling and nodding to his acquaintances as he went. The people had been slightly suspicious beforehand and feared that something had gone wrong with the arrangements for the day's entertainment. They were cheered, and their confidence was fully restored when they saw Dr. O'Grady was not in the least depressed. He smiled at Mary Ellen as he passed her and winked at Constable Moriarty.

Mrs. Gregg, as soon as she caught sight of him, rushed to meet him.

"Oh, Dr. O'Grady," she said, "isn't it terrible? What are we to do? I wouldn't mind so much only that Mrs. Ford is delighted. But you'll be able to do something, won't you?"

"The first thing to be done," said Dr. O'Grady, "is to stop those children pulling the clothes off Mary Ellen. Would you mind, Mrs. Gregg, just running over and setting her shawl straight? Fix it with a pin. It's horrid the way it is."

Mrs. Gregg went over to Mary Ellen. She was deeply interested in the girl's costume, and she still cherished a hope that Dr. O'Grady might manage somehow, even without the Lord-Lieutenant, to arrange for a ceremonial unveiling of the statue.

"Well, O'Grady," said Major Kent maliciously. "I suppose we may as well take down that statue. It's no particular use where it is, and it doesn't seem likely to help you to plunder the public funds."

"There will have to be slight alteration in our plans," said Dr. O'Grady, "but I don't see any reason for postponing the unveiling of the statue."

"Do you know that the Lord-Lieutenant's not coming?" said Father McCormack.

"I had a telegram from his private secretary," said Dr. O'Grady. "I must say I think he might have let us know a little sooner. I was out early and I didn't get the message till an hour ago. Where's Doyle?"

"Doyle's making Thady Gallagher drunk in the hotel," said the Major.

"Good," said Dr. O'Grady. "That's much the best thing to do with Thady. But I wish he'd be quick about it, for I want to speak to him."

"Here he is coming now," said Father McCormack.

Doyle, who had himself taken half a glass of whisky, approached Dr. O'Grady with great courage and determination.

"If the Lord-Lieutenant isn't coming," he said, "and I can see by the look of you that you know he's not, who's going to pay for the statue and the rest of the foolishness you're after buying? That's what I'd like to know."

"Don't you fret about that, Doyle," said Dr. O'Grady. "That will be all right."

"How can it?" said Doyle. "If the Lord-Lieutenant doesn't come, and he won't, who's going to give us the money?"

"Leave that entirely in my hands," said Dr. O'Grady. "It'll be perfectly all right."

"That's what you're always saying," said Doyle sulkily. "'It'll be all right. It'll be all right.' Haven't you been saying it to me for the last two years? 'All right,' says you, and, 'It's all right,' whenever the money you owe me is mentioned."

"More shame for you then, Doyle, for mentioning it so often. I wouldn't say 'All right' or anything else about it if you didn't force me to."

"I'm dead sick of your 'All rights' anyway," said Doyle.

"Be quiet now," said Father McCormack. "Isn't the doctor doing the best he can for you? Is it his fault that the Lord-Lieutenant isn't here?"

"If you'll only stop growling, Doyle, and co-operate with me in bringing off the day's entertainment successfully——"

"Surely to goodness, O'Grady, you're not going on with the statue farce?"

"Of course I am. The only chance we have now of getting the money——"

"It's a damned poor chance," said Doyle.

"On the contrary," said Dr. O'Grady, "it's a remarkably good chance. Don't you see that if we unveil the statue successfully, in spite of the way, the really scandalous way, the Lord-Lieutenant has treated us——"

"I wash my hands of the whole business," said the Major.

"You can wash them afterwards," said Dr. O'Grady, "but at present you'll stand in with the rest of us. After the way the Lord-Lieutenant has treated us over the statue he'll have to give us a rattling good pier. He won't be able to refuse. Oh, hang it! Here's Mrs. Gregg again."

Mrs. Gregg had settled Mary Ellen's shawl. She had spoken sternly, with an authority borrowed from her husband's official position, to Sergeant Colgan. She was filled with curiosity and excitement.

"Someone must get her out of this," said Dr. O'Grady. "I can't settle things with her babbling at me.

"If there was a chance that she'd be wanting a drink," said Doyle, "but them ones wouldn't."

"Mrs. Gregg," said Dr. O'Grady, "excuse my mentioning it; but there are three hooks in the back of your blouse that aren't fastened. It's an awfully nice blouse, but as you have it on at present it's rather—rather—well dégagé."

"I started in such a hurry," said Mrs. Gregg. "The moment I heard——"

"If you go into the hotel," said Dr. O'Grady, "you'll find a looking-glass. You'll be able to inspect the bouquet too. It's in a jug of water under the counter in——— You take her, Father McCormack, and find the bouquet for her."

Father McCormack was not listening. He was looking at a large motorcar which had just drawn up at the far end of the street, leading into the square.

"It's him after all," he said.

"It's who?" said Dr. O'Grady, turning round.

The crowd which was pressing round the statue began to edge away from it. Men were standing on tiptoe, straining their necks to see over their fellows' heads. Everybody began to move towards the motorcar. A loud cheer burst from the people nearest to it.

"It's him sure enough," said Father McCormack.

"It's the Lord-Lieutenant," said Doyle excitedly. "Bedamn, but this is great! We'll be all right now."

"It can't possibly be the Lord-Lieutenant," said Dr. O'Grady. "He'd never change his mind twice in the same morning."

A tall man, very well dressed in a long frock-coat and a shiny silk hat, stood up in the motor. The crowd cheered again with tumultuous enthusiasm.

"It must be the Lord-Lieutenant," said Mrs. Gregg ecstatically. "Oh, will someone please hook up my blouse?"

"There's nobody else it could be," said Doyle. "Come on now, till we go to meet him. Come on, Father. Come you, Major. Doctor, will you go first? It's you knows the proper way to speak to the likes of him."

But Father McCormack had a strong sense of his own dignity, and was convinced that the Church had a right to precedence on all ceremonial occasions. He walked, hat in hand, towards the stranger in the motorcar. The people divided to let him pass. Major Kent and Doyle followed him. Dr. O'Grady stood still. Mrs. Gregg ran over to Mary Ellen and begged her to hook up the back of the dégagé blouse. Young

Kerrigan mustered the town band. The members had strayed a little through the crowd, but at the summons of their leader they gathered in a circle. Kerrigan looked eagerly at Dr. O'Grady awaiting the signal to strike up "Rule Britannia." Dr. O'Grady, unable to make himself heard through the cheering of the people, signalled a frantic negative. The stranger stepped out of his motorcar. Father McCormack, bowing low, advanced to meet him.

"It is my proud and pleasant duty," he said, "to welcome your Excellency to Ballymoy, and to assure you——"

"I want to see a gentleman called O'Grady," said the stranger, "a Dr. O'Grady."

"He's here, your Excellency," said Father McCormack, "and there isn't a man in Ballymoy who'll be more pleased to see your Excellency than he will."

"I'm not His Excellency. My name is Blakeney, Lord Alfred Blakeney. I'm aide-de-camp to the Lord-Lieutenant, and I particularly want to see Dr. O'Grady."

CHAPTER XIX

Lord Alfred Blakeney walked up the street and crossed the square with great dignity. He made no acknowledgment whatever of the cheers with which the people greeted him. They still thought that he was the Lord-Lieutenant, and, expectant of benefits of some sort, they shouted their best. He glanced at the veiled statue, but turned his eyes away from it immediately, as if it were something obscene or otherwise disgusting. He took no notice of Mary Ellen, though she smiled at him. Father McCormack and Doyle followed him, crestfallen. Major Kent, who seemed greatly pleased, also followed him. Half way across the square Lord Alfred Blakeney turned round and asked which was Dr. O'Grady. Father McCormack pointed him out with deprecating eagerness, much as a schoolboy with inferior sense of honour when himself in danger of punishment, points out to the master the real culprit. Lord Alfred Blakeney's forehead wrinkled in a frown. His lips closed firmly. His whole face wore an expression of dignified severity, very terrible to contemplate. Dr. O'Grady seemed entirely unmoved.

"I'm delighted to see you," he said, "though we expected the Lord-Lieutenant. By the way, you're not the Lord-Lieutenant, are you, by any chance?"

"My name is Blakeney, Lord Alfred Blakeney."

"I was afraid you weren't," said Dr. O'Grady. "Father McCormack and Doyle insisted that you were. But I knew that His Excellency must be a much older man. They couldn't very well make anybody of your age Lord-Lieutenant of Ireland, though I daresay you'd do very well, and deserve the honour quite as much as lots of people that get it."

Lord Alfred Blakeney had been at Eton as a boy and at Christchurch, Oxford, afterwards as a young man. He was a Captain in the Genadier Guards, and he was aide-de-camp to the Lord-Lieutenant of Ireland. It seemed quite impossible that an Irish dispensary doctor could be trying to poke fun at him. He supposed that Dr. O'Grady was lamentably ignorant.

"I am here," he said, "at His Excellency's express command— —"

"Quite so," said Dr. O'Grady. "We understand. You're his representative. He was pretty well bound to send somebody considering the way he's treated us, telegraphing at the last moment. We're quite ready to make excuses for him, of course, if he's got a sudden attack of influenza or anything of that sort. At the same time he ought to have come unless he's very bad indeed. However, as you're here, we may as well be getting on with the business. Where's Doyle?"

Doyle was just behind him. He was, in fact, plucking at Dr. O'Grady's sleeve. He leaned forward and whispered:

"Speak a word to the gentleman about the pier. He's a high up gentleman surely, and if you speak to him he'll use his influence with the Lord-Lieutenant."

"Be quiet, Doyle," said Dr. O'Grady. "Go off and get the bouquet as quick as you can and give it to Mrs. Gregg."

Lord Alfred Blakeney, who had gasped with astonishment at the end of Dr. O'Grady's last speech to him, recovered his dignity with an effort.

"You evidently don't understand that I have come here, at the Lord-Lieutenant's express command——"

"You said that before," said Dr. O'Grady.

"To ask for—in fact to demand an explanation of——"

"I should have thought that you'd have offered some sort of explanation to us. After all, we've been rather badly treated and——"

"An explanation," said Lord Alfred sternly, "if any explanation is possible, of the extraordinary hoax which you've seen fit to play on His Excellency."

A group of spectators formed a circle round Dr. O'Grady and Lord Alfred. Father McCormack, puzzled and anxious, stood beside Mrs. Gregg. The Major was at a little distance from them. Mary Ellen stood almost alone beside the statue. The children of the town, attracted by some new excitement, had left her, and in spite of Sergeant Colgan, were pushing their way towards Lord Alfred. Dr. O'Grady looked round him and frowned at the people.

Then he took Lord Alfred by the arm and led him away to a corner of the square near the police barrack where there were very few people.

"Now," he said, "we can talk in peace. It's impossible to discuss anything in the middle of a crowd. You seem to think that the Lord-Lieutenant has some sort of grievance against us. What is it?"

"You surely understand that," said Lord Alfred, "without my telling you. You've attempted to play off an outrageous hoax on the Lord-Lieutenant of Ireland. At least that's my view of it."

"Quite a mistaken one!"

"The Lord-Lieutenant himself hopes that there may be some other explanation. That is why he sent me down here. He wants to give you the chance of clearing yourselves if you can. I may say frankly that if he'd asked my opinion I should——"

"You'd have put us in prison at once," said Dr. O'Grady, "and kept us there till we died. You'd have been perfectly right. We'd have deserved it richly if we really had——"

"Then you are prepared to offer an explanation?"

"I'll explain anything you like," said Dr. O'Grady, "if you'll only tell me what your difficulty is. Oh, hang it! Excuse me one moment. Here's that ass Doyle coming at us again."

Doyle had brought the bouquet out of the hotel and given it to Mrs. Gregg. He had warned Constable Moriarty not to allow the people to press against the statue. He was crossing the square in the direction of the police barrack when Dr. O'Grady saw him and went to meet him.

"Doctor," said Doyle, "will you keep in mind what I was saying to you this minute about the pier? Get a promise of it out of the gentleman."

"It's utterly impossible for me," said Dr. O'Grady, "to do anything if you keep interrupting me every minute. I'm in the middle of an extremely difficult negotiation, and unless I'm allowed a free hand there'll certainly be no pier."

"If there's no pier," said Doyle angrily, "it'll be the worse for you. Don't you forget, doctor, that you owe me a matter of £60, and if I'm at the loss of more money over this statue——"

Constable Moriarty's voice rang out across the square. He was speaking in very strident tones.

"Will you stand back out of that?" he said. "What business have you there at all? Didn't I tell you a minute ago that you weren't to go near the statue?"

Dr. O'Grady and Doyle turned round to see what was happening. A man from the crowd, a well-dressed man, had slipped past Constable Moriarty and reached the statue. He had raised the bottom of the sheet which covered it and was peering at the inscription on the pedestal.

"Doyle," said Dr. O'Grady, "that's the American again. That's Billing."

"Bedamn!" said Doyle excitedly. "You're right. It's him sure enough."

"Go and seize him. Take him into the hotel. Drag his subscription out of him if you have to use a knife to get it. Whatever happens don't let him go again."

Doyle realised what his duty was before Dr. O'Grady had stopped speaking. He ran across the square to the statue. Mr. Billing, heedless of Moriarty's threats, was lifting the sheet still higher. He had read the inscription and wanted to inspect the statue itself. Doyle seized him by the shoulder.

"Come you along with me," he said, "and come quiet if you don't want me to give you in charge of the police."

Dr. O'Grady, watching from a distance, saw Mr. Billing marched off towards the hotel. Then he turned to Lord Alfred again.

"I must apologize," he said, "for running away from you like that. But we couldn't have talked with that fellow, Doyle, pestering us. You don't know Doyle, of course. If you did, and if you happened to owe him a little money you'd realise how infernally persistent he can be."

Lord Alfred had also been watching the capture of Mr. Billing. He wanted to understand, if possible; what was going on round about him.

"What is your friend doing with the other man?" he asked.

"Only capturing him," said Dr. O'Grady. "You needn't feel any anxiety about that. The other man is an American and a thorough-paced swindler. Nothing will happen to him that he doesn't deserve. But we mustn't waste time. We've still got to unveil the statue. You go on with what you were saying. You were just going to tell me what the Lord-Lieutenant's difficulty is."

"You invited His Excellency down here," said Lord Alfred, "to unveil a statue——"

"Quite right. And we have the statue ready. There it is." He pointed out the statue as he spoke.

"The statue," said Lord Alfred, "purports to represent General John Regan."

"It does represent him. There's no purporting about the matter. The General's name is on the pedestal. You'll see it yourself as soon as you unveil it."

"It now appears," said Lord Alfred coldly, "that there never was such a person as General John Regan."

"Well? Try and get along a little quicker. I don't see yet where the insult to the Lord-Lieutenant is supposed to come in."

"You asked the Lord-Lieutenant to unveil a faked-up statue, and you have the amazing assurance to say now that you don't see that you've done anything wrong."

"I don't."

"But there never was a General——"

"Do you mean to say," said Dr. O'Grady, "that the Lord-Lieutenant supposed that the General really existed?"

"Of course he supposed it. How could there be a statue to him if he didn't? We all supposed it. It wasn't until His Excellency began to prepare the speech he was to make that we found out the truth. He wrote to the British Museum and to the Librarian at the Bodleian——"

"I'm sorry he took all that trouble. We didn't expect anything of the sort."

"What did you expect?"

"Oh, I don't know. A few words about the elevating nature of great works of art—particularly statues. You know the sort of thing I mean. How the English nation occupies the great position it does very largely because it flocks to the Royal Academy regularly every year. How the people of Ballymoy are opening up a new era for Ireland. But I needn't go on. You must have heard him making speeches scores of times. That was all we wanted, and if we'd had the slightest idea that he was taking a lot of trouble to prepare a learned lecture we'd have told him that he needn't."

"But how could he make any speech about a General who never existed?"

"My dear Lord Alfred! What has the General got to do with it? We didn't want a speech about him. We wanted one about his statue."

"But it isn't his statue. If there was no General there can't be a statue to him."

"There is," said Dr. O'Grady. "There's no use flying in the face of facts. The statue's under that sheet."

"It's not. I mean to say that there may be a statue there, but it's not to General John Regan. How can there be a statue to him when there was no such person?"

"Was there ever such a person as Venus?" said Dr. O'Grady. "There wasn't. And yet every museum in Europe is half full of statues of her. Was there ever such a person as the Dying Gladiator? Was there ever a man called Laocoon, who strangled sea serpents? You know perfectly well that there weren't any such people, and yet some of the most famous statues in the world are erected in memory of them."

"But His Excellency naturally thought——"

"Look here," said Dr. O'Grady, "if we'd asked him to unveil a statue of Hercules in Ballymoy, would he have gone round consulting the librarians of London and Oxford to find out whether there was such a person as Hercules or not? Would he have said he was insulted?

Would he have sent you here to ask for an apology? You know perfectly well he wouldn't."

Lord Alfred seemed slightly puzzled. Dr. O'Grady's line of argument was quite new to him. He felt sure that a fallacy underlay it somewhere, but he could not at the moment see what the fallacy was.

"The case of Hercules is quite different," he said feebly.

"It's not in the least different. It's exactly the same. There was no such person as Hercules. Yet there are several statues of him. There was no such person as our General, but there may be lots of statues to him. There's certainly one. There's probably at least another. I should think the people of Bolivia are sure to have one. We'll ask Billing when we see him."

"Is he the priest who mistook me for the Lord-Lieutenant?"

"Oh, no. He's the swindler whom Doyle caught. By the way, here's Doyle coming out of the hotel again. Do you mind if I call him?"

Doyle crossed the square very slowly, because he stopped frequently to speak to the people whom he saw. He stopped when he came to Father McCormack and whispered something to him. He stopped when he came to Major Kent. He stopped for a moment beside Mrs. Gregg. He seemed to be full of some news and eager to tell it to everybody. When he saw Dr. O'Grady coming to meet him he hurried forward.

"I have it," he said, "I have it safe."

"The cheque?" said Dr. O'Grady.

"Better than that. Notes. Bank of Ireland notes."

"Good," said Dr. O'Grady. "Then it won't make so much matter if we don't get the pier. I'm having a hard job with Lord Alfred. It appears that the Lord-Lieutenant is in a pretty bad temper, and it may not be easy to get the pier. However, I'll do my best. I wish you'd go and fetch the illuminated address. Is Thady Gallagher safe?"

"He's making a speech this minute within, in the bar, and Mr. Billing's listening to him."

"Good. Get the illuminated address for me now as quick as you can."

Doyle hurried off in the direction of the hotel. Dr. O'Grady turned once more to Lord Alfred.

"By the way," he said, "before we go on with the unveiling of the statue would you mind telling me this: Have you got an ear for music?"

Lord Alfred had recovered a little from the bewildering effect of Dr. O'Grady's argument. He reminded himself that he had a duty to perform. He regained with an effort his original point of view, and once more felt sure that the Lord-Lieutenant had been grossly insulted.

"I've listened to all you have to say," he said, "and I still feel, in fact I feel more strongly than ever, that an apology is due to His Excellency."

"Very well," said Dr. O'Grady, "I've no objection whatever to apologising. I'm extremely sorry that he was put to such a lot of unnecessary trouble. If I'd had the least idea that he wouldn't have understood about the General— — but I thought he'd have known. I still think he ought to have known. But I won't say a word about that. Tell him from me that I'm extremely sorry. And now, have you an ear for music?"

"That's not an apology," said Lord Alfred. "I won't go back to His Excellency and tell him— — hang it! I can't tell him all that stuff about Venus and Hercules."

"I wish you'd tell me whether you have an ear for music or not. You don't understand the situation because you haven't met Thady Gallagher. But I can't ask you to unveil the statue until I know whether you've an ear for music or not."

"I don't know what you mean, but— —"

Dr. O'Grady made a click with his tongue against the roof of his mouth. He was becoming very impatient.

"Well, I haven't," said Lord Alfred. "I don't see what business it is of yours whether I have or not; but anyhow, I haven't."

"None at all? You wouldn't know one tune from another?"

"No, I wouldn't. And now will you tell me— —"

"I'll tell you anything you like when this business is over. I haven't time to enter into long explanations now. The people are beginning to get very impatient."

Young Kerrigan, with his bandsmen grouped around him, was standing a little below the police barrack. Dr. O'Grady walked quickly over to him. He told him to be ready to begin to play the moment he received the signal.

"And— — listen to me now," he said. "You're to play some other tune, not the one I taught you."

"I'm just as glad," said young Kerrigan. "It's equal to me what tune I play, but Thady Gallagher—What tune will I play?"

"Anything you like," said Dr. O'Grady. "Whatever you know best, but not the one I taught you. Remember that."

He left young Kerrigan, and hurried over to where Major Kent, Father McCormack and Mrs. Gregg were standing together near the statue.

"We're now going to unveil the statue," he said, "and everybody must be ready to do his part. Father McCormack, I want you to take charge of Mary Ellen. In the absence of the Lord-Lieutenant she'll pull the string. You're to see that she does it when I give the word. Then you must go across to the door of the hotel and keep a look out for Thady Gallagher. If he tries to make any sort of disturbance quell him at once."

"I'm willing to try," said Father McCormack, "and so far as Mary Ellen is concerned I'm right enough. She's a good girl, and she'll do as I bid her. But it'd take more than me to pacify Thady when he hears the band."

"It's all right about that the band won't play that tune at all. As it happens Lord Alfred has no ear whatever for music. That lets us out of what was rather an awkward hole. Young Kerrigan can play anything he likes, and so long as we all take off our hats, Lord Alfred'll think it's 'God Save the King.' Thady won't be able to say a word."

"If that's the way of it," said Father McCormack, "I'll do the best I can with Thady."

"Mrs. Gregg," said Dr. O'Grady, "you can't present that bouquet, so the best thing for you to do is to step forward the moment the sheet drops off and deposit it at the foot of the statue. Major— —"

"You may leave me out," said Major Kent. "I'm merely a spectator."

"You'll support Mrs. Gregg when she's paying her floral tribute to the memory of the dead General."

"I'll do no such thing."

"You must, Major. You can't let poor Mrs. Gregg go forward alone."

"Please do," said Mrs. Gregg. "I shall be frightfully nervous."

"But—but—hang it all, O'Grady, how can I? What do you mean?"

"It's perfectly simple. Just walk forward beside her and smile. That's all that's wanted. The band will be playing at the time and nobody will notice you much. Now, I think everybody understands thoroughly what to do, and there's no reason why the proceedings shouldn't be a flaming success in spite of the conduct of the Lord-Lieutenant."

"What about the Lord-Lieutenant?" said Father McCormack. "I'd be glad if I knew what the reason is of his not coming to us when he promised."

"The reason's plain enough," said the Major. "He evidently has some common sense."

"As a matter of fact," said Dr. O'Grady, "the exact contrary is the case. What Lord Alfred says is that he wouldn't come because he found out at the last moment that there was no such person as General John Regan. I don't call that sensible."

"I was thinking all along," said Father McCormack, "that there was something queer about the General."

CHAPTER XX

Doyle came out of the hotel bringing the illuminated address. Dr. O'Grady took it from him and carried it over to Lord Alfred.

"Just take this," he said.

Lord Alfred looked at the address doubtfully. It was very large, and seemed an awkward thing to carry about.

"What is it?" he said.

"It's an illuminated address. We intended to present it to the Lord-Lieutenant, but of course we can't when he isn't here. You're to take it, and hand it over to him next time you see him."

He pushed the address into Lord Alfred's arms as he spoke.

Many men would have made some resistance, would have put their hands into their pockets, perhaps, and so forced Dr. O'Grady either to hold the frame himself or drop it on the ground. But Lord Alfred Blakeney had been aide-de-camp to the Lord-Lieutenant for several years. He knew something of the spirit which must animate all viceroys. It is their business to commend themselves, their office and the party which appoints them to the people over whom they reign. In private a Lord-Lieutenant with a sense of humour—no good Lord-Lieutenant ought to have a sense of humour—may mock at the things he has to do, but in public, however absurd the position in which he finds himself, he must remain gravely suave. His aides-de-camp must never under any circumstances do anything which could possibly cause offence to any part of the community. Dr. O'Grady was certainly a very important and influential part of the community of Ballymoy. Lord Alfred allowed the illuminated address to be pushed into his arms. He attempted no more than a mild protest.

"Can't I lay it down somewhere?" he said. "It's so huge."

"Better not. If you do it's sure to be forgotten, and then we'll have to forward it by post, which will involve us in a lot of extra expense."

"But it's so absurd to be lugging a great picture frame about in my arms all day, and I can't carry it any other way. It's too big."

Dr. O'Grady, having made over the address to Lord Alfred, was not inclined to listen to any complaints about its size. He took off his hat and stepped forward towards the statue.

"Ladies and gentlemen— —" he said.

The few people who could see Dr. O'Grady stopped talking in order to hear what he was going to say.

"Ladies and gentlemen— —" he said again.

This time, the nearer people having stopped talking, his voice carried further than it did at his first attempt. Very many more people turned round and began to listen.

"Ladies and gentlemen— —" he said.

This third beginning secured him a large audience. Nearly half the people in the square were listening to him. He felt justified in going on with his speech.

"Ladies and gentlemen," he said, "we are now going to proceed with the unveiling of the statue of General John Regan. Mary Ellen, whom most of you know— —"

He paused and the crowd cheered. A crowd nearly always cheers anyone who is mentioned by name in a speech, unless it is quite plain that the speaker means to be abusive.

"Mary Ellen," said Dr. O'Grady, "who is the nearest living relative of the great General, will perform the ceremony. Now, Mary Ellen," he went on, in a lower tone, "pull the string. Father McCormack, give her the string. She doesn't seem able to find it."

Father McCormack handed the end of the string to Mary Ellen. She chucked at it in a timid, doubtful way. Nothing happened.

"Pull harder," said Dr. O'Grady.

Sergeant Colgan, who was a benevolent man, and therefore anxious that the ceremony should be a success, stepped to Mary Ellen's side and laid his hand on hers. He pulled hard. The sheet fluttered to the ground. The crowd cheered delightedly.

"There now," said Dr. O'Grady to Lord Alfred Blakeney, "I told you there really was a statue under that sheet. Next time I say something to you I hope you'll believe it."

He held up his hand, and young Kerrigan, who was watching for the signal, began to play at once. The tune he chose was an attractive one which had achieved some popularity in a Dublin pantomime the year before. Mrs. Gregg glanced dubiously at Dr. O'Grady, and then walked towards the statue with the bouquet in her hand. When she had gone five or six yards she stopped and looked round to see what had happened to Major Kent. He was hanging back, but the piteous appeal in her eyes moved him. He scowled ferociously at the doctor, and then with clenched teeth and closely pressed lips joined Mrs. Gregg. Everybody cheered. The Major, in spite of being a landlord, was very popular in the neighbourhood. The cheers made him still more uncomfortable. He frowned with embarrassment and anger. Mrs. Gregg laid her hand on his arm. Still frowning, he led her forward, very much as if he were taking her in to dinner. Mrs. Gregg was frightened and nervous. She had only the vaguest idea of what she was expected to do. When she reached the base of the statue she curtseyed deeply. The people cheered frantically. Major Kent dropped her arm and hurried away. He was a gentleman of an old-fashioned kind, and, partly perhaps because he had never married, was very chivalrous towards women. But Mrs. Gregg's curtsey and the cheers which followed it were too much for him. His position had become intolerable. Mrs. Gregg, suddenly deserted by her escort, dropped the bouquet and fled. Sergeant Colgan picked it up and laid it solemnly at the foot of the statue. Young Kerrigan, stimulated by the cheers, worked the band up to a fortissimo performance of his tune.

Dr. O'Grady held his hat in his hand. He signalled frantically to Father McCormack. He took off his hat, whispering to Major Kent as he did so. The Major, who was utterly bewildered, and not at all sure what was happening, took off his hat. Several other bystanders, supposing that it must be right to stand bare-headed before a newly unveiled statue, took off theirs: Lord Alfred Blakeney looked round him doubtfully. Most of the people near him had their hats in their hands. He took off his.

The unusually loud noise made by the band reached Thady Gallagher in the bar of the hotel. He stopped abruptly in the middle of a speech which he was making to Mr. Billing. After a moment's hesitation he rushed to the door of the hotel. The sight of the people, standing bare-headed and silent while the band played, convinced him that Dr. O'Grady was in the act of perpetrating a treacherous trick upon the sincerely patriotic but unsuspecting inhabitants of Ballymoy. Standing at the door of the hotel he shouted and waved his arms. Mr. Billing stood behind him looking on with an expression of serious interest. Nobody could hear what Gallagher said. But Father McCormack and Doyle, fearing that he would succeed in making himself audible, hurried towards him. Doyle seized him by the arm, Gallagher shook him off angrily.

"It shall never be said," he shouted, "that I stood silent while an insult was heaped upon Ballymoy and the cause of Nationalism in Ireland."

"Whisht, now whisht," said Father McCormack. "Sure there's nothing to be angry about."

"There is what would make any man angry, any man that has the welfare of Ireland at heart. That tune— —"

"It isn't that tune at all," said Father McCormack. "It's another one altogether."

"It's not another," said Gallagher, "but it's the one I mean. Didn't Constable Moriarty say it was?"

"Oughtn't you to listen to his reverence," said Doyle, "more than to Moriarty? But if you won't do that, can't you hear the tune for yourself?"

"I can hear it; and what's more I can see the Major with his hat off and the young fellow that's down from Dublin Castle with his hat off, and the doctor— —"

"It's my belief, Thady," said Doyle, "that you're three parts drunk. It would be better for you to go back into the hotel."

He caught Gallagher by the arm as he spoke and held him fast Young Kerrigan reached the end of his tune with a triumphant flourish. Dr. O'Grady put on his hat again. One by one the various bystanders followed his example. Lord Alfred Blakeney looked round him, puzzled.

"Surely that wasn't the National Anthem?" he said.

"I thought," said Dr. O'Grady, "that you didn't know one tune from another."

"I don't; but, hang it all, a man can't be aide-decamp to His Excellency without getting to know the sound of the National Anthem. What tune was it and why did we all take off our hats?"

"You tell the Lord-Lieutenant when you get back," said Dr. O'Grady, "that we all, including Major Kent, who's a strong Unionist, stood bare-headed while the band played. He'll be able to guess what tune it was, and he'll be pleased."

"But it wasn't the— —"

"A speech will now be made," said Dr. O'Grady, addressing the crowd, "by Lord Alfred Blakeney as representative of the Lord-Lieutenant of Ireland."

"But I'm not," said Lord Alfred clutching at Dr. O'Grady. "His Excellency will be furious if he hears— —"

"Go on," said Dr. O'Grady pushing him towards the statue. "Stand on the pedestal."

"But I can't make a speech. I'm not prepared. I've nothing to say."

He was pushed forward remorselessly. At the very base of the statue he turned.

"I hope there are no reporters present," he said in a tone of despair.

"There probably are lots," said Dr. O'Grady. "Get up now and begin. The people won't stand here all day."

Lord Alfred Blakeney, still clasping the illuminated address in his arms, was hustled on to the lowest step of the pedestal. The people cheered encouragingly.

"Oh damn this great picture," said Lord Alfred. "Do hold it for me."

"Never mind it," said Dr. O'Grady. "It's all right as it is. Make your speech."

"Ladies and gentlemen," said Lord Alfred, "I find myself standing here to-day——"

"As representative of the Lord-Lieutenant," said Dr. O'Grady, prompting him.

"But I'm not. I tell you he'll be angry. I can't make this speech. I really can't."

"You can if you like," said Dr. O'Grady. "Go on."

"I stand here to-day," said Lord Alfred, "at the unveiling of this beautiful statue——"

"Hear, hear," said Doyle from the door of the hotel. "It's a grand statue surely."

"Go on," said Dr. O'Grady. "You're doing capitally. Say something about the grant from the Government for a new pier."

"About what?" said Lord Alfred.

"About a grant for a new pier," said Dr. O'Grady, speaking distinctly.

"But I've no authority. I can't."

"£500 will satisfy us," said Dr. O'Grady. "It's a mere trifle. After the shabby way the Lord-Lieutenant has behaved to us—but go on, anyway."

"I have much pleasure," said Lord Alfred Blakeney, "in declaring this statue—er—open—er—for public inspection."

The crowd cheered loudly. Dr. O'Grady whispered to Lord Alfred that he ought to say something about the value of the statue as a work of art. But this time Lord Alfred's will was stronger than the doctor's. He jumped off the pedestal and flatly declined to mount it again. He was crimson in the face with mortification and embarrassment. Then, when the cheering subsided a little, Mr. Billing's voice was heard, clear and incisive. He had pushed his way from the door of the hotel and was standing near the statue.

"That's a darned poor speech," he said.

It is extraordinary how close the primitive barbarian is to the most civilised man. No one could have been more carefully trained than Lord Alfred Blakeney. No one possessed more of that suave self-control which distinguishes a man of the governing classes from the members of the mob. Yet Lord Alfred collapsed suddenly under the strain to which he had been subjected. Mr. Billing's taunt threw him back to an earlier, a very early stage of development.

"Make a better one yourself, then," he said, "whoever you are."

"I'll make one that'll create a sensation, anyhow," said Mr. Billing.

He stepped jauntily up the two steps of the pedestal.

"Mr. Lord-Lieutenant, Right Reverend Sir, Ladies and Gentlemen," he said.

Lord Alfred Blakeney clutched Dr. O'Grady by the arm.

"I'm not the Lord-Lieutenant," he said desperately.

"I'm not even his representative. Do try to make him understand that."

"It doesn't in the least matter who you are," said Dr. O'Grady. "Listen to the speech."

"When I first set eyes on this town a month ago I thought I had bumped up against a most dead-alive, god-forsaken, one-horse settlement that Europe could boast."

The crowd, being as Gallagher always asserted intensely patriotic, was not at all pleased at this beginning. Several people groaned loudly. Mr. Billing listened to them with a bland smile. The people were still further irritated and began to boo. Thady Gallagher broke suddenly from Doyle's control, and rushed forward waving his arms.

"Pull the Yank down out of that," he shouted. "What right has he to be standing there maligning the people of Ireland?"

Father McCormack and Doyle were after him at once and closed on him, each of them grasping one of his swinging arms.

"Behave yourself, Thady," said Father McCormack, "behave yourself decent."

"Isn't it him that's paying for the statue," said Doyle, "and hasn't he a right to say what he likes?"

Mr. Billing seemed quite unimpressed by Gallagher's fiery interruption. He smiled benevolently again.

"I got bitten with the notion of speeding you up a bit," he said, "because I felt plumb sure that there wasn't a live man in the place, nothing but a crowd of doddering hop-toads."

The hop-toad is a reptile unknown in Ireland, but its name sounds disgusting. The crowd began to get very angry, and surged threateningly towards the platform. Sergeant Colgan felt that a great opportunity had arrived. He had all his life been looking for a chance of quelling a riot. He had it at last.

"Keep back, now," he said, "keep back out of that. Do you want me to draw my baton to you?"

"Well, gentlemen," said Mr. Billing, "I was mistaken and I own up. There is one live man in Ballymoy anyway. We haven't got a medical gentleman on our side of the Atlantic equal to Dr. Lucius O'Grady. He has run this show in a way that has surprised me considerable. He has erected a statue that will be an ornament to this town, and it's a pleasure to me to pay for it."

"Hear, hear," shouted Doyle.

The crowd, which had been booing a minute before, cheered heartily.

"He's fetched down the representative of the Lord-Lieutenant of this country to unveil the statue!"

"I'm not," said Lord Alfred feebly. "I wish I could get you to understand that I'm not his representative."

His protest was lost in a fresh burst of cheers.

"He has provided a charming grand-niece," said Mr. Billing, "a grand-niece that any man, living or dead, might be proud of—-"

"Get out," said Mary Ellen softly.

"For General John Regan," said Mr. Billing amidst tumultuous cheers, "and when I tell you that no such General ever existed in Bolivia or anywhere else, you'll be in a position to appreciate your doctor."

Doyle dropped Gallagher's arm and rushed forward. The crowd, too, astonished by Mr. Billing's last words, even to cheer, stood silent. What Doyle said was plainly heard.

"Be damn, doctor, but you're great, and I'd say that if it was the last word ever I spoke. Ask him for the price of the new pier now and he'll give it to you."

"Gentlemen," said Mr. Billing, "if 2,000 dollars will build the pier Mr. Doyle wants, I'll give it with pleasure, and I reckon that the show which Dr. O'Grady has run is cheap at the price."

Sergeant Colgan stepped forward with slow dignity. He beckoned to Constable Moriarty. His face wore an expression of steady determination.

"It would be better, doctor," he said, "if you and the other gentlemen present would move away. The demeanour of the crowd is threatening."

The demeanour of the crowd was, in fact, hilarious; but Dr. O'Grady understood that there are limits to the patience of the official guardians of law and order. The police—the fact is exemplified in their occasional dealings with the students of Trinity College—appreciate a joke as well as any men, and up to a certain point are tolerant of merriment. But it is possible to go too far, and there is a point at which fooling becomes objectionable. Dr. O'Grady took Mr. Billing by the arm.

"Come along," he said, "and let us have a drink of some sort, and something to eat. There's no reason why we shouldn't have something to eat. Doyle has a magnificent luncheon spread out in his hotel. Run in Doyle, and tell the cook to dish up the potatoes. Major, you bring Mrs. Gregg along with you. I'm sure Mrs. Gregg wants something to eat. Lord Alfred, I'm sorry we haven't a lady for you to take in, but Father McCormack will show you the way."

"If this business gets into the papers," said Lord Alfred, "the *Freeman's Journal* will make capital of it, and the *Irish Times* will say the Government must resign at once. Can't we square the reporters?"

"There aren't any," said Dr. O'Grady, "unless Gallagher's been taking notes. Come along."

The party, Doyle at the head of it, passed into the hotel. Sergeant Colgan turned and faced the crowd. His hand was on the baton at his side. His face and attitude were majestic.

"Get along home now, every one of yous," he said.

"Get along out of that!" said Constable Moriarty.

In twos and threes, in little groups of ten and twelve, silently obedient, the crowd slunk away. The statue of General John Regan was left looking down upon an empty market place. So the last word is spoken in the pleasant drama of Irish life. The policeman speaks it. "Get along home out of that, every one of you." So the curtain drops on our performances. In spite of our whirling words we bow to, in the end, the voice of authority.

THE END

* * *

Printed in Great Britain
by Amazon

62635488R20109